HARLEQUIN®
*Presents*

With Valentine's Day, February is always a romantic month. And we've got some great books in store for you....

*The High-Society Wife* by Helen Bianchin is the story of a marriage of convenience between two rich and powerful families.... But what this couple didn't expect is for their marriage to become real! It's also the first in our new miniseries RUTHLESS, where you'll find commanding men, who stop at nothing to get what they want. Look out for more books coming soon! And if you love Italian men, don't miss *The Marchese's Love-Child* by Sara Craven, where our heroine is swept off her feet by a passionate tycoon.

If you just want to get away from it all, let us whisk you off to the beautiful Greek Islands in Julia James's hard-hitting story *Baby of Shame*. What will happen when a businessman discovers that his night of passion with a young Englishwoman five years ago resulted in a son? The Caribbean is the destination for our couple in Anne Mather's intriguing tale *The Virgin's Seduction*.

Jane Porter has a dangerously sexy Sicilian for you in *The Sicilian's Defiant Mistress*. This explosive reunion story promises to be dark and passionate! In Trish Morey's *Stolen by the Sheikh*, the first in her new duet, THE ARRANGED BRIDES, a young woman is summoned to the palace of a demanding sheikh, who has plans for her future.... Don't miss part two, coming in March.

See the inside front cover for a list of titles and book numbers.

# *Sara Craven*

## THE MARCHESE'S LOVE-CHILD

# ITALIAN HUSBANDS

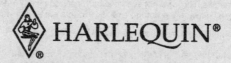

TORONTO • NEW YORK • LONDON
AMSTERDAM • PARIS • SYDNEY • HAMBURG
STOCKHOLM • ATHENS • TOKYO • MILAN • MADRID
PRAGUE • WARSAW • BUDAPEST • AUCKLAND

ISBN 0-373-12521-6

THE MARCHESE'S LOVE-CHILD

First North American Publication 2006.

# CHAPTER ONE

'YOU'RE going back to Italy?' There was outrage in Lily Fairfax's voice as she turned on her daughter. Anger too. 'Oh, I don't believe it. You can't—you mustn't.'

Polly Fairfax sighed soundlessly. 'Mother, I'm escorting an elderly lady to Naples, where she'll be met by her family, upon which—I catch the next flight home. I'll be gone for a few hours at most. Hardly *Mission Impossible*.'

'You said you'd never return there,' her mother said. 'You swore it.'

'Yes, I know,' Polly acknowledged wearily. 'But that was three years ago. And circumstances change. This is a work assignment, and there's no one else to do it. Since Safe Hands was featured on that holiday programme, we've been snowed under with requests.' She adopted a persuasive tone. 'And you enjoyed seeing me on television—you know you did.' She added a smile. 'So you can't complain if I'm in demand as a consequence.'

Mrs Fairfax wasn't pacified. 'Is this why this woman—this Contessa Whatsit wants you? Because you've been on television?'

Polly laughed. 'I shouldn't think so for a moment. She's far too grand to bother with anything so vulgar. And her name's the Contessa Barsoli.'

Her mother dismissed that impatiently. 'I didn't think you liked her very much.'

Polly shrugged. 'I don't particularly. She's been a total pain the whole week I've been with her. And I'm damned sure she doesn't care for me either,' she added musingly. 'She always looks at me as if I'm a slug in her salad. Believe me, I shan't be tempted to linger.'

'Then why did she choose you?'

'The devil she knows, perhaps.' Polly shrugged again. 'As opposed to some stranger. Anyway, she needs someone to see to her luggage, and make sure she's got all her documentation. Which is where Safe Hands comes in, of course.'

7

She leaned forward. 'To be honest, Mum, I don't know how much longer I can go on turning down jobs in Italy, just because of something that happened three years ago. I like my job, and I want to hang on to it. But Mrs Terence is running a business here, not an agency for people who've been crossed in love.'

'It was,' her mother reminded her tightly, 'rather more than that.'

'Whatever.' Polly bit her lip. 'But I can't pick and choose my clients, and I think Mrs T has made all the allowances over Italy that she's going to. So I have to treat it as just another destination from now on.'

'And what about Charlie?' Mrs Fairfax demanded fiercely. 'What's going to happen to him while you're gadding off?'

It hardly seemed to Polly that enduring another twenty-four hours in the company of a disdainful Italian autocrat counted as 'gadding'.

And her mother had never objected to her role as child-minder before, even when Polly was absent on other, much longer trips. In fact she'd declared that Charlie's presence had given her a new lease of life.

She looked out of the window to where her cheerful two-year-old was trotting about after his grandfather, picking up hedge clippings.

She said slowly, 'I thought he would stay with you, as usual.'

There were bright spots of colour in her mother's face. 'But it's not usual—is it? You're deliberately defying my wishes—yet again. I was totally against your taking that job in Sorrento three years ago, and how right I was. You came slinking home pregnant by some local Casanova, who didn't want to know about you any more. Can you deny it?'

'To be fair, Sandro had no more idea that I was expecting a baby than I did myself,' Polly said levelly. 'Although I agree it would have made no difference if he had known. But that's all in the past. I've—rebuilt my life, and he'll have moved on too.' She paused. 'All the same, I promise not to go within ten miles of Sorrento, if that will make you feel better.'

'I'd feel better if you didn't go at all,' her mother returned sharply. 'But if it really is just a day trip, I suppose I can't stop you.'

'You'll hardly know I've gone,' Polly assured her. 'Thanks, Mum.' She gave her a swift hug. 'You're a star.'

'I'm an idiot,' Lily Fairfax retorted, but she sounded slightly mollified. 'Are you going to stay for supper? I've made one of my steak pies.'

'It's good of you, darling,' said Polly, mentally bracing herself for another battle. 'But we must get back. I have this trip to prepare for.'

Mrs Fairfax gave her a tragic look. 'But I've got Charlie's favourite ice-cream for dessert. He'll be so disappointed.'

Only because you've already told him, Polly thought without pleasure.

Aloud, she said, 'You really mustn't spoil him like that.'

Her mother pouted. 'It's a sad thing if I can't give my only grandchild the occasional treat.' She paused. 'Why not leave him here—if you're going to be busy this evening?' she coaxed. 'It'll save you time in the morning if you have a plane to catch.'

'It's a kind thought.' Polly tried to sound positive. 'But I really look forward to my evenings with Charlie, Mum. I—I see so little of him.'

'Well, that's something your father and I wanted to discuss with you,' her mother said with sudden briskness. 'There's a lot of unused space in this house, and if we were to extend over the garage, it would make a really nice flat for you both. And it would mean so much less disruption for Charlie.'

She emptied the carrots she'd been scraping into a pan. 'We've had some preliminary plans drawn up, and, if you stayed, we could look at them over supper perhaps.'

Polly supposed, heart sinking, that she should have seen it coming—but she hadn't. Oh, God, she thought, is this the day from hell, or what?

She said quietly, 'Mum, I do have a flat already.'

'An attic,' her mother dismissed with a sniff, 'with a room hardly bigger than a cupboard for Charlie. Here, he'd have room to run about, plus a routine he's accustomed to. And we're in the catchment area for a good primary school, when the time comes,' she added. 'I think it's the perfect solution to all sorts of problems.'

My main problem, Polly thought wearily, is prising Charlie out of this house at the end of the working day. Of staking a claim in my own child. She'd seen trouble looming when her own former bedroom was extensively redecorated and refitted for Charlie, despite her protest that he wouldn't use it sufficiently to justify the expense.

Her mother must have had this in mind from the first.

She rallied herself, trying to speak reasonably. 'But I need my independence. I'm used to it.'

'Is that what you call the way you live? You're a single mother, my girl. A statistic. And this glamorous job of yours is little better than slavery—running around all over the place at the beck and call of people with more money than sense. And where did it lead? To you making a fool of yourself with some foreigner, and ruining your life.' She snorted. 'Well, don't come to me for help if you mess up your life a second time.'

Polly's head went back in shock. She said unsteadily, 'That is *so* unfair. I made a mistake, and I've paid for it. But I still intend to live my life on my own terms, and I hope you can accept that.'

Mrs Fairfax's face was flushed. 'I can certainly see you're determined to have your own way, regardless of Charlie's wellbeing.' She sent her daughter a fulminating glance. 'And now I suppose you'll take him with you, just to make your point.'

'No,' Polly said reluctantly. 'I won't do that—this time. But I think you have to accept that I do have a point.'

'Perhaps you'd send Charlie indoors as you leave.' Her mother opened a carton of new potatoes and began to wash them. 'He's getting absolutely filthy out there, and I'd like him to calm down before he eats.'

'Fine.' Polly allowed herself a small, taut smile. 'I'll pass the message on.'

As she went into the garden, Charlie headed for her gleefully, strewing twigs and leaves behind him. Polly bent to enfold him, the breath catching in her throat as she inhaled his unique baby scent. Thinking again, with a pang, how beautiful he was. And how painfully, searingly like his father...

Her mother had never wanted to know any details about his paternity, referring to Sandro solely as 'that foreigner'. The fact that Charlie, with his curly black hair, olive skin and long-lashed eyes the colour of deep topaz, was also clearly a Mediterranean to his fingertips seemed to have eluded her notice.

But it was the details that only Polly could recognise that brought her heart into her mouth, like the first time her son had looked at her with that wrenchingly familiar slow, slanting smile. His baby features were starting to change too, and she could see that he was going to have Sandro's high-bridged nose one day, and the same straight brows.

It would be like living with a mirror image before too long, Polly told herself, thinking forlornly that nature played cruel tricks at times. Why couldn't Charlie have inherited her own pale blonde hair and green eyes?

She smoothed the hair back from his damp forehead. 'Gran wants you to go inside, darling,' she whispered. 'You're sleeping here tonight. Won't that be fun?'

Her father came to join them, his brows lifting at her words. 'Will it, my love?' His voice was neutral, but the glance he sent her was searching.

'Yes.' Polly cleared her throat, watching Charlie scamper towards the house. 'It—it seems a shame to uproot him, when I have to start work early tomorrow.'

'Yes.' He paused. 'She means it all for the best, you know, Poll,' he told her quietly.

'He's my child, Dad.' Polly shook her head. 'I have to have an opinion on what's best for him, too. And that doesn't include moving back here.'

'I know that,' her father said gently. 'But I'm also aware how hard it must be raising a child without any kind of support from his father—and I'm not simply talking about the economics of it.'

He sighed. 'You were so precious to me, I can't imagine a man not wanting to involve himself with his own flesh and blood.'

Polly's lips moved in a wintry little smile. 'He didn't want to know, Dad—about either of us. It was best to leave it that way.'

'Yes, love,' he said. 'So you told me. But that hasn't stopped me from worrying—or your mother either.' He gave her a swift hug. 'Take care.'

Polly's thoughts were troubled as she rode home on the bus alone. Her mother's attempts to totally monopolise her grandson was becoming a seriously tricky situation, and she wasn't sure she had sufficient wisdom to resolve it.

The last thing she wanted was for Charlie to become a battle-ground, but even a mild suggestion that she should enrol him at a local nursery for a few hours a week so that he could mix with

other children had provoked such an injured reception from Mrs
Fairfax that she hadn't dared raise the subject again.

Her mother's hostile attitude to her work was a different thing.

Safe Hands had proved the job of her dreams, and she knew,
without conceit, that she was good at it.

The people who made use of the company were mainly female
and usually elderly, people who needed someone young, relatively
strong and capable to deal with their luggage, guide them through
airports and escort them safely round unfamiliar foreign cities.

Polly was the youngest of Mrs Terence's employees, but she
had a gift for languages, and her brief career as a holiday rep had
taught her patience and tolerance to add to her natural sense of
humour—qualities she soon found she needed in abundance.

She knew how to diffuse potentially explosive situations with
overseas Customs, find restaurants that were sympathetic to delicate digestions, hotels in peaceful locations that were also pictur-
esque, and shops prepared to deliver purchases to hotels, or post
them on to addresses abroad. She could also discover which art
galleries and museums were prepared to arrange quiet private tours
for small groups.

And she never showed even a trace of irritation with even the
most high-handed behaviour from her charges.

After all, she was being paid for acceding to their whims and
fancies, and part of her skill was in making them forget that was
how she earned her living, and persuading them that she was there
for the sheer pleasure of their company.

But with the Contessa Barsoli, it had been a struggle from day
one.

Polly had long accepted that not all her clients would like her,
but she did need them to trust her, and, from the start, her senses
had detected an inflexible wariness, bordering on hostility at times,
in the *contessa*'s attitude which she was at a loss to account for.

Whatever the reason, there had never been any real warmth
between them, so Polly had been genuinely astonished to hear that
the *contessa* had specifically requested her services again for the
homeward leg of her journey to southern Italy, and was prepared
to pay her a generous cash bonus too.

Surprised—but also alarmed enough to ask herself if the money
was really worth the damage to her nervous system.

Her previous visit—the first and last—had left her scarred—and scared. And there was no way she'd have dared risk a return, if there'd been the slightest chance she might encounter Sandro again. But the odds against such a meeting must run into millions to one. But irrational as it might seem, even the remotest possibility still had the power to make her tremble.

They said time was a great healer, but the wound Sandro had dealt her was still agonisingly raw.

She'd tried so hard to block out the memories of that summer in Sorrento three years ago. The summer she thought she'd fallen in love, and believed she was loved in return. But the images she'd hoped were safely locked away forever had broken free, and were running wild in her brain again.

Her room, she thought, wincing, during the hours of siesta, the shutters closed against the beat of the sun, and only the languid whirr of the ceiling fan and their own ragged breathing to break the silence.

And Sandro's voice murmuring soft, husky words of passion, his hands and mouth exploring her naked body with sensuous delight. The heated surge of his body into hers at the moment of possession.

She had lived for those shadowed, rapturous afternoons, and warm, moonlit nights, which made the pain of his ultimate betrayal even more intense.

What a gullible little fool I was, Polly thought with self-derision. And I can't say I wasn't warned. The other reps said that he was just looking for some easy summer sex, and cautioned me to be careful, but I wouldn't listen because I knew better.

I knew that he loved me, and that when the summer was over we were going to be married. I was convinced of it—because he'd said so.

I thought it was that innocent—that simple. I should have realised that he wasn't what he seemed. He told me he worked at one of the big hotels, but he always had too much money to be just a waiter or a barman. And these jobs were usually taken by younger men, anyway, while Sandro was thirty at least.

I knew from the first that there were depths to him that belied the seaside Romeo tag—and that the latent power I always sensed in him was part of his attraction for me.

But I liked the fact that he was something of an enigma. That there were questions about him still to be answered. I thought I would have the rest of my life to find out the truth.

Yes, I was a fool, but it never once occurred to me that I could be in any real danger. That there was another darker side to his life, far away from the sunlight and whispered promises.

Not until he got bored with me. Not until his friend arrived—the man in the designer suit with the smile that never reached his eyes. The man who came to tell me that it was all over, and to suggest, smiling suavely and icily, that it would be better for my health to get out of Sorrento, and away from Italy altogether.

The man who told me that I'd become an inconvenience, and that it would be much safer for me to quit my job and go back to England.

And that I should never try to contact Sandro, or come back to Italy again—ever.

In return for which I was to receive the equivalent of fifty thousand pounds.

Polly shuddered. Even now the memory made her shake inside. But what had crucified her then, and still hurt today, was that Sandro hadn't had the guts to come to her himself—to tell her in person that it was finished between them. And why...

She'd rejected his money with anger and contempt, unable to believe that he could insult her like that. Ordered his confederate out of her room.

But, all the same, she'd obeyed and left, because she was too heartbroken—and also too frightened to stay. She didn't know what Sandro could be involved with to afford a bribe of that size—and she didn't want to know. But something had reached out from the shadows around him, which had touched her life, and destroyed her hope of happiness.

She had been at home for several weeks before it dawned on her that she was pregnant—a knowledge born slowly from grief, bewilderment and unbelievable loneliness. At first she'd told herself that it could not be true—that they'd always been so careful—except for one night when their frantic, heated need for each other had outweighed caution.

And that, she had realised, stunned, must have been when it happened. Another blow to deepen the agony of pain and betrayal. Yet, although the prospect of single-motherhood had filled her with dread, she'd never once considered the obvious alternative and sought an abortion.

Her mother had thought of it, of course. Had urged her to do it, too, cajoling one minute, threatening the next. Railing at Polly for her stupidity, and for bringing shame on the family. Swearing that she would have nothing further to do with her daughter or the baby if the pregnancy went ahead. A resolution that had lasted no longer than an indrawn breath from the moment she had seen her newborn grandson.

Charlie had instantly taken the place of the son she'd always longed for. And there'd never been any question about who was going to look after him when Polly recovered and went back to work.

But, as Polly ruefully acknowledged, the arrangement had become a two-edged sword. Over the months, she seemed to have been sidelined into playing an elder sister's role to Charlie. Any slight wail, bump or graze brought her mother running, leaving Polly to watch helplessly while Mrs Fairfax hugged and comforted him. And that was not good.

She had to admit that her mother had not been too wide of the mark when she'd described Polly's flat as an attic. It had a reasonable-sized main room, a basic bathroom and a minuscule kitchen opening out of it, plus Charlie's cubby-hole. Polly herself slept on the sofa bed in the living room.

But she couldn't deny it was a weary climb up steep and badly lit stairs to reach her front door, especially when she was encumbered with Charlie, his bag of necessities and his buggy, which she didn't dare leave in the entrance hall in case it was stolen.

Once inside, she kept her home space clean and uncluttered, the walls painted in cool aqua. Most of the furniture had been acquired at auction sales, including the sofa bed, for which she'd bought a new cover in an Aztec print of deep blue, crimson and gold.

It wasn't flash, but the rent was reasonable, and she always felt the place offered comfort and a welcome as she went in.

And tonight she was in sore need of both.

It was a warm evening, so she unlocked the living-room window and pushed up the lower sash, sinking down onto the wooden seat beneath. There was some cold chicken and salad in the fridge, and it would be a moment's work to put a potato to bake in her second-hand microwave.

But she was in no hurry to complete her supper preparations. She felt tired and anxious—and more than a little disheartened. It seemed strange not to hear the clatter of Charlie's feet on the stripped boards as he trotted about, or his incessant and often unintelligible chatter.

She missed, too, his sudden, unsteady gallop to her arms. That most of all, she thought, her throat tightening.

I should have brought him home, she told herself restlessly, and not let myself be out-manoeuvred like that.

She felt, she realised, totally unsettled, for all kinds of reasons, so maybe this would be a good time to review her life, and see if she needed to make some changes.

And, first and foremost, she needed to be able to spend more time with Charlie.

When she began working again, after he was born, Safe Hands had seemed ideal, more of a career choice than an ordinary job. Having her cake, and eating it—or so she'd thought then.

She had been able to go on with the travelling she loved, and, as well as her salary, the majority of the clients paid her a cash bonus as well. Even at London prices, she could afford to live, and provide Charlie with what he needed, although there was never much left over for extras.

But his needs were changing, and so, she realised, were hers.

For one thing, it wasn't essential to work, or even live, in London. In fact, it would be sheer relief to be able to say goodbye to those stifling journeys on the underground and buses.

She could move to a totally different area altogether, away from the south-east of England. Deliberately select a place where it would be cheaper to live, and find a job in local tourism. Something strictly nine-to-five, with no time away from home, so that she could spend her leisure hours with her son.

During the day she'd need a minder for him, of course. There was no way out of that. But she'd look for someone young and lively, caring for other children too, so that Charlie would have playmates. Maybe, in time, she could even get a foot on the housing ladder—find somewhere small and manageable, hopefully with a garden. Something she would never be able to afford in London.

She would miss this flat, she thought, sighing, and it would be a wrench leaving Safe Hands but reason was telling her it would be for the best.

I have, she thought, to make a life for us both. For Charlie and myself. I need to build a proper relationship with him. And I can't do that if we stay here. Because I won't be allowed to.

But she wasn't delusional enough to think she could strike out on her own without a struggle, she told herself, wrinkling her nose. Her mother would fight her every step of the way, coming up with every possible reason why she should not do this thing—and a few impossible ones, too.

And when she saw Polly could not be moved, she would be very bitter. There might even be an open breach between them.

But that won't last forever, she thought. Whatever Mum thinks of me, she'll still want to maintain contact with Charlie.

She got to her feet. She would eat now, and when supper was over she'd use her laptop to go internet-exploring, looking at house prices in different parts of the country. Now that she'd made up her mind, there was no time to be lost.

Strange, she thought, how I can suddenly be so sure of that.

Yet the pressure on her to accept the Italian assignment must have contributed to her decision. It had left her feeling uneasy—and awoken too many bad memories.

A clean break with the past was what she needed. New job—new home—new friends.

She would never be able to forget, of course, that Sandro was Charlie's father. But in time, it might begin to hurt less. And she might even be able to stop being afraid. One day.


'See Naples and die, eh?' The man in the adjoining seat emphasised the originality of his remark with a slight dig in Polly's ribs, as their plane descended towards Capodichino Airport. 'That's what they say, isn't it?'

Polly gritted her teeth as she gave a wintry smile in acknowledgement.

But I don't care what 'they' say, she told herself fiercely. Naples is going to be my jumping-off point for a whole new life. And I plan to live every moment of it.

She couldn't say she'd enjoyed the flight. The *contessa* might need her physical assistance, but she certainly hadn't wanted her company. Which was why she was seated in first class, while Polly herself was in economy, with a neighbour who considered her presence his personal bonus.

Never mind, she thought. In a few moments I'll never have to see him again, or the *contessa* either.

She'd sipped mineral water throughout the flight, in spite of her fellow traveller's unceasing efforts to buy her what he called a proper drink. And the irony was that she'd have welcomed some alcohol, to dispel the shaky chill which had settled in the pit of her stomach. The closer they had got to their destination, their progress cheerfully marked by the captain, the more nervous she'd become.

I shan't relax until I'm safely back in Britain, she thought.

On the surface, she was calmness itself. She was wearing the company uniform of a slim-fitting, button-through dress in navy linen, with the distinctive silver brooch showing a pair of clasped hands pinned to her left shoulder. Her pale hair was in a loose knot on top of her head, and she wore her usual dusting of powder, and soft pink lipstick.

As they touched down, and the plane began to taxi to its stand, Polly reached under the seat, and extracted the navy leather satchel which held the travel documents and a few basic necessities in case of delay. Her client, she was sure, would have an eagle eye for the slightest lapse in efficiency.

Her companion nudged her again. 'Dangerous city, they say,' he whispered. 'If you're on your own tonight, I'd be happy to show you around.'

'Tonight,' she told him, 'I intend to be back in London.' And left him gaping.

Contessa Barsoli was a tall woman, rake-thin, with immaculately coiffed white hair and still handsome in a chilly way. A member of the cabin staff was permitted to help her descend the aircraft steps while Polly followed, instinctively lifting her face to the brilliant warmth of the southern sun.

Once inside the terminal, she found her charge a chair, retrieved her luggage and guided her through the formalities.

'There has been a small change of plan,' the older woman informed her abruptly. 'I am too tired to undertake a long car journey down to the Campania, so my cousin has arranged a suite for me at the Grand Hotel Neapolitana. You will accompany me there.'

Polly knew resignedly that she shouldn't be surprised. Most of the arrangements she'd made for the *contessa* during her stay in Britain had been subject to alteration, usually at the last moment. Why should this time be any different?

But this wasn't just irritating, she reminded herself, schooling her expression. It was seriously inconvenient. She had a return flight to catch, and the *contessa* knew it.

'Do you wish me to get us a taxi?' she asked quietly. If she could find a driver who knew a few short cuts through Naples' crowded streets, she might still be in with a chance.

'A taxi?' The *contessa* made it sound like a tumbrel. 'My cousin has sent a car and chauffeur for us. Oblige me by finding him.'

That was easily achieved. Transferring the *contessa* and her luggage to the roomy depths of the limousine was a completely different matter. The lady liked to take her time, oblivious to Polly's simmering frustration as the minutes ticked past.

The traffic was a nightmare, and when they did reach the hotel at last, Polly accepted that she probably wouldn't make it back to the airport in time for her flight.

I haven't a prayer, she told herself resignedly. It'll take me half an hour to get her to the lift.

But to her astonishment, the *contessa* suddenly became quite sprightly. She conducted her own registration at the desk, waving Polly regally away, and made no fuss about the prompt unloading of her luggage.

An under-manager escorted her, bowing, to the lift, where Polly caught up with her.

She said awkwardly, 'I need to say goodbye now, *contessa*, if I'm to get my flight.'

She got a severe look. 'But I wish you to accompany me to the suite, *signorina*. I have ordered coffee and *biscotti* to be served there. Besides,' she added, seeing that Polly was on the verge of protest, 'there is still the question of the money I offered you. I do not conduct such transactions in the foyers of hotels. If you want to be paid, you will come with me now.'

Groaning silently, Polly stood beside her as the lift made its way upward. They emerged onto a crimson-carpeted corridor, opposite a heavily carved door.

The under-manager produced a key with a flourish, and unlocked the door, and, still bowing, showed them ceremoniously into the suite.

Polly found herself in a large drawing room, shaded by the shutters which had been drawn over the long windows to combat the force of the mid-June sunlight. She had a confused impression of brocaded sofas and fresh flowers in elaborate arrangements, their scent hanging languidly in the air.

And realised suddenly that the room wasn't empty as she'd first thought. Because someone was there—someone standing by the windows, his figure silhouetted against the slatted light. Someone tall, lean and unforgettably—terrifyingly—familiar.

Even before he spoke, Polly knew who he was. Then his voice, low-pitched and faintly husky, reached her, and there was no longer room for any doubt. Or any hope, either.

He said, 'Paola *mia*. So, you have come to me at last.'

He moved—came away from the window, and walked towards her with that long, lithe stride she would have known anywhere, his shadow falling across the floor as he approached.

She tried to speak—to say his name, but her trembling mouth could not obey her and shape the word.

Because this could not be happening. Sandro could not be here, in this room, waiting for her.

As he reached her, she cried out and flung up her bare and unavailing hands in a desperate effort to keep him at bay. Only to find the shadows crowding round her, welcoming her, as she slid helplessly downwards into the dark whirl of oblivion.

# CHAPTER TWO

AWARENESS returned slowly, accompanied by an acrid smell that filled her nose and mouth with its bitterness, making her cough and mutter a feeble protest.

She lay very still, fighting against a feeling of nausea, hardly daring to open her eyes. Her senses told her that she was cushioned on satiny softness, and that she was not alone. That in the real world behind her closed eyelids, there was movement—people talking. And the heavy noise of traffic.

She propped herself dizzily on one elbow, and looked around her. She was lying in the middle of a vast bed, covered in deep gold embroidered silk. She was shoeless, she realised, and the top buttons of her dress had been unfastened.

The first person she saw was the *contessa*, as she stepped back, replacing the stopper in a small bottle. Smelling salts, Polly thought, dazedly. The older woman always insisted on having some handy in case travel motion upset her.

And, standing in silence a few yards away, was Sandro, head bent, his face in profile.

Not a figment of her imagination, as she'd hoped, but a nightmare that lived and breathed, and would not go away.

And not the laughing, dishevelled lover, wearing frayed shorts and an old T-shirt, and badly in need of a haircut, that she'd once known and desired so passionately, but that other, hidden man whose identity she'd never even suspected as she lay in his arms.

This other Sandro wore a dark suit that had clearly emanated from a great Italian fashion house. The dark curling hair had been tamed, to some extent at least, and there wasn't a trace of stubble, designer or otherwise, on what she could see of the hard, tanned face, only a faint breath of some expensive cologne hanging in the air.

His immaculate white shirt set off a sombre silk tie, and a thin platinum watch encircled his wrist.

Whatever path he'd chosen to follow, it had clearly brought him

21

serious money, Polly thought, anger and pain tightening her throat. And she didn't want to contemplate how it might have been obtained. Who said crime didn't pay?

Nor was he staying silent out of weakness, or any sense of guilt. Instinct told her that. He was simply exercising restraint. Under the stillness, Polly could sense his power—and the furious burn of his anger, rigorously reined in. Could feel the violence of his emotions in the pulse of her blood and deep within her bones, just as she'd once known the naked imprint of his skin on hers, and the intimate heat of his possession.

As if, she thought with a sudden sick helplessness, she lived within his flesh. Part of him. As she had once been.

Now that the impossible had happened, and she was face to face with him again, she was shocked by the intensity of her physical reaction to him. Ashamed too.

She had to make herself remember the cruel brutality of his rejection. The cynical attempt to buy her off, and the explicit threat that had accompanied it.

She needed to remind herself of the abyss of pain and loneliness that had consumed her after she'd fled from Italy. And, most important of all, she had to get out of here, and fast.

She sat upright, lifting a hand to her head as the room swayed about her.

The movement riveted everyone's attention, and Sandro took a hasty step forward, pausing when Polly flinched away from him involuntarily, his mouth hardening in an icy sneer.

'No,' he said. 'It is not pretty. You should have been prepared in advance, perhaps. Warned what to expect.'

As he came closer, Polly saw his face clearly for the first time. Saw the jagged scar that had torn its way from the corner of his eye, across the high cheekbone and halfway to his jaw.

For a brief moment she was stunned, as shocked as if she had seen some great work of art deliberately defaced.

He looked older too, and there was a weariness in the topaz eyes that had once glowed into hers.

Oh, God, she thought, swallowing. He thinks that I find him repulsive, and that's why I turned away just now.

A pang of something like anguish twisted inside her, then she took a deep breath, hardening herself against a compassion he did not need or deserve.

Let him think what he wanted, she thought. He'd chosen his life, and however rich and powerful he'd become he'd clearly paid violently for his wealth. And she'd been fortunate to escape when she did, and keep her own wounds hidden. That was all there was to be said.

She looked away from him. 'I don't understand.' Her voice was small and strained. 'What am I doing here? What—happened?'

'You fainted, *signorina*.' It was the *contessa* who answered her. 'At my cousin's feet.'

'Your cousin?' Polly repeated the words dazedly, her mind wincing away from the image the older woman's words conjured up of herself, unconscious, helpless. She shook her head, immediately wishing that she hadn't. 'Is that supposed to be some kind of joke?'

The *contessa* drew herself up, her brows lifting in hauteur. 'I do not understand you, *signorina*. There is no joke, I assure you. Alessandro is the son of my husband's late cousin. Indeed, his only child.'

'No,' Polly whispered. 'He can't be. It's not possible.'

'I am not accustomed to having my word doubted, Signorina Fairfax.' The *contessa*'s tone was frigid. She paused. 'But you are not yourself, so allowances must be made.' She handed Polly a glass of water. 'Drink this, if you please. And I will ask for some food to be brought. You will feel better when you have eaten something.'

'Thank you, but no.' Polly put down the empty glass and moved to the edge of the bed, putting her feet to the floor. She was still feeling shaky, but self-preservation was more important than any temporary weakness.

She'd fainted—something she'd never done in her life before, and a betraying sign of vulnerability that she could ill afford.

She spoke more strongly, lifting her chin. 'I would much prefer to leave. Right now. I have a flight to catch.'

'You are not very gracious, Paola *mia*.' Sandro's voice was soft, but there was a note in it that made her quiver. 'Especially when I have had you brought all the way from England just to see you again.'

*Had you brought...* The words echoed in her head, menacing her.

'Then you've wasted your time, *signore*.' Was that how you

addressed the supposed cousin of an Italian countess? Polly had no idea, and didn't much care. 'Because I have no wish to see you.'

There was a bitter irony in this, she thought. This was supposed to be the first day of her new life, and instead she seemed to have walked into a trap.

Ironic, inexplicable—and dangerous too, she realised, a shiver chilling her spine.

The *contessa* had deliberately set her up, it seemed. So she must be in Sandro's power in some way. But however scaring that was, it couldn't be allowed to matter, Polly reminded herself swiftly. She didn't know what was going on here, nor did she want to know. The most important thing, now, was to distance herself, and quickly.

'"*Signore*"?' Sandro questioned, his mouth twisting. 'Isn't that a little formal—for us, *bella mia*?'

Her pulses quickened at the endearment, putting her instantly on the defensive.

'To me this is a formal occasion,' she said tautly. 'I'm work-ing—escorting the *contessa*. And there is no "us",' she added. 'There never was.'

'You don't think so?' The topaz eyes were watchful. 'Then I shall have to jog your memory, *cara*.'

'I can remember everything I need to, thanks.' Polly spoke fiercely. 'And it doesn't change a thing. You and I have nothing to say to each other. Not now. Not ever again.' She took a deep breath. 'And now I wish to leave.'

Sandro shook his head slowly. 'You are mistaken, *carissima*.' His voice was soft. 'There is a great deal to be said. Or else I would not be here. But perhaps it would be better if we spoke alone.'

He turned to the *contessa*. 'Would you excuse us, Zia Antonia?' His tone was coolly courteous. 'I think Signorina Fairfax and I should continue our conversation in private.'

'No.' Polly flung the word at him, aware that her voice was shaking. That her body was trembling too. 'I won't stay here— and you can't make me.'

He looked at her, his mouth relaxing into a faint smile. 'You don't think so, Paola *mia*? But you're so wrong.'

'*Contessa!*' Polly appealed as the older woman moved towards

the door. 'You had no right to do this. Don't leave me alone—
please.'

The *contessa* gave her a thin smile. 'You require a chaperone?'
she queried. 'But surely it is a little late for that?' She paused,
allowing her words to sting, then turned to Sandro. 'However,
Alessandro, Signorina Fairfax might feel more at ease if you conducted this interview in the *salotto*. A suggestion, merely.'

'I bow to your superior wisdom.' Sandro spoke briskly.

Before Polly could register what he intended, and take evasive
action, he had stepped forward, scooping her up into his arms as
if she were a child. She tried to hit him, but he controlled her
flailing hands, tucking her arms against her body with insulting
ease.

'Be still,' he told her. 'Unless, of course, you would prefer to
remain here.' He glanced significantly back at the bed.

'No, I would not.' She glared up into the dark, ruined face. 'But
I can walk.'

'When you are shaking like a leaf? I think not.'

In spite of her continuing struggles, Sandro carried her back
into the now deserted drawing room. The *contessa* had disappeared, Polly realised with a stab of panic, and, although neither
of them were her company of choice, it meant that she and Sandro
were now alone. Which was far worse...

'This was easier when you were unconscious,' he commented
as he walked across the room with her. 'Although I think you have
lost a little weight since our last meeting, Paola *mia*.'

'Put me down.' Polly was almost choking with rage, mingled
with the shock of finding herself in such intimately close proximity
to him. 'Put me down, damn you.'

'As you wish.' He lifted a shoulder nonchalantly, and dropped
her onto one of the sofas flanking the fireplace. She lay, winded
and gasping, staring up at him.

'You bastard,' she said unevenly, and he clicked his tongue in
reproach as he seated himself on the sofa opposite.

'What a name to call the man you are going to marry.'

'Marry?' The word strangled in her throat. Polly struggled to
sit up, pulling down the navy dress which had ridden up round
her thighs. 'You must be insane.'

He shrugged. 'I once asked you to be my wife. You agreed.'
He watched as she fumbled to re-fasten the buttons he'd undone,

his lips slanting into faint amusement. Looking so like Charlie that she almost cried out. 'That makes us *fidanzato*. Or am I wrong?'

'You're wrong,' she bit back at him, infuriated at her own awkwardness, and at the pain he still had the power to cause her. 'Totally and completely mistaken. And you know it, as well as I do, so let's stop playing games.'

'Is that what we're doing?' Sandro shrugged again. 'I had not realised. Perhaps you would explain the rules to me.'

'Not rules,' she said. 'But laws. Laws that exist to deal with someone like you.'

'*Dio*,' he said. 'So you think our government interests itself in a man's reunion with his woman? How enlightened of them.'

'Enlightened enough to lock you up for harassment,' Polly said angrily. 'And I am not your woman.'

He grinned at her, making her realise that the scar had done little to diminish the powerful sexual charisma he'd always been able to exert, which was as basic a part of him as the breath he drew. He was lounging on the sofa opposite, jacket discarded and tie loosened, his long legs thrust out in front of him, totally at his ease. Enjoying, she thought bitterly, his control of the situation. While she remained shaken and on edge, unable to comprehend what was happening. Or why. Especially why...

'No? Perhaps we should have stayed in the bedroom after all, *cara mia*, and continued the argument there.' The topaz eyes held a familiar glint.

'You dare to lay a hand on me again,' Polly said, through gritted teeth, 'and I'll go straight to the police—have you charged.'

'With what offence? The attempted seduction of my future bride?' He shook his head regretfully. 'A girl who once spent a summer as my lover. I don't think they would take you seriously, *carissima*.'

'No,' she said. 'I expect they have to do what you want—like the *contessa*. And where is she, by the way?'

'On her way back to Comadora, where she lives.'

'But she was supposed to be staying here.'

He shook his head. 'No, Paola *mia*. I reserved the suite for myself.' He smiled at her. 'And for you to share with me.'

'If this is a joke,' Polly said, recovering herself from a stunned silence, 'I don't find it remotely funny.'

'And nor do I,' Sandro said with sudden curtness. 'This is no game, believe me. I am entirely serious.' He paused. 'Do you wish to test my determination?'

He hadn't moved, but suddenly Polly found herself remembering the strength of the arms that had held her. Recognised the implacable will that challenged her from his gaze and the sudden hardening of the mobile, sensuous mouth which had once stopped her heart with its caresses.

She bit her lip, painfully. 'No.'

'You begin to show sense at last,' he approved softly.

'Not,' she said, 'when I agreed to come to Italy today. That was really stupid of me.'

'You must not blame Zia Antonia,' he said. 'She shares your disapproval of my methods.' He shrugged. 'But if you and I had not met again tonight, then it would have been at some other time, in some other place. Or did you think I would simply allow you to vanish?'

She said coldly, 'Yes, of course. In fact, I counted on it.'

His head came up sharply, and she saw the sudden tensing of his lean body. 'You were so glad to be rid of me?'

*You dare to say that—to me? After what you did?*

The words trembled on the tip of her tongue, but she fought them back. He must never know how she'd felt in those dazed, agonised weeks following his rejection. How she'd ached for him, drowning in bewilderment and pain. Pride had to keep her silent now. Except in defiance.

She shrugged in her turn. 'Do you doubt it?' she retorted. 'After all, when it's over, it's over,' she added with deliberate *sang-froid*.

'You may think that, *mia cara*.' His voice slowed to a drawl. 'I do not have to agree.'

She looked down at her hands, clamped together in her lap. 'Tell me something,' she said in a low voice. 'How did you find me?'

'I was at a conference on tourism. A video was shown of a British company which looks after single travellers. You were its star, *cara mia*. I was—most impressed.'

Polly groaned inwardly. Her one and only television appearance, she thought, that her mother had been so proud of. It had never occurred to her that it might be shown outside the UK.

She said coldly, 'And you were suddenly overwhelmed by nostalgia, I suppose.'

'If so,' Sandro said with equal chill, 'I would have sighed sentimentally and got on with my life. But it reminded me that there are issues still unresolved between us.' He paused. 'As you must know, also.'

She moistened her dry lips with the tip of her tongue. 'I need to say something. To tell you that—I've never talked about you. Never discussed anything that happened between us. And I wouldn't—I give you my word...'

He stared at her, frowning. 'You wished to wipe me from your memory? Pretend I had never existed? But why?'

She swallowed, her throat tightening. *Because it hurt too much to remember,* she thought.

'Once I discovered your—your background,' she said, 'I realised it was—necessary. The only way...'

His gaze became incredulous. 'It disturbed you to find that I was rich. You'd have preferred me to be a waiter, existing on tips?' He gave a short laugh. *'Dio mio.'*

Polly sat up very straight. She said coldly, 'It was the way you'd acquired your money that I found—unacceptable. And your—connections,' she added bravely, controlling a shiver as she remembered the man who had confronted her. The scorn and menace he'd exuded.

'Unbelievable,' he said slowly. 'But if you expect me to apologise for my family, Paola, you will wait a long time.' The look he sent her was hard—unrelenting. 'I am what I am, and nothing can change that. Nor would I wish it to.'

He was silent for a moment. *'Certamente,* I hoped—at one time—that you would find it possible to live in my world. Understand how it works, and accept its limitations.'

But you soon changed your mind about that, Polly thought painfully. In fact, once you realised that I'd never be suitable, you were willing to pay a small fortune to get me out of your life altogether—and I should be grateful for that. Relieved that you sent me away, and saved me from an impossible moral dilemma. Prevented me from making a choice I might have hated myself for later, when I was sane again...

And knowing that has to be my salvation now. Has to...

She said stiltedly, 'That could—never have happened. It was better—safer for us to part.'

'You think so?' He drew a harsh breath. 'Then how is it I have been unable to forget you, Paola *mia*, no matter how hard I have tried? Or how many other women there have been in my life since you?'

She lifted her chin, resisting the sudden anguish that stabbed her. 'Am I supposed to feel flattered?'

'You ask me about your emotions?' Sandro asked derisively. 'What did I ever know about your thoughts—your feelings? I saw what I wished to see—believed what I needed to believe.'

He shook his head. '*Madonna,* how many times in these long months I have wished I could simply—dismiss you from my mind.' He paused. 'Forget you as easily as you have rejected the memory of me.'

Oh, God, Polly thought numbly, how little you know...

She tried to speak evenly. 'Life doesn't remain static. It moves on—and we have to go with it.'

'Do you go alone?' Sandro enquired, almost negligently studying his fingernails. 'Or do you have company on your journey?'

Polly tensed. 'That,' she said, 'is no concern of yours.'

'Then let us make it my concern,' he said softly. 'Because I wish to know the truth. Do you live alone?'

The question seemed to hang in the air between them while her mind ran in frantic circles, looking for a way out.

Useless to go on telling him it was none of his business. That would not deter him. On the other hand, it would be a humiliation to admit that since him, there had been no one in her life. That she existed in self-imposed celibacy.

She could invent a lover, but she'd always been a terrible liar, and the risk of him seeing through her story was too great.

And then, as if a light had dawned, she realised there was no need for invention after all.

Polly lifted her chin, and faced him. 'No,' she said, very clearly. 'I don't live alone.'

It was no more than the truth, she thought. And it might just set her free...

Sandro was very still suddenly, little golden fires leaping in his eyes as his gaze met hers. He said, 'And, naturally, your companion is male?' He watched her swift, jerky nod.

There was another silence, then he said harshly, 'Do you love him?'

Unbidden, an image of Charlie's small sleeping face invaded

her mind, and her mouth curved involuntarily, instinctively into tenderness.

'Yes,' she said. 'And I always will.'

As soon as she spoke the words, she knew they were a mistake. That she'd snatched at a means of escape from him, without fully considering the consequences. And that she could have gone too far.

'You dare to tell me that?' His voice crackled with suppressed anger.

Her heart jolted nervously, but she knew that she had to finish what she'd started. That she had no other choice.

She tilted her chin defiantly. 'What did you expect? That I'd stay single in memory of you? Like you remained celibate for me?' she added scornfully. 'Dream on—please.'

Sandro's eyes were fixed on her, a slow flame burning in their depths. 'And how long has he been part of your life? The truth.'

She touched the tip of her tongue to her dry lips. 'Two years—or so.'

'So,' he said slowly. 'You went from my arms to his.' His gaze went over her, measuring and contemptuous. 'I see you wear no ring.'

She swallowed. 'That's my own choice.'

'And have you whispered the same promises to him that you once made to me?' His voice was quiet. Compelling.

She hesitated, choosing her words with care. 'He knows that I'll—always be there for him.'

'How touching,' Sandro said softly. 'Yet you left him to come to Italy.' His sudden smile was cool. Dangerous. 'And to me.'

'I believed I was working for the *contessa*,' Polly returned fiercely, trying to conceal the fact that she was shaking inside, nearing the edge of panic. 'I had no idea that she could be a relation of yours—or that you were even in the region. If I'd known, I wouldn't be here.'

She flung back her head. 'So, how did you persuade her to do your dirty work? Bribery—or blackmail?'

His mouth thinned. 'You are not amusing, *carissima*. Be very careful.'

'Why?' she challenged recklessly. 'I already know the lengths you're prepared to go to—when there's something you want.'

*Or when you've stopped wanting...*

*You sent me away,* she thought. *So why are you here now, tormenting me like this—reviving all these unwanted memories?*

Her throat ached suddenly at the thought of them. But that was a weakness she couldn't afford, because the room seemed to be shrinking, the walls closing in, diminishing the space between them. A space she needed to maintain at all costs.

'I wonder if that's true.' Sandro's voice was quiet—reflective. 'Perhaps you don't know me as well as you think.'

'Well,' she said, 'that hardly matters any more.' She paused. 'And I don't think there's much point in continuing this discussion either.'

His smile twisted. 'Then we agree on something at last.'

'So, if you can tell me where to find my shoes and jacket, I'll go.'

'Back to him? Your *innamorato*?'

'Back to my life,' Polly said, lifting her chin. 'In which you have no part, *signore*.'

'I can hardly argue with that,' Sandro shrugged. 'You will find your belongings in the bedroom, Paola *mia*.'

He did not, she noticed, offer to fetch them for her, as the Sandro she'd once known would have done.

Don't fool yourself, she thought as she trod, barefoot, into the bedroom and paused, looking around her. As he said—you never really knew him at all.

Her jacket and bag were on a small sofa by the window, her shoes arranged neatly beneath it. As she reached them she was aware of a sound behind her, and turned.

Sandro had followed her, she realised, her heart missing a beat. She hadn't been aware of his approach, because he too had discarded his shoes. But the noise she'd heard was the sound of the door closing behind him, shutting them in together.

And now he was leaning back against its panels, watching her with hooded eyes, his expression cool and purposeful as, with one hand, he began to unfasten the buttons on his shirt.

Polly felt the breath catch in her throat. With a supreme effort, she controlled her voice, keeping it steady. 'Another game, *signore*?'

'No game at all, *signorina*.' Cynically, he echoed her formality. 'As I am sure you know perfectly well.'

She had picked up her bag, and was holding it so tightly that the strap cut into her fingers. 'I—I don't know what you're talking about.'

Sandro tutted. 'Now you're being dishonest, *bella mia*, but I expected that.' He allowed his discarded shirt to drop to the floor, and began to walk towards her.

She swallowed. 'I think you must be going crazy.'

'Possibly,' he said with sudden harshness. 'And I want to be sane again.' He halted, the topaz eyes blazing at her. 'You are under my skin, Paola. In my blood, like a fever that refuses to be healed. And that is no longer acceptable to me. So, I plan to cure myself of you once and for all—and in the only possible way.'

'No.' She stared back at him, her appalled heart thudding frantically. 'No, Sandro. You can't do this. I—I won't let you.'

'You really believe you have a choice?' He gave a short laugh. 'I know better.'

She backed away until her retreat was cut off by the wall behind her. Until he reached her.

'Please, Sandro,' she whispered. 'Please let me go.'

He laughed again, touching a finger to her trembling lips, before outlining the curve of her jaw, and stroking down the delicate line of her throat to the neckline of her dress.

'Once I have finished with you, *carissima*,' he drawled insolently, 'you are free to go anywhere you wish.'

'Do you want me to hate you?' Her voice pleaded with him.

'I thought you already did.' Almost casually, he detached her bag from her grasp and tossed it to one side, his brows snapping together as he saw the marks on her skin.

He lifted both her hands to his lips, letting them move caressingly on the redness the leather strap had left.

'I had almost forgotten how easily you bruise.' His voice was low and husky. 'I shall have to be careful.'

Her whole body shivered at the touch of his mouth on her flesh, the aching, delirious memories it evoked. And the promise of further, dangerous delights in his whispered words.

A promise she could not allow him to keep.

She snatched her hands from his grip, and pushed violently at the bare, tanned wall of his chest, catching him off balance. As Sandro was forced into a step backwards, she dodged past, running for the door.

With no shoes and no money, she was going nowhere, but if

she could just get out of this bedroom it might be possible to reason with him—deflect him from his apparent purpose.

She flung herself at the door handle, twisted it one way, then the other, trying to drag the door open, but it wouldn't budge an inch, and she realised with horror that he must have locked it too—and taken the key.

'Trying to escape again.' His voice was sardonic, his hands hard on her shoulders as he swung her relentlessly to face him. 'Not this time, *bella mia*.' His smile mocked her. 'Not, at least, until you have said a proper goodbye to me.'

'Sandro.' Her voice cracked. 'You can't do this. You must let me go...'

'Back to your lover? Surely he can spare me a little of your time and attention first. After all, he has reaped the benefit of our previous association, wouldn't you say?' He paused. 'And, naturally, I am intrigued to know if your repertoire has increased since then.'

Her face was white, her eyes like emerald hollows, as she stared up at him, her skin seared by his words.

She said chokingly, 'You bastard.'

'If you insist on calling me bad names,' Sandro said softly, 'I have no option but to stop you speaking at all.' And his mouth came down hard on hers.

She tried to struggle—to pull away from him, so that she could talk to him—appeal, even on the edge, to his better nature. Tell him that his actions were an outrage—a crime. But what did that matter to someone who lived his life outside the law anyway? her reeling mind demanded.

Her efforts were in vain. The arm that held her had muscles of steel. At the same time, his free hand was loosening the dishevelled knot of her hair, his fingers twisting in its silky strands to hold her still for the ravishment of his kiss.

Her breasts were crushed against his naked chest. She could feel the warmth of his skin penetrating her thin dress. Felt the heat surge in her own body to meet it.

She heard herself moan faintly in anguished protest—pleading that this man, to whom she'd once given her innocence, would not now take her by force.

But Sandro used the slight parting of her lips for his own advantage, deepening the intimacy of his kiss with sensual intensity as his tongue invaded the moist sweetness of her mouth.

No sign now of the tenderness with which he'd caressed her fingers only moments ago. Just the urgency of a need too powerful to be denied any longer.

A fever in the blood, he'd called it, she thought in a kind of despair, her starved body craving him in turn. And how was it possible that she could feel like this? That she could want him so desperately in return?

When at last he raised his head, the scar on his face was livid against the fierce burn of colour along his taut cheekbones.

He said, 'Take off your dress,' his voice hoarse, shaken. And when he saw her hesitate, 'Or do you wish me to tear it off you?'

'No.' She sounded small and breathless. 'I—I'll do it.' She turned away from him, as her shaking fingers fought with the buttons. When half of them were loose, she pushed the navy linen from her shoulders, freeing her arms from the sleeves as she did so, and letting the dress fall to the floor.

She faced him slowly, her arms crossed defensively across her body, trying to conceal the scraps of white broderie anglaise that were now her only covering.

'But how delicious,' he said, softly. 'Bought for your lover?'

Polly shook her hair back from her face. 'I dress to please myself.'

'Ah,' he said. 'And now you will undress to please me. *Per favore*,' he added silkily.

She could hear nothing but the wild drumming of her own pulses, and the tear of her ragged breathing. See nothing but the heated flare of hunger in his eyes. A hunger without gentleness, demanding to be appeased.

And his hands reaching for her—like some ruthless hawk about to seize his prey.

Not like this, she thought in anguish. Oh, dear God, not like this. Not to lie naked in his arms and be taken—enjoyed for one night alone. To be used, however skilfully, just so that he could get her out of his system, only to find herself discarded all over again when his need for her was finally assuaged. And to be forced to go through all that suffering a second time—unappeased.

It was unthinkable—unbearable.

Her voice shook. 'Sandro—please—don't hurt me...'

She paused, knowing she was on the edge of complete self-betrayal here. Realising too that she must not let him see that he still had the power to inflict more misery on her.

The sudden silence was total. He was completely still, apart from a muscle which moved swiftly, convulsively in his throat.

When at last he spoke, his voice was hoarse. '*Dio mio*, you think that I'm going to rape you? That I might be capable of such a thing?' He shook his head. 'How could you believe that? It is an insult to everything we have ever been to each other.'

He lifted his hand, and touched the scar. 'This has only altered my face, Paola. It has not turned me into a monster.'

'I—I didn't mean...' Polly began, then bit her lip. This was a misunderstanding that she could not put right—not without the kind of explanation she was desperate to avoid, she told herself wretchedly.

'*Basta*,' Sandro said sharply. 'Enough.' He bent and retrieved his shirt from the floor, dragging it on with swift, jerky movements.

'Now dress yourself and go,' he instructed icily. 'And be quick. Otherwise I might lose all self-respect, and justify your low opinion of me. Punish you in the way you deserve,' he added grimly.

He went to the door, unlocked it, then turned.

'Remember this, *mia bella*.' His voice grated across her taut nerve-endings, just as his contemptuous gaze flayed her skin. 'Even if I had taken you there on the floor like the *sciattona* you are, it would still not have been rape.' He smiled at her with insolent certainty. 'You know it as well as I do, so do not fool yourself.

'Now, get out of my sight,' he added curtly, and left, slamming the door behind him.

# CHAPTER THREE

SHE had missed her plane, but eventually managed to catch the last flight of the evening, thanks to a no-show.

Her escape from the hotel had been easier than she could have hoped. She had dressed quickly, her shaking hands fumbling so badly with the buttons on her dress that she had to begin again.

Then she'd wasted precious moments listening tautly at the door for some sound from the room beyond. Dreading that Sandro might be waiting there for her, still angry and possibly vengeful.

But when she had finally risked taking a look, the room was completely deserted, and she left on the run. The hotel commissionaire had summoned a cab for her, allotting her dishevelled state a discreetly impassive glance.

She had prowled around the airport, her eyes everywhere. Terrified that he might change his mind, and come to find her. To prevent her from leaving. Even when she presented her boarding card, she was half expecting his hand to reach over her shoulder and take it from her.

When the plane finally took off, she was almost sick with relief. She ordered a double brandy from the stewardess, and fell asleep before she'd drunk half of it.

She took a cab from the airport to her flat, unlocking the door and falling inside in the same movement. There was a strange empty chill about the place that she had never experienced before, that seemed to match the cold hollow inside her.

A voice in her head whispered, 'You're safe—you're safe...' But somehow she couldn't believe it. She even found herself picking her way in the darkness to her living-room window, and drawing the curtains before she switched on the lights.

Then she sank down on the sofa, and tried to stop trembling.

I didn't suspect a thing, she thought. To me, the *contessa* was simply another very demanding client, nothing more—but it was all a trick.

She had to be deeply in Sandro's power to agree to something

36

like that, Polly told herself, and shivered as she remembered how nearly she'd surrendered to that power herself.

Oh, God, she thought. He only had to touch me...

But it had always been like that. From the first time his hand had taken hers as they walked together, her body had responded with wild yearning to his touch. She had hungered and thirsted for his mouth on hers—for the brush of his fingers over her ardent flesh. For the ultimate mystery of his body joined to hers.

Sandro had enraptured her every sense, and she had mistaken that for love. And he had cynically allowed that—had said the words she wanted to hear—whispered the promises that would keep her enthralled until he chose to leave her.

She'd been just one more girl in his bed, easily discarded, instantly replaced. Except that he'd caught a fleeting glimpse of her on television and discovered, for some inexplicable reason, that he still wanted her.

Sandro Domenico, she thought painfully. A man rich enough to pay for his whims, and powerful enough to pull the strings that would satisfy them.

And yet he'd let her go, outraged at the idea that he could rape her physically, but too arrogant to realise he'd already done far worse damage to her emotionally.

Still, it was over now, and she had nothing more to fear. She'd insulted his sense of honour, such as it was, and he would never come near her again.

In fact, she'd got off comparatively lightly, she told herself. Yes, she was bruised by his anger and disgust, but she'd recover from that—given time. And her future held plenty of that.

In some ways, it all seemed like a bad dream—some torment dredged up from the depths of her unconscious. But the faint lingering tenderness of her lips forced her to face reality.

Wincing, she touched her mouth with her fingertips, telling herself that it could all have been so much worse. That at this moment, she might have been in his bed, and in his arms, with a whole new cycle of heartbreak and regret to endure.

For all she knew he could be married to someone 'suitable'. A dynastic union from the criminal network he belonged to, she thought with a pang.

But she—she was all right, she rallied herself. She'd had a narrow escape, that was all.

Just the same, her vague plans for a change of location had become a firm resolve as a result of the past twenty-four hours.

She and Charlie would move, somewhere anonymous and preferably far away. And, to ensure she could never be so easily traced again, she'd find out the legal implications of changing her name.

Drastic measures, she thought, but, in view of her recent scare, perfectly justified.

She stripped in her tiny bathroom, putting her clothing in the laundry basket, then took a shower, scrubbing herself from top to toe, and even shampooing her hair to make sure she erased every trace of him.

She only wished she could wash away the memories of the heated pressure of his mouth, and the familiar, arousing scent of his skin just as easily.

Dear God, she thought, towelling her hair with more than necessary vigour, that is—frighteningly pathetic.

She put on her cotton housecoat, belting it securely round her slim waist, and trailed into the kitchen.

She needed a hot drink, but not with the additional stimulus of caffeine. She'd have enough trouble sleeping as it was through what little was left of the night.

No, she'd have a herbal tea instead, she decided. A *tisana* at bedtime was a habit she'd acquired in Italy. One of the good ones, she amended wryly.

While the kettle was boiling, she wandered back into the living room, and, for reasons she couldn't properly explain, crossed to the window, and pulled back the edge of the curtain slightly.

The road below seemed empty, or was there an added density among the shadows opposite, in a gateway just out of the range of the street light?

No, she thought, hurriedly letting the curtain fall back into place. It was simply her imagination. Sandro had traced her through her work, simply and easily, so there was no need for him to compile a complete dossier on her.

Because if he'd done so, he'd have realised at once that her 'live-in lover' was pure invention, and told her so. And he'd have known, too, about Charlie...

She turned her head, staring at the chest of drawers, and the framed photograph that occupied pride of place. Charlie, on his second birthday. His father's image smiling at her.

Sandro's out of your life, she told herself feverishly. He's gone.

Nevertheless, on the way back to the kitchen, Polly found herself taking Charlie's portrait off the chest, and stowing it in the top drawer instead.

Better, she thought, safe than sorry, and shivered again.

Polly slept badly, in spite of her *tisana*. When morning came, she telephoned Safe Hands, said quite truthfully that she felt like death, then crawled back into bed and slept until lunchtime.

She woke with a start, thinking of Charlie. Why was she wasting time, when she could have the bonus of a whole afternoon in his company without the distractions of shopping and housework?

She rang her mother's house but there was no reply, so she left a message on the answering machine to say she would be over to collect him in an hour.

She took a quick shower, then dressed in a casual blue denim skirt, topping it with a crisp white cotton shirt, and sliding her feet into flat brown leather sandals. She brushed her hair back from her face and secured it at the nape of her neck with a silver barette, and hung small blue enamel cornflowers on delicate silver chains from her earlobes.

She had some work to do with the blusher and concealer she kept for emergencies, or her mother would guess something was wrong. And Polly had enough bad news to give her without mentioning Sandro's shock reappearance in her life.

But that was all over, so there was no need to cause her further distress, she told herself firmly, applying her lipstick and attempting an experimental smile which, somehow, turned into a wry grimace.

Positive thinking, she adjured herself, and, grabbing her bag, she left.

The house seemed unusually quiet when she let herself in, and Polly paused, frowning a little. Surely her mother hadn't taken Charlie out somewhere, she thought, groaning inwardly. Was this the latest move in the battle of wits between them? She hoped not.

She kept her voice deliberately cheerful. 'Mum—Dad—are you there?'

'We're in the living room.' It was her mother's voice, high-pitched and strained.

Her frown deepening, Polly pushed open the door and walked in.

It wasn't a particularly large room, and her instant impression was that it had shrunk still further in some strange way.

The first person she saw was her mother, sitting in the chair beside the empty fireplace, her face a mask of tension, and Charlie clasped tightly on her lap.

The second was a complete stranger, stockily built with black hair and olive skin, who rose politely from the sofa at her entrance.

And the third, unbelievably, was Sandro, standing silently in the window alcove, as if he had been carved out of granite.

For a moment the room seemed to reel around her, then she steadied herself, her hands clenching into fists, her nails scoring her palms. She was *not*, under any circumstances, going to faint again.

She said hoarsely, 'What the *hell* are you doing here?'

'Is it not obvious?' The topaz eyes were as fierce as a leopard's, and as dangerous. His voice was ice. 'I have come for my son. And please do not try to deny his parentage,' he added bitingly. 'Because no court in the world would believe you. He is my image.' He paused. 'But I warn you that I am prepared to undergo DNA testing to prove paternity, if it becomes necessary.'

Polly stared at him, her stomach churning, her heart pounding against her ribs. 'You must be mad.'

'I was.' His smile was grim. 'Before I discovered quite what a treacherous little bitch you are, Paola *mia*. But now I am sane again, and I want my child.'

Her low voice shook. 'Over my dead body.'

He said softly, 'The way I feel at this moment, that could easily be arranged. Do not provoke me any further.'

'He's going to take him away from us,' her mother wailed suddenly. 'Take him to Italy. I'll never see him again.'

Horror caught Polly by the throat. She turned on Sandro. 'You can't do that.'

'And what is there to stop me?' His glance challenged her.

'It—it's kidnapping,' Polly flung at him. She took a breath. 'Although I suppose that's an everyday occurrence in your world.'

And it was more common than she wanted to admit in her own,

she thought numbly. There'd been numerous headlines in the papers over the past few years where children had been snatched and taken abroad by a parent. They called them 'tug of love' babies...

She looked with scorn at the other man, who had got quietly to his feet. 'And what are you—another of his tame thugs?'

His brows rose. 'My name is Alberto Molena, *signorina*, and I am a lawyer. I act for the *marchese* in this matter.'

Polly gave him a scornful glance. 'Don't you mean you're his *consigliere*?' she queried with distaste.

He paused, sending Sandro a surprised look. 'May I suggest that you sit down, Signorina Fairfax, and remain calm? It would be better too if the little boy was taken to another room. I think he's becoming frightened.'

'I have a better suggestion,' Polly flared. 'Why don't you and your dubious client get out of here, and leave us alone?'

His tone was still quiet, still courteous. 'I'm afraid that isn't possible. You must understand that your child is the first-born son, and thus the heir of the Marchese Valessi, and that he intends to apply through the courts for sole custody of the boy. Although you will be permitted proper access, naturally.'

He looked at Charlie, who was round-eyed, his knuckles pushed into his mouth. 'But, believe me, it would be better if the little boy was spared any more upset from this discussion. We have a trained nanny waiting to look after him.'

He walked to the door and called. A pleasant-faced girl in a smart maroon uniform came in and removed Charlie gently but firmly from his grandmother's almost frenzied grasp, talking to him softly as she carried him out of the room.

'Where's she taking him?' Polly demanded shakily.

'Into the garden,' the lawyer told her, adding less reassuringly, 'For the time being.'

She swallowed convulsively, turning to the silent man by the window. 'Sandro.' Her voice was pleading, all pride forgotten. 'Please don't do this. Don't try to take him away from me.'

'I have already been deprived of the first two years of his life,' he returned implacably. 'There will be no more separation.' His lip curled. 'How remiss of you, *cara mia*, not to inform me of his existence. Even last night, when we talked so intimately about your living arrangements, you said nothing—gave no hint that you had borne me a child. Did you really think you could keep him hidden forever?'

She moistened her dry lips. 'How—how did you find out?'

He shrugged. 'I employed an agency to trace you. They suggested broadening the scope of their enquiries.' His voice was expressionless. 'I received their full report last night after you left. It made fascinating reading.'

She stared down at the carpet. 'So there was someone watching me when I got back,' she said almost inaudibly.

'Can you wonder?' Sandro returned contemptuously. 'I have a beautiful son, Paola, and you deliberately barred me from his life. You preferred to struggle alone than ask me for help—or give me the joy of knowing I was a father.' His gaze was cold, level. 'How can such a thing be forgiven?'

'It was over between us.' Polly lifted her chin. 'What did you expect me to do—beg?'

'I think,' he said softly, 'that is something you may have to learn for the future.'

There was a silence. Polly could hear her mother weeping softly.

'No court in the world,' she said huskily, 'would take a baby away from his mother.'

'Yet it is his grandmother who has the care of him each day.' His tone was harsh. 'I was watching when you came into the room, and he did not try to go to you. Is he even aware that you are his mother?'

Polly gasped, and her head went back as if he had slapped her.

She said unsteadily, 'I go out to work to support us both. As the *contessa* has probably told you, the hours can be long and difficult. But I needed the money, so I had no choice.'

'Yes,' he said, his voice quiet and cold. 'You did. You could have chosen me. All that was needed was one word—one sign.'

There was an odd intensity in his voice, which startled and bewildered her. And also rekindled her anger.

He talks, she thought, as if I deserted him.

A sudden noise from her mother—something between a sigh and a groan—distracted her, and she went over and sat on the arm of her chair, putting an arm round her shoulders.

Oh, God, she thought. To think I was going to tell her that I was taking Charlie away. But how could I have guessed this was going to happen?

'It's going to be all right, Mum,' she said softly. 'I promise.'

'How can it be?' Mrs Fairfax demanded, almost hysterically. 'He's going to take my little treasure to Italy, and I can't bear it.' She reared up from Polly's sheltering arm, glaring venomously at Sandro, who was regarding her with narrowed eyes, his mouth hard and set. 'How dare you come here, ruining our lives like this?' she stormed. 'Get out of my house. And never come back.'

'You are not the only one to suffer, *signora*.' His tone was almost dismissive. He looked at Polly. 'But it would be better for my son to be looked after by someone else until the custody hearing. The nanny I have engaged will move in with you.'

'She can't,' Polly told him curtly. 'My flat is far too small for that.'

He shrugged. 'Then you will be found somewhere else to live.'

'I don't want that,' she said raggedly. 'I don't want anything from you. I just need you to go, and leave us in peace.'

'The *marchese* is being generous, Signorina Fairfax,' Alberto Molena intervened unexpectedly. 'He could ask for the child to be transferred to the care of a temporary guardian while the custody issue is decided.'

'And, of course, he's so sure he'll get custody.' Polly got to her feet, her eyes blazing. 'So bloody arrogant and all-conquering. But what court's going to hand over a baby to someone with his criminal connections? And I'll make sure they know all about his underworld background,' she added defiantly. 'Whatever the cost.'

There was a stunned silence. Then Sandro muttered, *'Dio mio,'* and turned sharply, walking back to the window, his fists clenched at his sides.

Signor Molena's voice was hushed. 'I think you're making a grave mistake, *signorina*. Since the death of his father, the *marchese* has become head of an old and much respected family in southern Italy, and chairman of a business empire with strong interests in the tourist industry among other things.'

He spread his hands almost helplessly. 'You must surely have heard of the Comadora chain of hotels? They are internationally famous.'

'Yes.' Polly had to force suddenly numbed lips to form the words. Her shocked gaze went from his embarrassed face to Sandro's rigid back. 'Yes, I know about them.'

Signor Molena paused, awkwardly. 'And *marchese* means

''marquis'' in your language. It is an aristocratic title, not what you seem to think.' He shook his head. 'To suggest that any member of the Valessi family has ever been linked with criminal elements would be a serious slander if it were not so laughable.'

Polly had never felt less like laughing in her entire life. If she'd been cold before, she was now consumed in an agony of burning humiliation, blushing from her feet to the top of her head.

She wrapped her arms defensively round her body. 'I—I'm sorry,' she mumbled.

Behind her, her mother moaned faintly, and sank back in her chair.

Sandro turned slowly and studied them both reflectively. When he spoke his voice was calm but there was no sign of softening in his attitude.

'That is what you thought?' he asked. 'What you really believed, in spite of everything? It almost defies belief. Almost,' he added quietly, 'but not quite. And it explains a great deal.'

He paused. 'I understand from the *signora*, your mother, that your father is at his office. Perhaps he could be fetched. I do not think that she should be alone.'

Polly shook herself into action. 'Yes—yes, I'll telephone him. And her doctor...' She went out into the hall, standing helplessly for a moment as she tried to remember the number. Realising her mind was a blank.

Sandro followed, closing the door of the living room behind him.

She didn't look at him, doggedly turning the leaves of the directory. 'What—what will happen now?'

'The legal process will begin. But for tonight you may take Carlino to sleep at your *appartamento*.'

'Thank you,' she said with irony.

'The *bambinaia*, whose name is Julie Cole, will accompany you to put him to bed,' he went on, as if she hadn't spoken. 'Then she will return in the morning at seven o'clock to take care of him.'

He spoke as if he was conducting a board meeting, Polly thought incredulously, rather than trying to destroy her life.

She said, 'We could all stay here, perhaps. There's—plenty of room.'

'No,' he said. 'This is not an environment I want for my son.' Why? she wanted to cry. Because it's an ordinary suburban house rather than a *palazzo*? Just as I was an ordinary girl, and therefore not deemed as a suitable candidate to become your *marchesa*?

She could see now why it had been so important to pay her off, in order to get rid of her. There was too much at stake dynastically to allow a mistake like herself to enter the equation.

The old pain was back like a knife twisting inside her. A pain that her pride forbade her to let him see. So she would never ask the question 'Why did you leave me?' because she now knew the answer to that, beyond all doubt.

Besides, it would expose the fact that she cared, and that he still had the power to hurt her. And she needed that to remain her secret, and her solitary torment.

Besides, at the moment she was faced with all the suffering she could handle.

Unless she could divert him from his purpose somehow, she thought. Unless...

She picked up the phone irresolutely, then put it down again. She said quickly, before her courage ran out, 'Sandro, it doesn't have to be like this. Surely we could work something out. Share custody in some way.'

His mouth thinned. 'I am expected to trust you? When you have deliberately kept our child from me and even claimed to have a lover to sustain the deception? How much do you think your word is worth?'

Polly swallowed. 'I don't blame you for being angry.'

'*Mille grazie.*' His tone was sardonic.

'And maybe doing my best to be Charlie's mother hasn't been good enough,' she went on, bravely. 'But he doesn't know you at all, and if he was just whisked off to another country among strangers, however well-meaning, he'd be disorientated—scared. He—he's shy with people at first.'

'A trait he shares with you, *mia bella*, if memory serves,' Sandro drawled with cool mockery.

She remembered too. Recalled how gentle and considerate he had been that first time in bed together. How he'd coaxed her out of her clothes and her initial inhibitions.

She flushed hotly and angrily. 'May we cut out the personal reminiscences?' she requested curtly.

He shrugged. 'It is difficult to see how. Making a child together is an intensely personal matter.' He paused. 'And by the time I take Carlino to Italy, we will be well acquainted with each other. I guarantee that. And my own old nurse, Dorotea, will be waiting to look after him. The transition will not be too hard.'

But it will be agony for me, she thought, her throat tightening convulsively. First I lost you, and now you're trying to take Charlie away. And already I feel as if I'm dying inside.

She said tonelessly, 'I'd better make those calls.'

He inclined his head courteously, and went past her, and out into the garden.

Presently, distant but gleeful, Charlie's laughter came to her on the light summer wind, and she stood, staring in front of her unseeingly, her teeth sunk so deeply into her lower lip that she could taste blood.

She wanted to hate Julie Cole, but it was impossible. She was too kind, too tactful, and she thought that Charlie was heaven on legs.

And if she knew that her job was more for security than enjoyment, she kept that to herself.

The creamy scrambled eggs she made for supper were good too, and Charlie loved the triangles of buttered toast that went with them, although Polly could barely force her portion past the sick, scared lump in her throat.

She had wanted to wait at the house to talk to her father, or perhaps just put her head down on his shoulder and cry out her fear, but suddenly there was a car and driver at the gate, and Sandro was insisting quietly but implacably that she should take Charlie home.

She'd begun a protest, but Sandro had simply looked at her, his brows lifted haughtily, questioningly, and the words seemed to stutter and die on her lips.

'You begin to learn,' he had approved coldly.

She had been shaken to find him carrying Charlie down to the car in his arms, and found herself hoping that the little boy would have one of his infrequent tantrums, kicking, screaming and reaching for her as proof that no one else would do.

He didn't; nor did he burst into tears when Sandro had gently but firmly removed his thumb from his mouth.

She had said defensively, 'He doesn't really do that any more. Only when he's tired—or frightened.'

'All the more reason, then, to take him home,' Sandro had retorted unarguably.

She could only imagine the kind of scene that would erupt once her father returned, and her mother had some solid support.

'I'll make your father sell the house,' she'd hissed at Polly as she was leaving. 'Marquis or not, I'm going to fight this man through every court in the land.'

Polly sighed silently. She really doesn't know what she's up against, she thought unhappily. And I'm only just beginning to find out, too.

Only twenty-four hours ago or less, she'd been planning for her life to change, but not to this extreme, catastrophic extent. She'd seen a period of struggle ahead, but never the bleak desert of loneliness that now threatened her.

'He may not win,' she thought. And only realised she'd spoken aloud when Julie said, 'Are you all right, Miss Fairfax?'

Polly jumped, then mustered an attempt at a smile. 'Yes, fine,' she lied.

Julie studied her dubiously. 'I saw some white wine in the fridge while I was getting the eggs. Why don't you sit down and put your feet up, while I do the dishes, and then I'll bring you a glass?'

I don't want a glass, thought Polly. I want a bottle, a cellar, a whole vineyard. I want the edges of my pain blurred, and to be able to stop thinking.

She cleared her throat. 'I know Sandro—the *marchese*—instructed you to put Charlie to bed, but I'd really like to do it myself, if you wouldn't mind.'

'Sure, Miss Fairfax.' Was that compassion in the other girl's voice? 'Anything you say.'

Charlie was tired, and more than a little grumpy, especially when he realised his usual playtime in the bath was going to be curtailed. By the time she'd wrestled him into his pyjamas, Polly felt limp, and close to tears.

'Let me take him.' Julie spoke gently behind her. 'You look all in.'

Polly submitted, standing in his doorway, while her grizzling son was tucked in deftly and firmly.

He'll never settle, she told herself with a kind of sour triumph, only to be confounded when he was fast asleep within five minutes.

She stood at the side of the cot, watching the fan of dark lashes on his cheek, and the small mouth pursed in slumber. She ached to snatch him up and hold him. To run with him into the night to a place where they would never be found.

But she was crying for the moon, and she knew it. Even if there was such a place, she hadn't enough money to go on the run, or enough skill to outwit Sandro for long. And she couldn't afford to provoke his wrath again. She needed to reason with him—to persuade—even to plead, if she had to. Besides, on a purely practical level, instinct warned her that if she attempted to leave, whoever waited in the shadows opposite would step out and prevent her from going.

She sank down onto the floor, and leaned her head against the bars of the cot, listening to Charlie's soft, even breathing. And thinking of all the nights of silence that could be waiting for her.

When she finally returned to the other room, she discovered gratefully that the sofa bed had been opened and made up for the night, and the glass of wine was waiting with a note that said, 'See you in the morning. J.'

She took a first sip, then carried the wine into the bathroom, and began to half fill the tub with warm water, softened by a handful of foaming bath oil. No shower tonight, she told herself. She wanted to relax completely.

She took off her clothes and slid with a sigh into the scented water, reaching for her wineglass.

It would help her sleep, she thought. And tomorrow, when she was more rested, things might seem better. After all, she knew now the worst that could happen to her, and there must be a way of dealing with it that would not leave her utterly bereft.

She leaned back, resting her head on the rim of the bath, and closing her eyes.

Yes, tomorrow she would make plans. Find out if she qualified for legal aid, and get herself a lawyer of her own. Someone who would negotiate with Sandro on her behalf, and allow her to maintain some kind of distance from him.

I really need to do that, she thought. To stay calm—and aloof. I can fight him better that way.

And at that moment, as if he were some demon she'd conjured

up from her own private hell, she heard his voice, low, mocking and far too close at hand.

'Falling asleep in the bath, *mia bella*? That will never do. Surely you don't wish Carlino to become motherless so soon?'

# CHAPTER FOUR

POLLY started violently, giving a strangled cry of alarm as the glass jerked and the wine spilled everywhere.

She looked round and saw Sandro leaning in the doorway, watching her with cool amusement.

She tried to sit up, remembered just in time that there weren't enough bubbles to cover her, slipped on the oily surface, and was nearly submerged. She grabbed the rim of the bath, gasping in rage, and saw Sandro walking towards her.

'Keep away from me.' Her voice rose in panic.

'I am coming to rescue your glass, nothing more,' he countered silkily. 'If it breaks, you could hurt yourself badly.' He took it from her hand. 'Besides, how shameful if I had to tell people that the mother of my child drowned while drunk,' he added, his mouth slanting into a grin.

'Just keep me out of your conversations,' Polly said hotly, aware she was blushing under his unashamed scrutiny. 'How the hell did you get in here?'

'I told Julie not to lock the door when she left.'

'You did what?' Polly almost wailed. 'Oh, God, how could you? You realise what she'll think?'

He shrugged. 'I am not particularly concerned.' He gave her a dry look. 'Anyway, I imagine one look at Carlino told her all that she needs to know. We cannot hide that we once had a relationship.'

'Yes,' she said. 'With the emphasis on the "once". But not now, and not ever again, so will you please get out of here? Before I call the police,' she added for good measure.

Sandro shook his head reprovingly. 'Your skills as a hostess seem sadly lacking, *cara mia*. Perhaps you feel at a disadvantage for some reason?'

'Or maybe I prefer company I actually invited here,' Polly threw back at him. 'And you'll never be on any guest-list of mine.'

'You entertain much, do you—in this box? I'm sure you find

the sofa that turns into a bed a convenience—for visitors who linger.'

'This is my home,' she said. 'And I assure you it caters for all my needs.' She paused. 'Now I'd like you to go.'

Quite apart from anything else, it was uncomfortable and undignified crouching below the rim of the bath like this. And the water was getting colder by the minute, she thought angrily.

His brows lifted. 'Without knowing why I am here? Aren't you a little curious, Paola *mia*?'

'I can't think of one good reason for you to inflict yourself on me again,' she told him raggedly. 'Can't you understand you're the last person I want to see?' She sent him a hostile glance. 'Unless you've come to tell me that you've had a change of heart, and you've decided not to proceed with the custody application.'

'No,' Sandro said gently. 'I have not. I simply felt that we should talk together in private. Maybe even in peace. Who knows?'

'I know.' Her voice was stormy. 'And we have nothing to discuss. You want to rob me of my son? I'm going to fight you every step of the way. And my parents will be behind me.'

'No.' Sandro inclined his head almost regretfully. 'They will not.' He raised the glass he was still holding. 'Now, I am going to pour you some more wine. I think you are going to need it.'

He allowed her to absorb that, then continued. 'So, I suggest you stop trying to hide in that inadequate bath, and join me in the other room.' He took a towel from the rail and tossed it to her, then walked out, closing the door behind him.

Polly scrambled to her feet, holding the towel defensively against her as she stepped out gingerly onto the mat. She began to dry herself with hasty, clumsy hands, keeping an apprehensive eye on the door in case Sandro chose to return.

Not that she could do much about it even if he did, she thought, grimacing. And it was ridiculous, anyway, behaving like some Victorian virgin in front of a man who'd seen her naked so many times before. Someone who'd kissed and caressed every inch of the bare skin she was now so anxious to conceal.

Instead of this burning self-consciousness, she should have pretended it didn't matter. Demonstrated her complete and utter indifference to his presence whether she was dressed or undressed.

Fine in theory, she thought. But much trickier in practice.

Especially if Sandro had interpreted her apparent sang-froid as provocation...

Her mouth felt suddenly dry, forcing her to abandon that train of thought for one just as disturbing. What was that comment about her parents meant to imply? What had been said in her absence—and, dear God, what pressure had been brought to bear?

She needed to find out, and quickly.

She looked down at the small pile of clothing she'd discarded earlier. Common sense suggested she should put it back on. Use it as part of the armour her instinct assured her that she was going to need.

But in the end, she opted for the elderly cotton robe hanging on the back of the door. It was plain and prim, without an ounce of seduction in its unrevealing lines, she thought, fastening the sash in a tight double bow. Her equivalent of a security blanket, perhaps.

Then, drawing a deep breath, she squared her shoulders and marched defiantly into the living room, only to halt, disconcerted, when she found it deserted.

The door to Charlie's room was ajar, however, and she ran, stumbling slightly on the skirts of her robe, and pushed it open.

Sandro's back was to the door, but he was bending over Charlie's cot, his hands reaching down, and she felt her heart miss a beat. Was he planning to snatch her baby while he thought she was safely in the bathroom?

'What are you doing in here?' she hissed. 'Don't touch him. Don't dare.'

Sandro straightened, and turned. 'I saw this on the floor.' He held up a small brown teddy bear. 'I was replacing it.' He paused. 'And I came in simply to watch my son sleep. A pleasure that has been denied me for the past two years,' he added coldly.

'And which you want to deny me permanently,' Polly flung at him, tight-lipped.

His smile was wintry. 'Just as you would have done to me, *mia cara*, if fate had not intervened,' he returned unanswerably.

He held the door, allowing her to precede him back into the living room.

He looked round him, his expression disparaging. 'And this is where you have allowed him to spend the beginning of his life? In this *conigliera*?'

'And what precisely does that mean?'

'A hutch,' he said. 'For rabbits.'

She bit her lip. The room did seem to have shrunk suddenly, or was it just the effect of Sandro's presence? And the bed being open and made up didn't help either. In fact it was a serious embarrassment.

'It was all I could afford at the time,' she said. 'And it works,' she added defiantly, thinking of the hours she'd spent painting the walls, and stripping and stencilling the small chest of drawers which held Charlie's things, and which just fitted into his room. He gave no credit, either, she thought bitterly, for the way she kept the place neat and spotless.

'One word from you,' he said harshly, 'one hint that you were *incinta*, and it would all have changed. My son would have come into the world at Comadora, in the bed where I was born, and my father and grandfather before me.' He took her by the shoulder, whirling her to face him. His voice was passionate. '*Dio*, Paola, why did you not tell me? How could you let me exist without knowing?'

'Because we were no longer together.' She freed herself from his grasp. 'I made a decision that my baby was going to be part of my life only, and that I wanted nothing from you.' She paused. 'Didn't I make that clear enough at the time?'

'More than clear.' His mouth twisted. 'What I could not understand was—why.' He frowned. 'You could not have truly believed I was Mafioso. That is impossible—*assurdo*.'

'Why not? It was evident there were things you hadn't told me,' Polly countered. 'Things you didn't want me to know.' She shrugged. 'What was I supposed to think?'

'Not, perhaps, to give me the benefit of the doubt?'

'No,' she said. 'Any more than you decided to tell me the truth. And I expect we both had our reasons.'

'*Sì,*' Sandro said quietly. 'But I also have regrets, which you do not seem to share.'

'You're wrong.' She looked down at the floor. 'I wish very much that I had never met you.'

'Unfortunately for us both, the situation cannot be changed.' His voice was a drawl. He picked up her refilled glass from the chest of drawers and handed it to her. 'Shall we drink to our mistakes?'

Polly realised she was holding the glass as if it might explode. 'This isn't a social occasion,' she reminded him tautly. 'You said you came here to talk.'

'And I would do so,' he said, 'if I thought you were in any mood to listen.' He paused. 'I had better fortune with your parents.'

Polly stiffened. 'What have you been saying to them? If you've threatened them...'

He gave her a weary look. 'With what? A cattle prod, perhaps?' His mouth curled. 'Once again, you are allowing your imagination to run away with you, *mia cara*.'

She flushed. 'You're trying to tell me they gave up without a fight. I don't believe it.'

'Your mother, I think, would have gone to any lengths to thwart me,' he said. 'Your father, however, was more reasonable.'

'He thinks I should simply hand Charlie over to you?' Her voice broke on a little sob. 'Oh, how could he?'

'No, he knows that even if he made the kind of sacrifices your mother was demanding, he would still not have the financial resources for a lengthy court battle.' His smile was brief and hard. 'Especially if it took place in Italy,' he added softly.

The colour deepened in her face. 'You'll go to any lengths— pull any dirty trick to win, won't you?' she accused in a stifled voice.

Sandro shrugged. 'I see little point in losing, *bella mia*,' he returned. 'But I am prepared to offer a draw—a negotiated settlement.'

She stared at him. 'Would it mean that Charlie stayed with me?'

'That would depend on you,' he said. 'Carlino is coming to Italy with me. As my son, he needs to learn about his heritage. I am merely inviting you to accompany him.'

'As what? Some kind of glorified nanny?' she demanded. She shook her head. 'I think I'd rather have my day in court.'

'He already has a nanny,' Sandro told her evenly. 'And another waiting in Italy to love him. But what he really needs is the stability of both parents in his life. So, Paola *mia*, I am asking you once again, as I did three years ago, to be my wife.'

For a long, dazed moment Polly was too shaken to speak.

At last, she said huskily, 'Is this some grotesque joke?'

'No,' he said. 'We are, if you remember, already engaged to each other,' he added cynically.

Her breathing quickened. 'Was I really supposed to believe that—that nonsense? I—I don't think so. And whatever happened between us, it was all over a long time ago, and you know it. You can't simply revive it—on a whim.'

'Very well, then,' Sandro returned equably. 'Let us forget it ever took place. Pretend that, for the first time, I am making you an offer of marriage, Paola *mia*.'

She shook her head. 'But you don't—you can't want to marry me.'

'I have no particular desire to be married at all,' he retorted. 'But there are good reasons why I should sacrifice my freedom.'

'Your freedom?' Polly almost choked. 'What about mine?'

He looked around him. 'You call this liberty? Working long hours. Living in little more than one room? I don't think so.'

'I could always sue you for child support.' She drew a breath. 'That would improve my circumstances by a hundred per cent.'

'But I am already offering to support our child—as the Marchese Valessi,' he said silkily. 'Besides, our marriage would remove any possible objections to Carlino's right to inherit when the time comes, and it would mean that his well-being and nurture becomes the concern of us both from day to day.' He paused. 'I suggest it as a practical alternative to a custody battle.'

'Which I might win,' she said swiftly.

'You might, but could you fight the appeal which would follow?' Sandro countered. 'Or the appeal against the appeal?' His smile was chilly. 'The case might last for years.'

'Or until I run out of money, of course,' she said bitterly. 'You don't need a cattle prod, *signore*.'

His brows lifted. 'You regard marriage to me as some kind of torture, *signorina*?' he asked softly. 'Then perhaps I should make something clear to you at once. What I am offering is only a matter of form. A way of legalising the situation between us. But it would not be a love match. Too much has taken place for that. We would share nothing more than a roof, if that is what concerns you.'

He gave her a level look. 'I accept now that any feelings we had for each other belong in the past. That we are different people, and we have both moved on.'

'You say that now.' Her voice was husky. 'Yet only last night you told me I was still in your blood.'

'But a lot has happened since then,' Sandro said harshly. 'And my feelings towards you have naturally changed as a result.' He paused. 'Now our child remains the only issue between us, and his ultimate welfare should be our sole consideration. You agree with that, I hope?'

Polly nodded numbly.

'*Bene,*' he said briskly. 'In return, I promise that your life as the Marchesa Valessi will be as easy as I can make it. You will be made a suitable allowance, and asked occasionally to act as my hostess.' His smile was hard. 'But you may spend your nights alone.'

She swallowed. 'And—you?'

'I hardly think that concerns you,' he said coldly. 'However, I will ensure that any liaisons I have are conducted discreetly.'

She bit her lip. 'As ours was?'

'*Davvero,*' he nodded. 'Precisely.'

She said with difficulty, 'And what about me—if I met someone?'

His brows lifted. 'I should require you to behave with equal discretion. I would tolerate no open scandal in my family.'

He paused. 'So what is your answer, Paola? Will you be my wife?'

'I don't know what to say.' Concealed by the skirts of her robe, her hands were clenched painfully into fists. 'I mean—you might want more children at some point.'

'I have a son to safeguard the inheritance. That was always my priority in such matters. As to the rest...' He shrugged again. 'I have cousins, both married with *bambini*. At times my house seems full of children. Although that, of course, will be good for Carlino,' he added thoughtfully. 'He does not talk as well as he should, and he hardly knows how to kick a ball. That must change.'

Polly's lips parted in sheer outrage. 'How—dare you? Last week you didn't even know you were a father. Now you're a bloody expert on child-rearing.'

'I made no such claim,' Sandro returned mildly. 'But Julie had concerns which she mentioned to me.'

'Then she had no right,' Polly flared. 'Charlie's absolutely beautiful, and he can do all kinds of things,' she added hotly, burying the memory of various clashes she'd had with her mother on that very subject.

'And could do far more, I suspect.' Sandro's smile was cold, 'if he was allowed to—and once keeping his clothes clean from every speck of dust is no longer a major priority.' He allowed her to absorb that, then went on, 'Can he swim?'

She reddened, still stung by his last comment, but honestly unable to refute it. He hadn't missed much during his first encounter with her mother, she thought ruefully.

'No, not yet,' she said in a subdued voice. 'I meant to take him to the local baths, but weekends are always so busy.'

'It's not a problem,' he said. He smiled at her for the first time that night without edge, the sudden unforced charm making the breath catch in her throat. 'I shall enjoy teaching him myself in our own pool.'

She caught her lower lip in her teeth, struggling to regain her equilibrium. Trying to disregard the image his words had presented. 'Yes—I suppose...'

'So,' he said, after a pause, 'shall we settle this thing now? Will you marry me, and come to Italy with our son?'

'I don't seem to have much of a choice,' she said in a low voice.

Something unreadable came and went in his face. 'And if you could choose? What then?'

'I would wish to be as far from you,' she said passionately, 'as it's possible to get.'

His head went back, and his eyes narrowed. 'Well, do not despair, *bella mia*,' he drawled scornfully. 'My home at Comadora is large, a *palazzo*, with thick walls, and many rooms. You should be able to avoid me easily.'

'Thank you,' she said huskily.

'Tonight, however, you will not be so fortunate,' he added.

She stiffened. 'What are you talking about?'

'I intend to spend the night here.'

She gasped. 'But—but you can't...' She tried not to look at the all too obtrusive sofa bed. 'There's no room.'

'It will be cramped,' he agreed. He took off his jacket, and began to loosen his tie. 'But it is only for one night.'

She said in a choked voice, 'You promised me—you swore this wouldn't happen. Oh, why did I think I could trust you?'

'The boot is on the other foot, *cara mia*.' He began unhurriedly to unfasten his shirt. 'I do not trust *you*. Who knows what you might be tempted to do, if you were left alone?

'But I have no intention of breaking my word,' he added. 'This armchair looks comfortable enough, so I shall use that.' His smile grazed her skin. 'And you can have that *congegno* quite undisturbed. I hope you sleep well.'

He draped his shirt over the back of the chair, sat down and removed his shoes and socks, while Polly watched in growing alarm. But when he stood up, his hands going to the waistband of his trousers, she intervened.

'Kindly stop right there,' she said grittily.

'You have some problem?'

'Yes.' Her green eyes were stormy. 'Of course I do.'

'Then deal with it.' He unzipped his trousers, stepped out of them, then placed them, folded, with the rest of his clothes. He was wearing brief silk shorts, and the rest of him was smooth tanned skin. For one burning moment of self-betrayal she found herself remembering the taste of him, and felt her body clench in uncontrollable excitement.

'Why, Paola, you are blushing,' he jeered softly. 'But not even to spare you will I sleep in my clothes. And you were not always such a prude,' he added drily. He indicated his shorts derisively. 'These, as you know, are a concession. But if the sight of me is still too much, you could always close your eyes.' He paused. 'Have you a towel I can use?'

Dry-mouthed, she muttered acquiescence, and went to the chest of drawers. As she reached for a towel, she uncovered Charlie's photograph.

'What is that?' Sandro came to her side, and took it from the drawer. He studied it for a moment, brows lifted, then turned to her. 'Is this where you usually keep it?'

'No,' she admitted reluctantly.

'You hid it,' he asked, incredulously. 'In case I came here?'

'Think whatever you wish,' she flung at him. 'I don't give a damn.'

He set the photograph carefully on top of the chest of drawers. 'And you wonder why I do not trust you,' he said silkily. He rescued the towel from her nerveless hand and went into the bathroom, closing the door behind him.

For a moment she stood irresolutely, trying to decide what to do. She could hardly go to bed in her robe, without exciting the kind of comment from him she most wished to avoid. And what nightgowns she possessed were far too thin and revealing.

However...

Polly knelt, opening the bottom drawer of the chest, searching with feverish fingers. There were some oddments of winter clothing here, she knew. Among them...

She drew out the pyjamas with a sigh of relief. They were worn out, washed out, and she'd never liked them, but they were good old-fashioned winceyette, and they covered her from her throat down to her feet.

She was just fastening the last button on the mandarin-style jacket when Sandro returned, and stopped dead at the sight of her.

'*Santa Madonna,*' he breathed, with a kind of fascinated horror. 'No wonder you sleep alone. I think I shall have to choose your trousseau myself, particularly the *biancheria intima.*'

'Thank you,' Polly returned icily. 'But I prefer to pick my own lingerie. And if you don't like the way I look, you can close your eyes too,' she added triumphantly.

'That is one solution,' he admitted musingly. 'But I can think of others that I would enjoy more.' He saw her blench, and grinned. 'Calm down, *cara mia.* I intend to keep my word. But sometimes to cover too much can be a mistake, because it excites the imagination.' He paused. 'I suppose a spare blanket is too much to hope for.'

She wanted to scream at him that she hoped he caught galloping pneumonia and died alone in a ditch. Instead she heard herself say unwillingly, 'Yes, there is one.'

She fetched it from the corner cupboard, pale blue and still in its wrappings. 'I bought it for Charlie,' she told him, gruffly. 'For when he moves into a bed instead of his cot.'

There was a silence. 'Then I am doubly grateful,' he said quite gently. 'Because this is a sacrifice for you. And I will make sure it goes with us to his new home.'

For a moment, there was a note in his voice that made her want to cry. She turned away hurriedly, and got into bed, pulling the covers over her, the metal base creaking its usual protest as she settled herself.

'*Dio,*' Sandro muttered. 'And that—atrocity will remain here.'

Well, she wasn't going to argue about that, Polly thought wearily. Aloud, she said, past the constriction in her throat, 'Will you turn the light off, please? When you're ready.'

'I am ready now.'

She lay, eyes tight shut, as he went past her, and the room was plunged into darkness. Waited for him to return to the chair.

Instead, she was aware of him standing beside her. He said quietly, 'Paola, do you ever wish you could turn back the clock? Wipe out what has been?'

'No,' she said. 'Because I know it's impossible, and I prefer to deal with reality.'

He sighed. 'Then could we not declare a truce for this one night? Be together for old times' sake?'

She wanted so badly to yield. To reach up and draw him down to her. She was starving for him, her body quivering with need, aching for him. Reminding her that she'd never shared a room with him before without eventually falling asleep in his arms in the drugged sweetness of sensual exhaustion.

But if she surrendered, she would be lost forever. And if she resisted, as she knew she must, at least she would retain what remained of her pride. Which might be all she had left to sustain her in the weeks, months, even years ahead.

'Even if I was in the mood for casual sex,' she said stonily, 'you gave me your word.' And paused. 'Besides, you flatter yourself, *signore*,' she added, coolly and distinctly. 'The old times weren't that special.'

She heard his swift intake of breath, and flinched, knowing she had gone too far. Waiting for a retribution which seemed inevitable.

But there was nothing.

She felt rather than heard the moment he moved away. Listened, all her senses tingling, as he wrapped himself in the blanket. Then, in the heavy silence which followed, she turned her face into the single pillow, and lay like a dead thing.


It had never occurred to her that she would sleep. She was too aware of his even breathing only a few feet away, demonstrating quite clearly, she realised, that her rejection couldn't have weighed too heavily with him after all.

She sighed silently, searching for a cool place on the pillow. She needed to look calm and rested in the morning, not wan and heavy-eyed.

Because Sandro must not be allowed to think that he still mattered to her.

That was what she needed to remember above all. Anything else would be a disaster, because, as those few moments in the darkness had proved all over again, it was going to be difficult to remain immune to the devastating allure of his sexuality.

But that, she thought, had always been her downfall from their first meeting. She had been too much in love, too blinded by the passion and glamour of him to ask the right questions and demand answers that made sense.

Her first major surprise had been his brilliant command of English, but when she'd asked him about it he'd simply said he'd had good teachers.

Polly had wondered, with a pang, whether he meant other women, and decided not to probe any further. Now she suspected that he'd gone to school in England, and probably university too, either here or in America.

He'd told her too that he worked at the Grand Hotel Comadora, but she'd never gone there to see him because its sheer expensive exclusivity discouraged casual visitors. The entrances were controlled by security guards, and the staff were subject to strict rules, so she'd stayed away. Otherwise she'd have soon found out that he wasn't simply an employee, but the owner. And that had been the last thing he wanted her to know.

Her own *naïveté* made her cringe now. The way she'd trusted him with all her small, loving dreams of their future.

'I'd like a tiny house,' she told him once. 'In one of the villages high above the sea, with a terraced garden, and its own lemon tree.'

'Mm.' He'd stroked her hair back from her love-flushed face with gentle fingers. 'And will you make me *limoncello* from our tree?'

He was talking about the lethally potent liqueur that was brewed locally, and she'd laughed.

'Well, I could try.'

God, what a fool she'd been, and how he must have been secretly amused at her, knowing full well that he was going to dump her once their warm, rapturous summer together was over.

He'd found himself an inexperienced virgin, and cynically turned her into an instrument for his pleasure.

I bet he couldn't believe his own luck. I must have been the perfect mistress, she thought, wincing. Easily duped, and ecstatically wanton. He didn't even have to kiss me. The sound of his voice—the warmth of his skin as he stood next to me were enough.

And, as she'd discovered tonight, they still were.

So how was she going to deal with the bleak sterility of the future that awaited her in Italy? A wife who was not a wife, she thought, living in a house that would never be her home. Her only link with Sandro, the child he had made in her body. A child, at the same time, who had driven them further apart than any years or miles could have done.

Sandro blamed her for keeping her pregnancy from him, but what else could she have done when she'd been dismissed so summarily from his life? And the accompanying threat might have been veiled, but it was real enough to have kept her from Italy ever since. Or until yesterday, at least.

And that had been all his own doing.

And now amazingly she was going to return to the Campania at his side. Somehow, she was going to have to learn to be his *marchesa*. To sit at his table, wearing the clothes and probably the jewellery he provided. To be pleasant to his family, and welcoming to his guests. And never by word, look or gesture let anyone suspect that she was bleeding slowly to death.

She supposed there would be compensations. She knew there would be heartbreak. And she was scared.

Scared of the inevitable isolation that awaited her—the power he still exerted over her trembling senses—and the ever-present danger of self-betrayal.

She needed to work on her anger—her bitterness at his desertion. They would protect her. Build a barrier that not all his sensual expertise could breach. That was the way she must go.

All the same, she found her mind drifting wistfully back to the tiny dream house and its lemon tree, and she saw herself walking beneath it with Sandro, her hand in his, as the sun glinted through the leaves.

And though her mouth smiled, there were tears on her face as she finally fell asleep.

# CHAPTER FIVE

SHE was weighed down, sinking into the depths of a dark and bottomless sea, unable to move or save herself.

Polly opened her eyes, gasping, to the familiar surroundings of the flat, bathed in early-morning light through the thin curtains, but the sensation of being pinned down persisted. Even increased.

Slowly, and with foreboding, she turned her head, and saw that Sandro was lying next to her, on top of the covers. The blue blanket was thrown lightly over him, and, she realised incredulously, Charlie's small pyjamaed form was also present, sprawled across his father's bare chest, his dark head tucked into the curve of his shoulder. Both of them were fast asleep.

For a moment Polly was transfixed by this unexpected tableau. And deep within her, she felt such a stir of tenderness that she almost cried out.

She swallowed deeply, reclaiming her self-control. Reminding herself that she would have to get accustomed to seeing them together, although not in such intimate circumstances. And, at the same time, knowing a pang of jealousy that Charlie, usually awkward with strangers, should have capitulated so readily. She overcame an impulse to snatch him back.

Slowly and stealthily, she began to ease her way towards the edge of the bed. It was still early, but her need for coffee was evenly matched with her desire to extract herself from a difficult situation.

Besides, she wanted both Charlie and herself to be ready by the time Julie arrived.

Julie, she thought, her mouth tightening, who was going to get a piece of her mind. And yet was that really fair to the girl, who'd only been doing the job she was hired for?

Yes, she had concerns, but so had Polly. She'd been worried about her mother's apparent resolve to keep Charlie a baby for as long as possible, and therefore more dependent than he should be at his age. Mrs Fairfax had lavished presents on 'my little prince' and 'Gran's sweet little man', most of them in the form of expensive clothing which she fussed to keep pristine. Even helping his grandfather to gather up hedge clippings seemed to be on the forbidden list, Polly recalled wryly. Hardly any wonder that Charlie didn't shine at outdoor activities.

And he was lazy about feeding himself, and doing simple tasks that Polly set him, probably because he was used to having everything done for him at other times.

I knew there were problems, she admitted as she slid with infinite care from under the covers, but at the same time I wanted to avoid another confrontation with my mother. So I have only myself to blame.

She stood up, then paused, suddenly aware of movement behind her. Stiffening as Sandro's voice said a husky, '*Buongiorno*'.

'Good morning.' She didn't look at him. 'I was going to make coffee—if you'd like some. I—I don't have espresso,' she added stiltedly.

'Coffee would be good,' he said. 'If I can free myself sufficiently to drink it.' She could hear the smile in his voice, and bit her lip.

'Shall I put him back in his cot?' she asked.

'Why disturb him for no cause?'

'Perhaps I should ask you the same thing.' Polly stared down at the floor. 'What is he doing here?'

'He was crying,' Sandro said shortly. 'He wanted a drink, which I gave him. Should I have left him thirsty?'

'He'd have needed changing too.' God, she thought, she sounded so carping—like a miserable shrew.

'I even managed that,' he returned. 'After a struggle. Although I do not guarantee my handiwork,' he added drily.

'You did that?' Polly turned then, staring down at him.

'But of course. He was uncomfortable.'

'Well—thank you for that,' Polly said reluctantly. She shook her head. 'I can't understand why I didn't hear him myself. I always do...'

'You were dead to the world.' His voice gentled a little. 'You did not even scream "rape" when I joined you on the bed. Perhaps you sensed Carlino was there to act as chaperone.'

'Maybe so,' she agreed stiffly.

'A friend warned me that when you have a child, the concept

of ''three in a bed'' takes on a new meaning,' he went on. 'I now know what he means.'

Polly looked away, her mouth tightening, and he sighed. 'That was a joke.'

'An inappropriate one,' she said, hating the primness in her voice. 'I'll get the coffee now. And—thanks again for helping with Charlie.'

'It was my pleasure,' he said, his voice faintly weary.

By the time she returned, Charlie had woken and was in a grizzly mood.

'You are sour in the mornings, *figlio mio*,' Sandro told him. He slanted a faint grin at Polly. 'Like your *mammina*.'

She sipped the strong, scalding brew she'd made. 'I'm sorry.' Her voice was defensive. 'But this isn't easy for me.'

'Or for me, *cara mia*,' he said. 'Or for me.'

He swallowed his own coffee with the complete disregard for its temperature that she remembered so well, then rose, swinging Charlie up into his arms. 'Come, my little grumbler. Come and take a bath with Papa and see if it improves your temper.' He glanced at Polly. 'You have no objections, I hope.'

'No,' she said. 'None.'

She occupied herself with stripping the bed and turning it back into a sofa, while attempting to ignore the noise of splashing and Charlie's gleeful squeals coming from the bathroom. Trying hard, too, not to feel envious and even slightly dejected, because that would get her nowhere.

Her path might have been chosen for her, but she had to follow it, whatever the cost.

What would happen next? she wondered. She supposed she would have to see Mrs Terence and tell her that Safe Hands would be losing her earlier than planned.

And she would have to visit her parents and break the news to them too—a situation which had all the makings of a Class A nightmare.

And if Sandro was serious about moving her into a larger flat, and so far he seemed to have meant everything he said, then she would have to pack.

She wandered into the tiny kitchen and poured herself some orange juice. She felt as if she needed all the vitamins she could get.

It was as if her life had been invaded by a sudden whirlwind, all her plans and certainties swept away.

And at some point she would have to stand beside Sandro in a church or registry office, and listen to him making promises he had no intention of keeping as he put his ring on her finger.

Three years ago, all my dreams were of marrying him, she thought unhappily. And now it's happening at last, but not in a way I could ever have hoped. Because I'm being offered the façade of a marriage, without its fulfillment. And, for Charlie's sake, I have to find some way—to endure.

She rinsed out her glass and put it on the draining board.

What was the old saying? she wondered drearily. Be careful what you wish for, in case your wish comes true?

Well, she had wished so hard to be Sandro's wife—once.

She gave a small wretched sigh, then went into Charlie's room to choose his clothes for the day, and that was where Sandro found her a few minutes later. He was fully dressed, while Charlie, capering beside him, was in a towel draped like a Roman toga.

'Do you have a mop, or a cloth, perhaps? I need to dry the bathroom floor.' Sandro's tone was faintly rueful.

'It doesn't matter,' Polly said too brightly. 'I'll clear up when I have my own bath.' She paused. 'You seemed to be having fun together,' she went on with an effort. 'Somehow—he's not shy with you.'

'Why should he be?' Sandro lifted a hand and touched his scarred cheek. 'Did you think, perhaps, that this would terrify him—make him run away from me screaming, and force me to think again?' he added sardonically.

'No—oh, no,' Polly stammered. 'But he can be tricky with people he's only just met. But not you.'

Sandro shrugged. 'Blood calling to blood, perhaps.'

'Yes,' she said. 'That must be it.'

He was watching her. He said quietly, 'Paola, I am not trying to take your place. You will always be his mother. But he needs us both.'

Her throat closed. She nodded, unable to speak, her hands restlessly folding and unfolding a little T-shirt.

His hand closed on her shoulder. His touch was gentle, but she felt its resonance through her blood and bone.

'Go and dress yourself,' he directed quietly. 'I will see to our son.'

She didn't want his kindness, his consideration, Polly thought wildly as she fled. She needed antagonism to feed her anger—her determination to stay aloof from him at all costs. To blank out forever the memories of those days and nights when her universe had narrowed to one room, and the bed where she lay in his arms.

She needed to hate him.

The state of the bathroom was a spur to that, of course. It looked as if it had been hit by a tidal wave, and it took ten minutes' hard graft with a mop and bucket, and a roll of paper towels, to render it usable again.

But even then the recollection of Charlie's crows of delight diffused her resentment.

And it occurred to her, too, that next time Sandro chose to play submarines or whatever with his son it would be someone else's task to do the clearing up after them.

It was clear that her life was going to change at all levels, not just the strictly personal. And would she be able to cope?

Although she would not be Sandro's wife in the accepted sense, she would have some practical role to play in his life, and maybe she should ask to have it defined.

She sighed. So many things she needed to know—not least how he'd acquired the scar on his face. Her own assumptions had been totally and embarrassingly wrong, of course, but she'd been offered no other explanation for an injury that must have gone dangerously deep.

She could only suppose that Sandro found the circumstances surrounding it too difficult and painful to discuss. So what could possibly have happened, and could she ever persuade him to talk about it?

Then there was his family. It seemed that he had other cousins apart from the *contessa*. How much did they know about her existence? she wondered. And what would they feel about her arrival—an interloper with a child?

Polly sighed again. She was just beginning to realise there were problems she hadn't even imagined awaiting her in Campania.

When she emerged from the bathroom, freshly attired in jeans and a pale blue shirt, she found Sandro standing by the window with

Charlie in his arms, apparently having a murmured conversation about the traffic in the street below.

'Have you pointed out the security men watching the flat?' Polly asked caustically.

'I sent them away last night,' Sandro told her, unfazed. 'From now on, *cara*, I shall be watching you myself.' He paused, watching the swift rush of colour to her face. 'So, what are your plans for the day?'

'Principally, giving up my job, and trying to calm my mother.' Polly thrust her hands into the pockets of her jeans in an effort at nonchalance. 'She's probably looking for a hit man right now to take you out of the equation.'

'What a pity I am not Mafioso as you thought,' he murmured. 'I could perhaps have suggested someone.'

Polly's mouth tightened. 'I suppose I should also start packing—if you really intend to move us out of here. Or was that simply a threat?'

'I do intend it,' he said. 'And as quickly as possible. But do not bring too much, *cara*. I plan to provide you and Carlino with everything you need, including new wardrobes.'

She lifted her chin. 'And I prefer to choose my own things.'

He looked her up and down, brows raised. 'Of which those are a sample?'

'There was a time,' Polly said, 'when you would have found these clothes perfectly acceptable.'

'But then we are neither of us the same people,' he said, gently. 'Are we, Paola?'

'No,' she said. 'We're not. And, as a matter of interest, who was the Sandro Domenico you once claimed to be?'

'You are interested?' His brows lifted mockingly. 'A step forward, perhaps. Domenico was the name of my late father, and was given to me as a second name at my christening. I used it when I did not wish to reveal my true identity.'

'Of course,' she said. 'Why didn't I guess?'

'So, will you allow me to make reparation for that, and accept that I wish to show my gratitude to you for agreeing to marry me, and how better than with a *corredo di sposa*?'

'I don't want your gratitude,' she said stonily. 'Or a trousseau of designer dresses. Just the space you promised me.'

'Does that exclude you from having lunch with me at my hotel—the Grand Capital? There are things we need to discuss.'

Polly bit her lip. 'If I must.'

Sandro shrugged. 'You overwhelm me,' he told her drily. 'Shall we say one o'clock in the bar?'

'Lunch in a restaurant?' Polly gave her angelically smiling son a dubious glance. 'I'm not sure Charlie could manage that.'

'He does not have to,' Sandro said briskly. 'I have arranged for him to spend some time with friends of mine, Teresa and Ernesto Bacchi, so we can talk without distraction.'

Polly drew a swift breath. 'That's very arbitrary,' she said mutinously. 'I might not like these friends of yours.'

'Well, you will meet them later today, so you can judge for yourself,' he said, shrugging.

'And it might upset Charlie, too.'

'I doubt that,' he said. 'They have twins his age. And he is more adaptable than you think.' Sandro smoothed the little boy's hair back from his forehead. 'Tell Mammina,' he whispered. He pointed to himself. 'Who am I?'

'Papa,' Charlie said promptly, and hid his face on his father's shoulder.

Polly made herself laugh and applaud. How easily Sandro had won him over, she thought. But why should she wonder at that?

Before he'd even spoken to her that first day in Sorrento, she'd been aware of the intensity of his gaze, her own mouth curving shyly—involuntarily—in response to his smile. Her heart had thudded in anticipation of the moment when he would come to her side.

Dear God, she thought wearily. She'd been seduced with just a look. A number-one, first-class pushover.

She turned away blindly, murmuring about finding her bag, and then the door buzzer sounded to announce Julie's arrival.

She'd decided it would be hypocritical to have a battle with the nanny over concerns that she actually shared, so she greeted her with a polite word, and smile instead.

She took herself into the kitchen to make more coffee while Julie received her instructions for the day.

At the moment Sandro ruled, and there was nothing she could do about it, she thought, leaning against the cramped work surface while she waited for the kettle to boil.

She was still inwardly reeling from the shock of his return, and its traumatic aftermath, but her confusion wouldn't last forever. Soon, she would be back in control of herself, and she'd make damned sure that more of a partnership was established over Charlie's parenting than existed at the moment.

Something that might be easier once she was officially Sandro's wife—and one of the few advantages of the forthcoming marriage, she thought painfully.

When she returned to the living room, Sandro came over to her, having relinquished Charlie to his nanny.

'I must go,' he said. He took out his wallet, and extracted what seemed to be an obscene amount of money, which he placed next to Charlie's photograph on the chest of drawers. 'For taxis,' he said. 'Tomorrow there will be a car and driver for your use.'

'Public transport has always been perfectly adequate,' Polly informed him loftily, conveniently forgetting how often she had cursed its delays and overcrowding.

Sandro shrugged. 'Then spend it as you wish,' he said. 'In this, at least, the choice is yours.'

Ignoring her mutinous glance, he took her hand and bowed over it.

'I will not kiss you, *bella mia*,' he said softly. He lifted her imprisoned fingers, drawing them lightly over his unshaven chin, the topaz eyes meeting hers in open challenge. 'I would not wish to mark your exquisite skin.'

Polly mumbled something incoherent, and withdrew her hand from his with more haste than courtesy, aware that Julie, in spite of her training, was watching open-mouthed.

And probably thinking every inch of me is grazed to the bone, she thought, cringing inwardly.

If you only knew, she told the other girl silently. If you only—truly—knew...

And found herself sighing under her breath.

She handed in her notice at Safe Hands, aware that she was causing a slight shock wave, but unable to explain or defend her decision. Far too tricky, she thought.

And then, of course, she had her parents to face.

She'd expected her mother to be instantly on the attack when she arrived at the family home, but Mrs Fairfax was upstairs, lying on her bed with the curtains drawn. The look she gave Polly was subdued, almost listless.

'So, he's persuaded you,' she said heavily. 'I supposed he would. A man like that. I—we didn't realise what we were taking on.'

Polly took her mother's cold hand in hers. 'It won't be so bad,' she said, wondering which of them she was trying to convince. 'And Italy's such a beautiful country. You'll be able to come and visit as often as you like. I'm sure Sandro will want that,' she added, mentally crossing her fingers.

'Crumbs from the rich man's table,' her mother said with a harsh laugh. 'How could I ever have imagined it would end like this—that he'd come to find you?'

'She'll be all right,' her father told Polly comfortingly as they went downstairs. 'I'm going to take her down to Cornwall for a few days. She loves it there, but we haven't been able to go recently.'

'No.' Polly bit her lip. 'Because you've been too busy looking after Charlie. Maybe the break will do her good—stop her brooding.' She hesitated. 'Dad—about the wedding—when it happens...'

'You want us to stay away?'

She shook her head vehemently. 'I'm counting on you to give me away, but how is Mum going to feel about it?'

'Let's cross that bridge when we come to it,' he said gently. He gave her a searching look. 'Sweetheart—tell me something.'

'If I can.'

'Charlie's father,' he said. 'Was it just a temporary fling, or did you really care about him?'

She looked away. 'I—cared,' she said in a low voice. 'But I discovered that—he didn't.'

'Well, at least he's trying to put things right now, no matter what your mother says.' He gave an awkward chuckle. 'Even asked my permission, which threw me.' He put his hand on her shoulder. 'It won't be easy, I know, but maybe you could try meeting him halfway?'

*But he would have to want that too,* she thought. *And he doesn't. Besides, how can I meet him anywhere when I don't even know who he is? And never did...*

She suppressed a sigh, and her little smile was wintry. 'Perhaps that's a bridge I have to cross.' She kissed his cheek. 'Good luck with Cornwall. I'll be in touch.'

She didn't want to be late for lunch, so she reluctantly spent some of Sandro's money on a taxi after all.

She hadn't changed into anything more formal for their meeting, just added her favourite pair of earrings—the tiny enamelled cornflowers on delicate silver chains. But she began to wish she had dressed more smartly as she walked across the Grand Capital's marble foyer, skirting the fountain and the groups of elegant women who'd gathered there to chat before lunch.

Sandro was already sitting at the bar when Polly entered. He was laughing at something the barman had said, and she hesitated, almost stunned, as the full force of his attraction hit her once more like a punch in the throat.

Nor was she the only one, she realised, recovering her breath. Women were sending him predatory looks from all over the room. No change there, then, she thought drily, remembering the same reaction every time she'd walked down a street with him in Sorrento.

And the scar on his cheek had not detracted from his appeal in any way. On the contrary, thought Polly, he looked like some Renaissance swordsman injured in a duel.

At that moment, he looked round and saw her. He slid off the stool, coming across to her, his mouth curling in faint cynicism as he registered her instant tension.

'Cara,' he said softly, and took her hand. 'So you have decided to join me. I could not be sure. But I am delighted.' He leaned towards her, his gaze travelling to her mouth, and Polly flinched, freeing her fingers from his grasp.

'Still no kiss?' His tone was mocking. 'Even though I have learned my lesson from this morning, and shaved more closely in anticipation?'

'I don't consider that any particular inducement,' Polly responded stonily. 'I've agreed to marry you, and I see no need for any—embellishments.'

'Now, there we disagree. I see I shall have to teach you the difference between public and private behaviour, my reluctant bride.' He smiled as he spoke, and only Polly was aware of the ice in his voice. 'But we will discuss that later.'

He took her to a corner table, and signalled to a hovering waiter. 'What would you like to drink. Is it still Campari and soda?'

More unwanted memories, she thought, biting her lip. She said coolly, 'Just a mineral water, please.'

'Last night you drank white wine.'

'Today I need to keep a clear head.'

He gave her a thoughtful look, then turned to the waiter. 'Mineral water, *per favore*,' he directed. 'For both of us.'

The waiter departed, leaving a silence behind him that Sandro was the first to break.

'Have you had a productive morning?' he asked.

'I suppose so.' Polly gave a slight shrug. 'I resigned from my job, and visited my parents, who are planning a holiday in Cornwall.'

'I have not been idle either,' he said. 'The legal requirements for our marriage are being fast-tracked, so I have decided it would be best if you moved here to my suite until the wedding.'

'I—move in with you?' she repeated blankly. 'What are you talking about?'

'Finding a flat to rent for such a short time could be a problem,' he explained. His mouth curled slightly. 'But do not be too disturbed, *cara*. The suite has two large bedrooms.'

She said in a hollow voice, 'There are three of us. Four with Julie.'

'The *bambinaia* will work only in the daytime. At night, we will care for Carlino ourselves. You have been doing that since he was born,' he added. 'So it is scarcely a hardship. He can decide whose room he shares each evening.' He gave her a cool smile. 'An excellent arrangement, don't you think?'

Her voice shook. 'You don't want to know what I think.'

'Probably not,' he agreed drily. 'But you will not be forced to endure my company for too long. We shall leave for Italy and Comadora immediately after our wedding, and, once there, I will do my best to keep out of your way. In view of my work commitments, it should not be too difficult.'

Polly gave him a pleading look. 'Can't we do a deal over this? As it's only for a short time, couldn't Charlie and I stay at the flat?'

'Unfortunately that is impossible.' His hand closed over hers, his thumb stroking her soft palm, sending tiny tremors through her senses which she was unable to ignore or control. 'You see, *carissima*, I need you near to me,' he whispered huskily. 'Especially at night. Just in case you decided to try and escape me after all.'

At that moment, the waiter arrived back with their drinks, and a colleague came hurrying with menus and a wine list.

Polly withdrew her hand from his clasp, not trusting herself to speak, longing for a sliver of ice long and sharp enough to pierce her tormentor to the heart.

She took refuge behind her menu while she regained her equilibrium.

Last night had been bad enough, she thought broodingly. She'd never envisaged having to move in with him, but she realised now that she'd been naïve. There were probably plenty of other options, but his will was paramount, and he was letting her know it.

Yet he'd been so different once; gentle, humorous, patient—and adoring, or so she'd believed.

Now, she thought, wretchedness gnawing at her, it seemed that treacherous, deceitful and arrogant were more accurate descriptions.

He'd simply played the part of the sincere lover, as a ploy to keep her in his bed, trusting and eager, all summer long.

Yet, while she knew this, how was it possible that his lightest touch still had the power to stir her to the depths of her being, reigniting needs and longing that should be dead?

It was madness, and she needed to become sane again, or her existence, even on the outskirts of his life, would become intolerable.

She'd never felt less hungry in her life, but she knew she should eat something, so decided on consommé and chicken in wine sauce to follow. Fuel, she thought, for the next battle.

'So,' Sandro said when they were alone again, 'you will stay here with me, and no more arguments?'

She nodded abruptly, and he smiled at her. 'I am charmed by your obedience,' he told her, and raised his glass. 'Shall we drink to marital harmony?'

'No,' Polly said grittily, 'thank you. Not even in water.'

'*Che peccato,*' he said lightly. 'What a shame. Then, instead, let us drink to your earrings.' He put a hand out as if to touch one of the little cornflowers, and Polly shrank back.

He stared at her, his brows snapping together. When he spoke, his voice crackled with anger. 'Tell me, Paola, do you intend to cringe each time I come near you?'

'Isn't that the whole point?' she demanded huskily. 'I don't want you near me. You've promised to keep your distance, but can I believe you?'

'And how can I make you see that some contact between us is inevitable, and that you must accept it?' he asked coldly. 'I am letting it be known among my family and friends that we are reunited lovers.'

She said thickly, 'You can't expect me to go along with that. Not after everything that's happened...'

'I do expect it,' he said harshly. 'In fact, I insist on it. There is bound to be talk—even scandal—when our marriage, and our child, become public knowledge. I wish to minimise that for Carlino's sake. Make people believe that we were victims of fate who have been given a second chance together.'

She gave him a scornful look. 'That is such hypocrisy.'

'You would prefer to have the whole truth broadcast?' His voice bit. 'I can tell you my cousin Emilio would be delighted. He publishes a whole range of cheap gossip magazines, exposing secrets that the rich and famous would prefer to remain hidden.

'Until yesterday, he considered himself my heir, and will not be pleased to find himself demoted,' he added cuttingly. 'If he finds out that ours is simply a marriage of convenience, then our sleeping arrangements will be headline news in every trashy publication he puts on the streets. Is that what you want?'

'Oh, God.' Polly put down her glass. 'He couldn't, surely.'

'Think again,' he said. 'We have never liked each other, so he would do it and revel in it. So I prefer to safeguard my pride and my privacy, *cara mia*. And you would be well advised to co-operate too, unless you wish to feature as a discarded mistress—and the unwanted wife that Alessandro Valessi threw out of his bed. Is that what you choose?'

'No,' she said, staring down at the table. 'I—I don't want that.'

'Then play your part, and stop behaving as if I were a leper,' he told her. 'Because it bores me.' He paused. 'It also makes me wonder,' he added softly, 'what you would do if, some night, I—tested your resolve. *Capisce?*'

'Yes.' Her voice was a thread.

'*Bene.*' He gave her a swift, hard smile. 'Now let us go, happily united, into lunch.'

# CHAPTER SIX

SHE walked into the restaurant beside him, moving like an automaton. His hand was under her arm as if she was in custody, as they followed the head waiter to yet another corner table.

'They have a new chef here,' Sandro told her as he took his place beside her. His sleeve, she realised, was only a few inches from her bare arm. Altogether too close for comfort. 'And the food is said to be very good,' he added.

'You seem to know a lot about it,' she said. 'Is this hotel part of the Comadora chain, by any chance?'

'We acquired it six months ago.'

'I see.' She played nervously with the cutlery. 'Will—will you tell me something?'

His gaze sharpened. 'If I can,' he said, after a pause.

'When we first met—why didn't you tell me who you really were? Why did you let me think you were simply a minor hotel employee?'

'Because that is exactly what I was,' he said. 'I had been travelling round all the hotels in the group to learn the trade, working in every department, so I could see what shape they were in.

'Traditionally my family has always been involved in agriculture and banking. The hotels were acquired in the nineteenth century by one of my ancestors who is said to have won them in a poker game.

'When my father inherited them, he wanted to get rid of them. He had no interest in tourism. But I felt differently. I thought managing the chain—updating and improving it—would be more interesting than citrus fruit and olive oil, or sitting in some air-conditioned office in Rome.

'So I was working incognito, and compiling a report that I hoped would convince my father to keep the hotels and invest in them.'

'But I wasn't involved with any hotels,' Polly protested. 'I

worked for an independent tour company. You could have told
me the truth.'

He said quietly, 'Paola, as the Valessi heir, I brought a lot of
baggage with me. We are a wealthy family, and there had been
women in my life whose sole priority was my money. I had
become—wary.'

He spread his hands. 'You had no idea who I was, and yet you
wanted me—for myself. For Sandro Domenico. I found that—
irresistible. Can you understand that?'

'I understand.' There was a constriction in her throat. 'But your
money must have been useful when you needed to be rid of—
someone.'

His mouth hardened. 'Yes,' he said. 'In the end, it usually came
down to—money.' He paused. 'Is that all you want to ask?'

'No.' She shook her head. 'I have a hundred questions. But I'm
not sure you'd be prepared to answer them all.'

'No?' He sent her a meditative look. 'Try me.'

She took a deep breath. 'Well—the scar on your cheek. I was
wondering how that happened.'

'I was in an accident,' he said expressionlessly. 'In the hills
above Comadora. My car left the road on a bend and plunged into
a ravine. I was thrown clear, but badly injured. My life was saved
by a local man who found me, and administered some rough first
aid before the ambulance got to me.'

It was a bald recital of the facts—something he'd clearly done
many times before. He spoke as if it no longer had the power to
affect him, but Polly could sense the tension in him.

She stared down at the immaculate white tablecloth. She said
quietly, 'You were—lucky.'

You could have died, she thought, the breath catching in her
throat. You could have been killed so easily. And I—I might never
have known just how much I had to mourn.

'Yes,' he agreed. 'Fortunate, indeed.' His eyes were hooded as
he looked at her. 'Do you require further details?'

Oh, God, Polly thought. I know what I have to ask—but I don't
want to hear the answer.

She took a deep breath. She said, 'When did it happen? Was
anyone else involved—in the crash?'

'Three years ago. I had a passenger,' he said levelly. 'A girl
called Bianca DiMario. She—did not get clear.'

Polly stared at him, aware of the sudden chill spreading through her veins. She said hoarsely, 'That's—terrible.'

She wanted to stop there—to ask nothing more. But that was impossible, of course.

I have to go on, she thought, steeling herself. I—I have to know.

'You—you were close? You knew her well?' *She was a casual acquaintance? You were just giving her a lift? Please say that's all it was—please...*

'I had known her for most of my life,' he said quietly. 'She came to live at the *palazzo* with her aunt, the *contessa*, at my father's invitation. Bianca's parents were both dead, and the *contessa* was a widow who had been left with little money.

'My father had a strong sense of family, and he considered it a duty and an honour to care for them both.' He paused. 'Bianca was also intended to be the next Marchesa Valessi,' he added, evenly. 'The announcement of our engagement had been planned for the week after the accident.'

Polly was reduced to stricken silence as the pain returned, twisting inside her. She could see so clearly now why he'd had to get rid of her with such indecent haste—and offered such a high price to achieve that.

She'd become an embarrassment, she thought. Their affair an insult to his future wife.

She bent her head. 'I—I'm sorry,' she said huskily. 'It must have been utterly ghastly—to lose the girl you were going to marry in such a way.'

'Yes,' he said. 'It was the worst time of my life. Something I cannot let myself forget.' His faint smile was grim. 'So I keep the scar to remind me how I was robbed forever of my chance of happiness.'

How can I listen to this? she asked herself imploringly. How can I let him hurt me all over again? She wanted to throw herself at him, hitting him with her fists, and screaming that she mattered too.

She wanted to weep until she had no tears left.

With a supreme effort, she mastered herself.

'The accident,' she said. 'Does anyone know what caused it?' How could she speak normally—discuss this terrible thing when she was falling apart inside? When she had to face all over again that everything he'd ever said to her—promised her—had been a lie?

Sandro shrugged. 'The inquiry found a burst tyre on my car, so I was—exonerated. But I still have to live with the memory.'

And I, Polly thought, shall have to live with your betrayal of me—and I don't know if I can do that. I think you may be asking the impossible.

She met his gaze. 'Bigamy,' she said clearly. 'Is that another Valessi family tradition? Because you seem to have been engaged to two women at one time.'

He sighed harshly. 'I should never have let things go so far, and I know it.' His mouth twisted. 'Believe me, I have been well punished for my silence.'

'Bianca.' She forced herself to say the name. 'Did she—know about me?'

A muscle moved beside his mouth. 'Yes.' One small, uncompromising word.

'I see,' she said. She was silent for a moment. 'So—I was the only fool.'

'No,' he said. 'I meant to tell you everything. To explain, and ask you to forgive me. But then the crash came, and after that—everything changed.' His smile was icy. 'As you know.'

'Yes,' Polly said almost inaudibly. She paused. 'It must have been awful for the *contessa* too—to lose her niece.' She forced a smile. 'No wonder she doesn't like me.'

He sighed again. 'Paola *mia*, Bianca has been dead for three years. Zia Antonia has to accept that.'

'And she still lives at the *palazzo*—in spite of it all?'

'Of course,' he said. 'I could hardly ask her to leave. Besides, I am often away, and she currently manages the house and estate for me.'

'So she's bound to have constant reminders of Bianca.' Polly hesitated. 'And three years isn't all that long—when you care deeply for someone.' She took a breath. 'After all, you must think about her too.'

She saw his face harden, his hand lift as if to touch his scarred cheek, then fall again.

'*Sì*,' he said harshly. 'I think about her. And three years can seem an eternity.'

I asked for that, Polly thought wretchedly. A self-inflicted wound.

She said in a low voice, 'I'm sorry. I shouldn't have pried.'

'You had to know,' he said. 'And I wished to explain. But up to now, you have shown no curiosity about the past.' His mouth twisted. 'Who knows? I might have spent all these years in the Regina Coeli prison for robbery with violence.' He put his hand briefly over hers. 'So, is there nothing else you wish to ask me?'

For a moment, she thought she detected a note of pleading in his voice. But that was ridiculous. Sandro had never pleaded in his life.

And there were questions teeming in her brain, falling over themselves to escape. But she knew she could not bear to hear the answers. The news about Bianca had been as much as she could take today.

She shook her head. 'There's nothing I need to know. After all, it's not as if ours will be a real marriage. It's just an arrangement, for Charlie's sake. So, it's better if we can keep our lives separate—and private.'

He was silent for a moment, then he inclined his head almost wryly. 'As you wish.'

The food when it came was delicious, but Polly might as well have been chewing sawdust. She had to force every mouthful past the tightness in her throat, helped down by the Orvieto Classico he'd chosen. Because she couldn't allow Sandro to glimpse her inner agony.

He broke my heart once, she thought. I can't allow him to do that again. Especially when I know that he could—all too easily. And she sighed quietly.

When the largely silent meal was finally over, Polly found her next ordeal was accompanying Sandro up to the penthouse to inspect her temporary home.

She'd hoped she would find some insoluble problem with the accommodation, but the bright, airy rooms with their masses of fresh flowers seemed just about perfect.

To her unspoken relief, the bedrooms were well apart, facing each other from opposite sides of the large and luxurious drawing room. And each had its own bathroom, so she could hardly complain about a lack of privacy.

'Will you be comfortable here?' he asked, watching her prowl around. 'I hope it has everything you want.'

'Everything,' she said. 'Except the freedom to make decisions, and live my own life.'

'A trifle, surely.' Sandro's tone was solemn, but his eyes were glinting in sudden amusement. 'When the cage you occupy is so beautifully gilded. Also unlocked.' He produced a key from his pocket. 'For your bedroom door,' he said. 'In case I walk in my sleep.'

Her heart missed a beat, but she spoke lightly. 'You'd soon wake up when Charlie started yelling.' She glanced at her watch. 'When are we picking him up from your friends? Time's moving on, and I still have to go back to the flat and pack our things.'

'I have arranged for two of the girls from Administration here to do that for you,' Sandro said calmly, meeting her fulminating gaze head-on. 'I told them to bring the minimum. I will have the remainder suitably disposed of.'

'My God,' she said furiously. 'You take a lot upon yourself. Is this part of your campaign to force me to buy new clothes?'

He smiled at her. 'No, I am relying on Teresa to do that,' he said. 'She cannot wait to take you shopping.'

'I can buy my own damned things,' Polly threw at him. 'And I don't need a minder.'

'I hope she will be much more than that,' he told her with a trace of chill. 'Her husband is one of my greatest friends, and I was best man at their wedding. They have been—good to me in return.'

He paused. 'You are going to a new life, Paola, with its own demands. As my wife, you will be expected to patronise Italian designers. How many do you know? What formal clothes will you need? How many dinner dresses—how many ballgowns?

'This is a world Teresa knows, and you can trust her advice.' He paused. 'She can also help you in another way. Before she married Ernesto, she worked as a linguist. So you may practice speaking Italian to her. Start to regain your former fluency.'

Her face warmed suddenly as she recalled precisely how that proficiency had been acquired during those long, hot afternoons a lifetime ago. The things he had whispered to her as she lay in his arms—and taught her to say to him in return.

She was suddenly aware that he was watching her, observing

the play of embarrassed colour on her skin, before he added softly
and cynically, 'But with a rather different vocabulary, *carissima*.'

She said with deliberate coldness, 'Do you have any other
orders for me?'

He was unfazed. 'If I think of any, I will let you know.'

'How nice it must be,' she said, 'to always get your own way.
Think about it.' She ticked off on her fingers. 'You need an heir—
you have one ready-made. You require somewhere convenient to
keep us—and you own a hotel with a vacant suite. You don't wish
to be married—and you find a wife who doesn't want to be anywhere near you either. You're ahead on all points.'

'Am I, *bella mia*?' His tone was cordial. 'How interesting that
you should think so. But perhaps you should refrain from mentioning my good fortune to Teresa and Ernesto. They might not
agree with you.'

He paused. 'One more thing before we go to meet them.' He
reached into the inside pocket of his jacket and extracted a small
velvet box.

As he opened it, Polly drew an unsteady breath at the
coruscating fire from the enormous diamond it contained.

'Give me you hand.' It was a command, not a request, but she
still hesitated.

'Surely—this isn't necessary...'

'On the contrary, it is essential,' Sandro contradicted her. 'So—
*per favore...*'

Mutely, reluctantly, she allowed him to slide the ring onto her
finger. A moment, she thought in anguish, that she'd imagined so
many times during the summer of their love. But not like this.
Never like this.

Her voice shook slightly. 'It's—beautiful.'

At the same time its dazzling brilliance seemed almost alien on
her workaday hand, she thought, making her feel like some latter-
day Cinderella.

But Sandro was no Prince Charming, she reminded herself soberly. And his diamond was altogether too magnificent a symbol
of the cold, sterile bargain they had made with each other.

As if Sandro had read her thoughts, he said quietly, 'You will
soon accustom yourself to wearing it.'

She bent her head. 'Along with everything else, it seems.'

'There will be compensations,' he told her. 'Tomorrow I shall open a bank account for you.'

She shook her head almost violently. 'I don't want that.'

'*Dio mio.*' His voice was weary. 'Paola, do you have to fight me each step of the way? Do you wish our child to be brought up in a battlefield?'

She looked away. 'No, of course not.'

'Then please try and accept the arrangements that must be made.'

'I can—try,' she said unsteadily. 'But it's not easy when your whole world has suddenly been—turned upside down.'

'You think you are alone in that?' There was a note of harsh derision in his voice. 'I too am obliged to make—adjustments.'

'But you don't have to.' She faced him with new determination, hands clenched at her sides. 'I—I understand that you need to see Charlie, to spend time with him, and I swear I'll co-operate in any way over this. But why tie yourself to an unwanted marriage when you could meet someone to love—someone who knows how to be a *marchesa*?' She paused. 'Someone the *contessa* might even approve of.'

'You think that is an essential quality in my bride?' His mouth twisted.

'I think that, otherwise, there'll be problems,' Polly said flatly. 'You must see that. After all, she runs your home—and she'll see me as an interloper. A poor substitute for the girl she loved.'

'Then she too will have to adjust.' His voice hardened. 'Believe this, Paola. My son will grow up in my home with the knowledge that his mother is my wife. Nothing else will do—either for him, or for the world at large.'

He walked to the door, and held it open. 'Now begin to play your part. My friends expect to meet a girl happily reunited with her lover—so pretend,' he added flatly. '*Avanti.*'


The serial killer was on the move, and the heroine was alone in her apartment, with a thunderstorm growling overhead. Any minute now she was going to run herself a bath or take a shower, Polly thought wearily, because that was what always happened.

I need, she thought, blanking out the television screen with one terse click of the remote control, to be distracted, not irritated.

She also wanted to relax—but her inner tensions were not so easily dispelled.

Besides, she could do without artificial horrors. Her mind was full enough already of disturbing sounds and images—bleached rock in the blazing sun, the squeal of tyres, the screech of brakes and wrenched metal. A girl screaming in fright, and then an even more terrifying silence, with Sandro lying unconscious and bleeding under a pitiless sky.

Perhaps this was why she was still up and restless, when common sense suggested she should be in bed, with Charlie fast asleep in his cot near by. She'd wondered if he would react badly to his new surroundings, but he'd settled with little more than a token protest.

Perhaps I should be more like him, Polly thought with a grimace. Learn to deal with six impossible things before breakfast.

However, liking Teresa and Ernesto had not proved impossible at all. She was tall, and slim as a wand, with long dark hair and laughing eyes. And although she was the epitome of chic, that did not stop her indulging in a rough-and-tumble on the floor with Charlie and the twins.

Ernesto was quieter, with a plain, kind face, observing his wife and children with doting fondness through his silver-rimmed glasses.

In other circumstances, Polly would have loved to have them as friends. As it was, she felt a total fraud. And sitting next to Sandro on one of the deeply cushioned sofas in their drawing room, with his arm draped casually round her shoulders, had proved unnervingly difficult.

Blissfully married herself, Teresa, left alone with Polly, had made it clear that she thought Sandro was glamorous and sexy beyond belief, in spite of his scarred face, and that she was assisting at the romance of the century.

And even if I told her that marrying Sandro was simply a rubber stamp on a legal arrangement I want no part of, Polly thought sadly, she wouldn't believe me.

'Ah, but shopping will be such fun, *cara*,' Teresa had told her buoyantly. 'Particularly as Alessandro has put no limit on our spending,' she added with glee.

And although she must have been brimming with curiosity

about Sandro and Polly's former relationship, she nobly refrained from asking questions that her guest might find difficult to answer.

There had been only one awkward moment, when Teresa had been admiring Polly's engagement ring. 'A diamond?' she exclaimed. 'But I thought...' She encountered a swift glance from Ernesto, and hastily went on, 'I thought, as your bride has green eyes, you would have chosen an emerald for her. Or do you believe they are unlucky? Some people do, I think. And a diamond is forever, no?'

Sandro had smiled lazily. 'Forever,' he agreed.

But Polly found herself wondering what Teresa had meant to say.

'So, was that such a hardship?' he'd asked as their chauffeur-driven car took them back to the hotel, with Charlie bouncing between them.

'No,' she admitted. 'They were lovely. I hate making fools of them like this.'

He gave her a dry look. 'Do not underestimate Teresa, *cara*. She is a shrewd lady.'

Is she? Polly thought. Yet she clearly thinks Sandro and I will be having an intimate dinner for two in our suite, followed by a rapturous night in each other's arms. How wrong can anyone be?

'Then I'll take care to be extra-careful,' she said. She paused. 'Why did she query my engagement ring being a diamond?'

'You noticed,' Sandro gave a shrug. 'She would expect you to wear the Valessi ruby, which is traditionally passed to each bride.'

'But not to me.'

'No,' he said, his mouth hardening. 'It was found in the wreckage of the car. My father had it buried with Bianca.'

'I see.' She swallowed. 'Well, that's—understandable.' She paused, desperate for a change of subject. 'I—I wonder if the box containing my life has been delivered yet?'

He looked at her thoughtfully. 'That has made you angry,' he said. 'Which was not my intention. I thought I had simply relieved you of a tedious job.'

'It would have been,' she admitted. She forced a smile. 'I'm just accustomed to my independence.'

'Then it may please you to know that you will not be burdened with my presence at dinner tonight,' he told her drily. 'I am going out. Would you prefer to dine in the suite, or go down to the restaurant?'

'I'll stay in the suite. It will be better for Charlie.'

'As you wish. I will arrange for Room Service to bring you a menu.'

Polly wondered where he was planning to spend the evening, but knew she could never ask. Because she did not have the right. This was the life she had agreed to for Charlie's sake. A life of silences. No questions asked, or information volunteered. A life where to be blind and deaf might be a positive advantage.

'I shall come to say goodnight to Carlino before I leave,' he added. 'If you permit, of course.'

'I can hardly prevent you.'

'You have a key to your room,' he reminded her. 'There could be a locked door between us.'

Yes, Polly had thought, her mouth drying. But would that really keep you out, if you wanted to come in?

Remembering that now, she got up with a shiver, and, walking over to the long glass doors which opened on to the balcony, she pushed them open and stepped out into the sultry night, tightening the sash on the towelling robe as she did so.

Her elderly, much-loved cotton dressing gown had not survived the Great Pack, so she'd had to use the one hanging on the bathroom door in its plastic cover. She missed her old robe badly. She'd had it for years—even taken it to Italy with her, when she worked for the travel company, and now it was gone. Like a symbol of her old life, she thought sadly.

But at least they'd brought Charlie's blue blanket—and the brown teddy bear, both of them now adorning his cot. She would have to find something else to comfort herself with.

How peaceful everything looked in the moonlight, she thought, leaning on the stone balustrade. How normal. And how deceptive appearances could be.

She would not be welcome at Comadora, and she knew it. The *contessa* would be bound to resent her savagely, but at least she knew she had not imagined the older woman's hostility to her.

It was probable that Bianca had confided her hurt over Sandro's affair to her aunt. And now the *contessa* had to watch the hated mistress elevated to wife.

I'd hate me too, she thought soberly. But it's still going to be a problem.

She turned restlessly to go back inside, and cannoned into Sandro, who had come, silent and completely unsuspected, to stand behind her.

She recoiled with a little cry, and immediately his hands gripped her arms to steady her.

'Forgive me,' he said quietly. 'I did not mean to startle you.'

She freed herself, her heart thudding. 'I—I didn't expect to see you.'

His brows lifted. 'You thought I would celebrate our *fidanzamento* by staying out all night,' he asked ironically.

Polly lifted her chin. 'Even if you did,' she said, 'it would be no concern of mine. Do whatever you want.'

'You are giving me permission to stray, *cara mia*?' Sandro drawled. 'How enlightened of you, but totally unnecessary. Because I shall, indeed, do as I please.' He paused. 'I thought you would be in bed.'

'I'm just going,' she said hastily.

She wanted to escape. With his arrival, the night was suddenly too warm and the balcony too enclosed as if the balustrade and surrounding walls had shrunk inwards.

And Sandro was too close to her, almost but not quite touching. She felt a bead of sweat trickle between her breasts, and dug her nails into the palms of her hands.

'Then before you do, perhaps you will allow me to steal another look at my son.'

'Of course,' Polly said, edging past him into the living room. 'And he's my son too,' she added over her shoulder.

'I have not forgotten,' he said. 'What were you doing out there, Paola? Gazing at the moon?'

'Just—thinking.' She paused, looking down at the floor. 'Will—will the *contessa* be returning for the wedding?'

'No,' he said. 'She will remain at the *palazzo* to make sure everything is ready for our arrival.'

'And afterwards?'

He paused. 'She will stay, at least until you are ready to take over the running of the household.'

'Or even longer?' She still did not look at him.

'Perhaps.' He sighed. 'Paola, my father promised her a home.

Out of respect for his memory, I cannot honourably deprive her of it, unless she wishes to go, no matter what has happened.' He paused. 'I hope you can accept that.'

'It seems I shall have to.' *And more easily than she will ever accept me...*

She turned and walked into her dimly lit bedroom. Sandro followed, and stood by the cot, an expression of such tenderness on his face that her heart turned over.

She thought, Once he looked at me like that, and winced at the wave of desolation that swept over her. Ridiculous reaction, she told herself fiercely. Unforgivable, too.

She went back to the door and waited, her arms hugged defensively round her body.

Sandro looked at her meditatively on his way past to the living room.

'Yes?' She felt suddenly nervous, and her voice was more challenging than she intended. 'You have something to say?'

'Our son,' he said quietly. 'How curious to think we should have made a child between us, when, now, you cannot even bear to stand next to me.' His voice changed suddenly—became low, almost urgent. 'How can this have happened, Paola *mia*? Why are you so scared to be alone with me? So frightened that I may touch you?'

'I'm not scared,' Polly began, but he cut across her.

'Do not lie to me.' There was a hard intensity in his tone. 'You were a virgin when you came to me, yet, even then, you never held back. From that first moment, you were so warm—so willing in my arms that I thought my heart would burst with the joy of you.'

Oh, God, she thought wildly. *Oh, dear God...*

She could feel the slow burn of heat rising within her at his words, at the memories they engendered, and had to fight to keep her voice deliberately cool and clear.

'But that,' she said, 'was when I was in love with you. It—makes—quite a difference.'

Her words seemed to drop like stones into the sudden well of silence between them. The air seemed full of a terrible stillness that reached out into a bleak eternity.

Polly felt her body quiver with tension. She had provided the lightning flash, and now she was waiting for the anger of the storm to break.

But when he spoke, his voice was calm. 'Of course,' he said. 'You are right. It—changes everything. I am obliged to you for the reminder. *Grazie* and goodnight.'

She was aware of him moving, turning away. Then, a moment later, she heard his own door open and close, and knew she was alone. And safe again.

Her held breath escaped her on a long, trembling sigh.

She'd had a lucky escape and she knew it. Now all she had to deal with was the deep ache of traitorous longing that throbbed inside her.

But she could cope, she told herself, shivering. She had things to do. Clothes to buy. Italian lessons to learn. Long days with Charlie to enjoy for the first time since he was a baby.

So much to keep her busy and banish all those long-forbidden thoughts, and desires. And, for her own sake, she should make a start at once. Telephone Teresa in the morning. Make a list of all the books she'd not had time to read. She could even have parcels of them, she thought, sent to her in Italy. She might even book for a theatre matinée, now that she had a nanny. Go to the cinema. Something. Anything.

While, at the same time, she underwent the painful process of turning herself into some stranger—the Marchesa Valessi. The wife that no one wanted—least of all Sandro himself.

# CHAPTER SEVEN

'So,' TERESA said, 'in two days you will be married. It is exciting, no?'

'Wonderful,' Polly agreed in a hollow voice.

She didn't feel like a bride, she thought, staring at herself in the mirror, although the hugely expensive cream linen dress which Teresa had persuaded her to buy, and which would take her on to the airport and her new life after the ceremony, was beautifully cut and clung to her slenderness as if it adored her, managing to be stunning and practical at the same time. While her high-heeled strappy shoes were to die for.

It wasn't just the usual trappings of tulle and chiffon that were missing, she thought. It was radiance she lacked.

And at any moment, Teresa would be ordering her to relax, because otherwise the tension in her body would spoil the perfect line of her dress. But the other girl would never understand in a million years that this was not merely bridal nerves, but sheer, blind panic.

Since their confrontation on her first night in the hotel Sandro had taken her at her word and left her strictly to her own devices, except when they were with Teresa and Ernesto, when he continued to play the part of the charming, attentive bridegroom.

On the other occasions when they encountered each other, he was polite but aloof. But these were rare. Except for the sacrosanct hours he devoted to Charlie, he spent very little time at the hotel.

Well, she could not fault him for obeying her wishes, she thought. But she alone knew that she was lonely, and that her sense of isolation would only increase once she reached Comadora.

'Now take the dress off and hang it away,' Teresa cautioned. 'Sandro must not see you in it before the wedding.' She paused. 'Is all well with you, Paola? You are quiet today.'

Polly stepped out of the dress, and slipped it onto a padded hanger. 'Well, for one thing, there's Julie.'

'Oh?' Teresa's eyes twinkled. 'Has she fallen in love with Alessandro?'

'No, of course not,' Polly said. 'At least, I don't think so.'

Teresa giggled. 'They all do. I had a nanny from Australia when the twins were born, and each time Alessandro came into the house she would go pink—like a carnation—and refuse to speak for hours.'

Polly's brows lifted. 'And how did he react?'

'*Ahime*, he did not even notice.' Teresa shrugged. 'It is endearing how little vanity he has in such matters.'

'Well, his arrogance in other ways more than compensates for that,' Polly said crisply, zipping herself into a pretty blue shift dress.

'You would not think so if you had known his father, the Marchese Domenico,' said Teresa. 'Now, there was a supreme autocrat. And of course that old witch he brought to the house after his wife died encouraged him to think he could do no wrong. She and Bianca, her secret weapon.'

Polly put her wedding dress away in the wardrobe. She said, 'What was she like—Bianca? Was she beautiful?'

'An angel.' Teresa waved a languid hand. 'A dove. Submissive and so sweet. I longed to bite her and see if there was honey in her veins instead of blood. And taught by nuns,' she added darkly. 'She wore her purity like a sword—every inch of her being saved for the marriage bed.'

She sighed. 'No wonder Alessandro looked for amusement elsewhere.' She stopped dead, clapping a hand over her mouth, looking at Polly in round-eyed horror. '*Dio*, Paola. My mouth will be my death. Forgive me—please.'

Polly sat down at her dressing table, and ran a comb through her hair. She said quietly, 'There's nothing to forgive. I'm really under no illusion about Sandro—or myself.'

'*Cara*,' Teresa shot off the bed where she'd been sprawling, and came to kneel beside Polly. 'Listen to me. Ernesto—myself—every friend Sandro has—we are so happy that you are together. And that you have given him a son that he adores. Let the past rest. It does not matter.'

'Bianca died,' Polly said. 'That makes it matter.'

'You think he wished to marry her?' Teresa demanded. 'No, and no. It was the *contessa*, who saw to it that Bianca had the old *marchese* twisted round her little finger. With Sandro, he was always harsh, but Bianca was his sweetheart, his darling child. And Bianca wanted Alessandro.'

'Yet you say they weren't lovers.'

Teresa gave her a worldly look. 'But whose choice was that? Ernesto, who has known Alessandro since they were children, told me that she used to watch him constantly—try always to be near him. He said—forgive me, this is not nice, and Ernesto is never unkind—that she was like a bitch on heat.' She shrugged. 'And for her, he was unattainable.'

'Then why did he agree to marry her?'

'His parents' marriage had been an arranged one,' Teresa said. 'It was made clear to him what was expected of him in turn. And perhaps he felt it was a way to please his father at last. He was only twelve when his mother died, and after that his relationship with the *marchese* became even more troubled. And Sandro was wild when he was younger,' she added candidly.

She gave Polly a serious look. 'But you can understand, *cara*, why his relationship with Carlino is so important to him. Why he wishes to make his own son feel loved and secure.'

'Yes,' Polly said quietly. 'I can—see that.'

Teresa got to her feet, brushing the creases from her skirt. 'But you were telling me of Julie. There is some problem?'

'She's having some time off this afternoon to go for a job interview.' Polly sighed. 'Apparently, she's only on a temporary contract with us, which lasts until we get to Italy and then Sandro's staff take over, and she flies back. I—I'm going to miss her badly, and so will Charlie. And she's someone I can talk to in my own language.'

'Then ask him if you may keep her on.' Teresa shrugged. 'It is quite simple.' She gave Polly a wicked grin. 'I am sure that you can persuade him, *cara*. Do as I do. Wait until you are in bed, and you have made him very happy. He will give you anything. And the rest of the servants will be pacified when they have your other *bambini* to care for.'

Polly's blush deepened painfully, but she made herself speak lightly. 'That's the kind of cunning plan I like.'

The way things were between them, he was more likely to fire Julie instantly, she thought ruefully when Teresa had gone. But she could always ask, although it wouldn't be in the way the other girl had suggested.

Not that she had the opportunity for the rest of the day. In the afternoon, she went to visit her parents in a last-ditch effort to get them to come to the wedding.

But Mrs Fairfax, still in her dressing gown and looking pale and wan, was adamant, insisting she wasn't well enough to go, and needed her husband with her in case of emergency.

And she alarmed Charlie by hugging him too tightly, and weeping.

Polly got back to the hotel feeling as if she'd been run down by a train, her only comfort her father's quiet, 'She'll come round, sweetheart. She just needs time.'

Sandro was out, and, although she planned to tackle him about Julie on his return, he was still missing by the time she eventually admitted defeat and went to bed.

He was spending the eve of his wedding with Teresa and Ernesto, who were going to act as their witnesses, so she would just have to catch him first thing in the morning before he left, she told herself.

Charlie had already been collected by Julie, and taken down to the dining room for breakfast, when she woke, so she had the bathroom to herself.

She bathed and put on one of her new dresses—primrose silk with a scooped neck, and slightly flared skirt. Nailing her colours to the mast, she thought with faint defiance as she crossed the drawing room to his door.

'Avanti.' The response to her knock was cool and casual, and Polly, drawing a deep breath, opened the door and went in.

The curtains were drawn back, filling the room with sunlight, and Sandro was in bed, lying back against the piled-up pillows, reading a newspaper and drinking coffee from the breakfast trolley beside him. His skin looked like mahogany against the pristine dazzle of the white bed linen.

He glanced up, his brows snapping together as he saw her.

'Buongiorno,' he murmured after a pause. 'You will forgive me if I do not get up,' he added, indicating the sheet draped over his hips which was quite clearly his only covering. 'Would you like coffee?'

'No, thank you.' Polly shifted uneasily from one foot to the other, praying she would not blush, and wondering if it was possible to look at someone without actually seeing them. And certainly without staring. And particularly without feeling that treacherous excitement slowly uncurling inside her. 'I've had breakfast.'

'How virtuous of you, *cara*,' he drawled. 'They bring an extra cup each morning, presumably because they hope I will eventually get lucky. I think I shall have to tell them to stop.' He refilled his own cup. 'So—to what do I owe this extraordinary pleasure?'

Polly gritted her teeth. 'I—I've come to ask you a favour.'

His brows rose. 'You fascinate me, *bella mia*. Especially when you choose my bedroom to make your request.'

'Well, don't read anything into that,' Polly said shortly. 'It's just that I seem to see so little of you these days.'

Sandro moved, stretching slowly and indolently, letting the concealing sheet slip a little. 'You are seeing enough of me this morning, *carissima*,' he drawled. 'Or do you want more?'

She glared at him. 'No.'

'You disappoint me,' he murmured. 'But if it is not my body, I presume it is money. How much do you want?'

'Money?' Polly repeated in bewilderment. 'Of course it isn't. I haven't spent half the allowance you made me.'

'I would not grudge more.' Folding his arms behind his head, Sandro studied her through half-closed eyes, frankly absorbing the cling of the silk to her body, a faint smile curving his mouth. 'You seem to be spending it wisely.'

She flushed under his scrutiny. 'Thank you—I think.'

*'Prego.'* He continued to watch her. 'I hope you do not wish me to persuade your mother to attend the wedding. I should hate to disappoint you.'

She bit her lip. 'No. I've accepted that it's a lost cause. Besides, she wouldn't listen to you. You—you seem to make her nervous.'

*'Mi dispiace,'* he returned without any real sign of regret. 'I seem to have the same effect on you, *cara mia*. So—what is it?'

She swallowed. 'I'd like Julie to stay in Italy with us, and go on looking after Charlie—please.'

Sandro moved slightly, adjusting the sheet to a more respectable level. He sent her a meditative look.

He said, 'Paola, I have a houseful of staff who are dancing for joy at the prospect of looking after the future *marchese*. He will not lack for attention, I promise you.'

'No,' she said. 'But he's used to Julie, and he likes her. Anyway, the others will speak Italian to him, and he might feel lost at first.' She hesitated. 'And I like Julie too, and I can talk to her in English. In spite of Teresa's coaching, I'm going to feel pretty isolated.'

'*Davvero?*' His tone was sardonic. 'You do not feel that you could talk to me, perhaps?'

That was what Teresa had said, she thought, biting her lip again. She looked at the floor. 'That isn't very likely,' she said constrictedly. 'After all, we're not marrying for any kind of companionship, but for Charlie's sake.'

'Does one rule out the other?' He was frowning slightly.

'I think it has to,' Polly countered, with a touch of desperation. 'And after all, you—you won't always be there,' she added, feeling dejectedly that she was losing the argument. 'You have your work—your own life to lead.'

'No,' he said, quietly. 'That is true.' He shrugged a naked shoulder. '*Va bene*. If that is what you want, I agree.'

'Oh.' Polly found herself blinking. 'Well—thank you.'

'Is that all? I am disappointed.' The topaz eyes glinted at her. 'I was hoping for a more—tangible expression of gratitude.'

Polly stiffened. 'I don't think I understand.'

'And I think you do.' He smiled at her, and held out a hand in invitation. 'Is one kiss too much to ask?'

She wanted to tell him to go to hell, but there was too much riding on this transaction.

She said coldly, 'You're not as generous as I thought.'

'And nor are you, *carissima*,' he said gently. 'Which is why I have so far asked for so little. Besides, you will have to kiss me tomorrow at the wedding. It is tradition.' His smile widened. 'And you certainly need the practice.'

There was a taut silence, then Polly trod awkwardly to the side of the bed. Ignoring his proffered hand, she bent to brush his cheek with swift, unyielding lips.

But before she could straighten, Sandro had grasped her wrists in an unbreakable hold, and she was being drawn inexorably downwards, losing her balance in the process. She found she was being turned skilfully, so that she was lying across his body, the outrage in her eyes meeting the mockery in his. Mockery mingled with something altogether more disturbing. Something that, in spite of herself, every pulse in her body leapt to meet.

He said softly, 'But I will not settle for as little as that, Paola *mia*.'

And her instinctive cry of protest was stifled by the warmth of his mouth on hers.

He kissed her deeply and thoroughly, holding her imprisoned in one arm, while his other hand twined in her hair to hold her still, defeating any attempt she might make to struggle. Forcing her to endure the sensuous and unashamedly possessive invasion of his tongue, as his mouth moved on hers in sheer and unashamed enticement.

Robbing her, she realised numbly, of any real desire to fight him. Awakening very different memories—and longings.

The heat of the sun pouring through the window—the unforgettable scent of his naked skin—the pressure of his lithe, muscular body against hers sent the last three years rolling back, and they were lovers again, their bodies aching and melting to be joined together in the ultimate intimacy, yet deliberately holding back to prolong the sweetness of the final moments.

He had always wooed her with kisses, she remembered dazedly, arousing her with a patient, passionate tenderness that splintered her control, and sent her reason spinning, so that she clung to him mutely imploring his possession.

Why else had she been unable to see that bringing her to eager, quivering acquiescence was the work of a practised seducer?

Yet even now, it seemed, she was unable to resist him, or the sensual magic of his lips.

When he lifted his head she was breathless, her heart thudding unevenly against her ribcage—which he must have known, because his hand had moved and was gently cupping her breast, his thumb stroking her hardening nipple to a rapturous peak through the silk of her dress.

He looked down at her, his eyes glittering and intent, asking a question which she was too scared and confused to answer. She only knew that if he kissed her again, she would be lost. And as he bent to her once more, a soft moan, half-fear, half-yearning, parted her lips.

And then, swiftly and shockingly, it was over, as the telephone beside the bed suddenly rang, its stridency shattering the heated intensity within the room like a fist through a pane of glass.

Sandro swore softly and fluently, but his hold on her relaxed, and she forced herself out of his embrace and off the bed, and ran to the door.

She flew across the intervening space, snatching at the door handle to her own bedroom, but as she did so it opened anyway, and she half fell into the room beyond.

As she struggled to recover her balance, there was a cry of 'Mammina' and Charlie, looking angelic, came scampering towards her from the bathroom, with Julie close behind.

'He had a little accident with his cereal this morning,' she told Polly, trying to look severe. 'I've just had to change his top and trousers. You wouldn't believe how far he can spread one small bowl.'

As Polly bent to him, fighting for calm, the door opposite was flung wide, and Sandro came striding towards them, his face like thunder, tying the belt of a robe he'd clearly thrown on as an afterthought.

Polly scooped Charlie up in her arms, and turned to face him defensively.

He halted, staring at her, his ominous frown deepening. He said in Italian, 'We need to talk, you and I. Now.'

'There's nothing to talk about,' Polly said, nervously aware that Julie had vanished with discreet haste back into the bathroom. She reverted to her own language. 'I should have known I couldn't trust you.'

His mouth twisted contemptuously. 'No,' he said. 'I think, my beautiful hypocrite, that you realised you could not trust yourself. It is that simple. So why, for once in your life, can't you be honest?'

He took a step towards her, and she recoiled, still clutching Charlie, who was beginning to wriggle. She said hoarsely, 'Don't touch me. Don't dare to come near me. You—you promised to leave me alone.'

'That will be my pleasure,' Sandro hit back. 'Now, be silent. You are frightening our son.' Charlie was squirming round, his lip trembling, holding out his arms to his father, and Sandro took him from her, soothing the little boy quietly.

He said, 'He will spend the day with me. I will telephone to say when he may be collected.' He carried him back to his own room, where he turned and looked back at Polly, his eyes icy with warning.

He said too softly, 'And, as long as you live, *signorina*, never—never again use our child as a barrier between us.'

The door closed behind them both, leaving Polly shaking and alone in the middle of the room.

'Are you all right, Miss Fairfax?' Julie was regarding her anxiously from the doorway.

Polly mustered her reserves. 'Yes,' she lied. 'Fine. A—a misunderstanding, that's all.'

'I thought at first that the *marchese* had come to give you the good news,' Julie said. 'He spoke to me as I was going off duty yesterday evening, and suggested that I should go to Italy as well, to help Charlie to settle in. Isn't that great? I was going to tell you myself, first thing, only his lordship there did his trick with the cereal.'

Polly's hands slowly curled into fists. He knew, she thought, fury uncurling inside her. He knew exactly what I was going to ask, and used it against me. A ploy to get me into bed with him. And—dear God—I was almost fool enough to fall for it. To give in.

'Miss Fairfax?' Julie was looking puzzled. 'I thought you'd be pleased.'

'Yes,' Polly said, summoning a hurried smile. 'I'm delighted. That's—absolutely wonderful. Just what we both wanted.'

She paused. 'And Charlie's spending the day with his father, so you have some free time to go and pack for the Campania. Mind you take a couple of bikinis too,' she added over-brightly. 'Apparently the *palazzo* has a pool.'

Julie's face lit up. 'Well—if you don't mind...'

When the other girl had gone, Polly walked over to one of the sofas and sat for a long time, with her face buried in her hands.

She was angry, but her anger was mixed with guilt too. It was wrong of her to use Charlie like that, but the truth was she hadn't dared allow Sandro to touch her again. Or come within a yard of her, for that matter.

As it was, she felt sick with shame at how easily he'd drawn a response from her. And how her unfulfilled body now felt torn apart by frustration. Like the first time he had made love to her, she thought wretchedly, when she'd been wild for him, his caresses exciting her to the point of desperation. When, at last, he'd entered her, her body had been molten with need, and there'd been no pain.

Just a rapturous sense of total completion, she thought wretchedly. And what she'd believed was utter love.

I know better now, she told herself, her mind raw. I know he was just using me for sex—nothing more, but that's something I'll learn to live with.

But I can't let it happen ever again—and I won't.

She hadn't taken his money, she thought harshly. Nor would she accept the false coin of his lovemaking, no matter what the cost to her as a woman. And no matter how she might ache for him, as she did now.

The next day, she married Sandro in a ceremony so brief she could hardly believe it was legal. As they were pronounced man and wife, and he turned to her, she closed her eyes, bracing herself for the promised kiss, only to feel his lips brush her cheek swiftly and coldly.

As she stepped back she glimpsed Teresa and Ernesto exchanging astonished glances, and moved to them to be hugged with real warmth. Teresa drew her to one side. 'A little gift, *cara*,' she whispered, handing her a flat parcel, wrapped in silver tissue with violet ribbons. 'Do not open it now. Wait until tonight.'

Polly forced a smile of thanks, and put the package in the soft leather shoulder bag which served as her hand luggage.

There were no problems on the flight itself. Polly had never travelled first class before, and sitting in comfort, being served champagne, at least gave a veneer of celebration to the day's proceedings.

Charlie chatted in wonder about 'big planes', gave an imitation of a jumbo jet taking off, then fell asleep, but he awoke grouchily when they reached Naples, and the subsequent journey soon disintegrated into nightmare.

Polly discovered, dismayed, that her son did not enjoy travelling by car, even an air-conditioned limousine, and that he was constantly and miserably sick throughout the trip.

Every few miles they were forced to stop, so that Charlie could

be cleaned up and comforted, and eventually Julie, who'd borne
the brunt of the little boy's misery, was sent to sit in the passenger
seat beside the chauffeur, and Sandro took her place, cradling
Charlie on his lap and talking to him gently.

'Why not give him back to me?' Polly suggested, aware that
her linen dress was already ruined. 'I'm worried that he'll spoil
your beautiful suit,' she added awkwardly.

He gave her a look of faint impatience. *'Che importa?'* he
demanded, and Polly subsided, biting her lip and turning to look
out of the window.

Up till now, she'd been totally unaware of the scenery she was
passing through, all her attention given to Charlie's woes. But now
she had a breathing space to take in the reality of her surroundings.
The road they were travelling had been carved out of the rock-
face which towered above them. On the other side was the eternal
blue of the Mediterranean, serene today, reflecting the cloudless
sky. And straight ahead, nestling in the curve of the bay, a cluster
of terracotta roofs round a boat-studded marina.

Beyond it, a rocky promontory jutted into the sea, dominated
by a large rectangular building with faded pink walls, made even
more imposing by the tower at each of its corners.

She did not need Sandro's quiet 'Comadora at last' to recognise
that this place, more a fortress than a palace, was to be her home,
and Charlie's inheritance.

She said, 'It—it looks a little daunting.'

'That would have been the intention, when it was built,' he
agreed drily. 'This coast was often attacked by pirates.'

'Yes,' she said, her tone subdued. 'That was part of the local
history I had to learn when I was here—before.' She hesitated. 'I
suppose I must learn not to mention that.'

*'Perche?'* His brows lifted. 'Why should you think so?'

She said stiffly, 'I didn't think you'd want your family to know
that your wife used to be a travel rep.'

'Why, Paola,' he said softly, 'what a snob you are.'

Polly bit her lip. 'How did you explain why I was back in your
life? It might be better if I knew.'

He shrugged. 'After the crash, I suffered memory problems for
a while, something they all know. Once I recovered fully, you had
disappeared, and it took time for me to find you.' He looked at

her over Charlie's sleeping head, his smile mocking. 'And now we are together again—united in bliss forever.'

Polly drew a breath. 'Your restored memory seems to have been pretty selective.'

'You have a better version?'

'No,' she admitted unwillingly. 'But no one's ever going to believe that we're—blissfully happy.'

'Then pretend, *cara mia*.' There was a sudden hard note in his voice. 'Pretend like you did three summers ago, when you let me believe you found pleasure in bed with me.'

'Sandro—please...' She felt her face warm, and turned away hurriedly, her body clenching in swift, intimate yearning.

That jibe of hers, uttered purely in self-defence that first night at the flat, seemed to have hit a nerve, she thought unhappily. But it didn't mean anything. After all, no man liked to have his expertise as a lover challenged.

'Do I embarrass you?' he asked coldly. 'My regrets.'

There was a silence, then he said, 'Will you tell me something, Paola? When you went back to England, did you already know that you were carrying my child?'

'No,' she said. 'No, I didn't.'

'Ah,' Sandro said quietly.

The car turned in between tall wrought-iron gates, and negotiated the long winding drive which ended in a paved courtyard before the main entrance to the *palazzo*.

It was bright with flowers in long stone troughs, and in the middle was a fountain sending a slender, glittering spire of water into the air.

Thank God, Polly thought as the car drew up. Peace at last. She stretched, moving her aching shoulders, longing for a bath and a change of clothing, hopefully with a cold drink included somewhere too.

The car bringing their luggage would have arrived ages ago, she thought.

It seemed that if she was going to be unhappy, at least it would be in comfort. But for now, that thought brought no solace at all.

The massive arched double doors opened, and a man, short and balding, dressed in an immaculate grey linen jacket came hurrying across the courtyard to meet them, looking anxious.

He looks like the bearer of bad news, thought Polly. Perhaps there's been another accident and our luggage is all at the bottom of the Mediterranean.

Clearly Sandro was concerned, because he deposited Charlie on her lap and got out.

The little man, hands waving, launched himself into some kind of diatribe, and Polly watched Sandro's expression change from disbelief to a kind of cold fury, and he turned away, lifting clenched fists towards the sky.

When he came back to the car, he was stony-faced as he opened Polly's door.

'The *contessa*,' he said, 'has decided to surprise us with a welcome party, and has filled the *palazzo* with members of my family, including my cousin Emilio,' he added with a snap. 'Tonight, Teodoro tells me, there will be a formal dinner, followed by a reception for some of the local people.'

'Oh, God, no.' Polly looked down in horror at her stained and rumpled dress. 'I can't meet people like this. Is there no other entrance we could use?'

'There are many,' he said. 'But the Marchesa Valessi does not sneak into her house through a back door. Give me Carlino, and we will face them all together.'

Stomach churning, she obeyed, pulling her dress straight and pushing shaking fingers through her dishevelled hair.

Then Sandro's hand closed round hers, firmly and inflexibly, and she began to walk beside him towards the doorway of the *palazzo*. As they reached it, she lifted her chin and straightened her shoulders, and was aware of his swift approving glance.

She was fleetingly aware of a hall hung with tapestries, and a wide stone staircase leading up to a gallery. A clamour of voices abruptly stilled.

People watching her, eyes filled with avid curiosity or open disapproval, a few smiling. And, for a moment, she almost froze.

Then Charlie lifted his head from his father's shoulder, and looked at all the strange faces around him. In a second his expression had changed from bewilderment to alarm, and he uttered a loud howl of distress, and began to sob.

Polly felt the atmosphere in the great hall change instantly. Censure was replaced by sympathy, and the marked silence that had greeted them changed to murmurs of, 'Poor little one, he is tired,' and, 'He is a true Valessi, that one.'

The crowd parted, and a small, plump woman, her hair heavily streaked with grey, came bustling through. Arms outstretched, voice lovingly scolding, she took Charlie from his father's arms and, beckoning imperiously to the wilting Julie to follow, disappeared just as rapidly, the sobbing Charlie held securely against the high bib of her starched apron.

'That was Dorotea,' Sandro said quietly, his taut mouth relaxing into a faint smile. 'Don't worry, Paola, she has a magic touch. Carlino will be bathed, changed, fed and in a good mood before he knows what is happening. And Julie also,' he added drily.

Lucky them, Polly thought, and groaned inwardly as the crowd parted again for the *contessa*.

'*Caro* Alessandro.' She embraced him formally. 'Welcome home. As you see, your family could not wait to meet your beautiful wife.'

'I am overwhelmed,' Sandro said politely. 'But I wish you had allowed Teodoro to give me advance warning of your plans.'

She gave a tinkling laugh. 'But then there would have been no surprise.'

'No,' he said. 'That is precisely what I mean.'

He looked about him. 'I am delighted to welcome you all,' he began. 'But as you can see we have had a bad journey with a sick child, and my wife is exhausted. She will meet you all when she has rested.' He turned to Polly. 'Go with Zia Antonia, *carissima*, and I will join you presently.'

Polly was aware of an absurd impulse to cling to his hand. 'Don't leave me with her,' she wanted to say. Instead she forced a smile and nodded, and followed the *contessa*'s upright figure towards the stairs.

From the gallery, they seemed to traverse a maze of passages until they arrived at last at another pair of double doors, elaborately carved.

The *contessa* flung them open and motioned Polly to precede her. 'This is where you are to sleep,' she said.

Polly paused, drawing a deep breath. She had never imagined occupying such a room, she thought dazedly. It was vast and very old, its ceiling beamed, and the walls decorated with exquisite frescos.

It was dominated by one enormous canopied bed, with crimson

brocade curtains and a magnificent bedspread in the same colour, quilted in gold thread, but little other furniture.

'That door is to the bathroom.' The *contessa* pointed a manicured hand. 'I think you will find all you need.' And the sooner the better, her tone of voice seemed to indicate. 'The other leads to the dressing room, where your clothes have been unpacked for you.' She paused. 'Would you like some tea to be brought to you?'

'That would be kind.' Polly hesitated. 'If it's not too much trouble—as you have all these other guests, I mean.'

'How can it be a difficulty?' The thin lips wore a vinegary smile. 'After all, *cara* Paola, you are the mistress of the house now, and your wish is our command.' She indicated a thick golden rope. 'Pull the bell, if you wish for the services of a maid to help you dress. Or perhaps your husband will prefer to assist you himself— as this is your *luna di miele*.'

'I can manage,' Polly said quietly, conscious of the faint sneer in the older woman's voice, and the swift pang of alarm that her words engendered. 'But I would like to make sure my son is all right, and I don't know where the nursery is.'

'I will instruct Dorotea to take you to him later.' She looked Polly up and down with faint disdain. 'Now, I recommend that you do as Alessandro suggests, and take some rest. After all, this will be your wedding night, officially at least,' she added, with another silvery laugh, and left the room, closing the door behind her.

Left to herself, Polly walked over to the long windows and opened the shutters. She knelt on the embrasure, lifting her face to the heavy golden warmth of the late afternoon.

If the *contessa* had deliberately plotted to present her at her worst, she could not have done a better job, she thought bitterly. But there was no way the older woman could have known how badly Charlie would react to the long journey from the airport.

I wish I could stay here, she thought, because I think I've already got *'null points'* from the jury downstairs.

Instead, she had to put on one of the evening dresses Teresa had made her buy, and play her unwanted role as *marchesa* with whatever style and grace she could summon. And undo, if possible, that first unfortunate impression.

And talking of Teresa... Polly fetched her shoulder bag, and retrieved the parcel it contained. As she undid the ribbons, the tissue parted to reveal a cascade of the finest black lace.

Polly's eyes widened as she examined it. It was a nightgown, she realised, low-necked, split to the thigh on one side, and almost transparent. Provocation at its most exquisite. An expensive, daring tease.

Any girl who wore it would feel irresistibly sexy. And any man who saw it couldn't fail to be aroused.

It seemed clear that Teresa had sensed the tensions in her relationship with Sandro, and decided the honeymoon could need a kick-start.

As Sandro said, you're shrewd, Polly addressed her friend silently, bundling the delicate fabric back into its wrappings, and wondering where she could hide it. But this time you've misread the situation badly.

She left the package on the bed for the time being, and went to investigate the bathroom. The room itself probably dated from the Renaissance, she thought, but the plumbing was strictly twenty-first century, and luxurious in the extreme.

The walls were tiled in shades of blue, interspersed with mother-of-pearl, which gave the impression that the room was under shimmering water.

There was a deep sunken bath, and a capacious shower cubicle in the shape of a hexagon, with a pretty gilded roof.

Thankfully Polly slipped out of her clothes, and stepped behind its glass panels. There was a corner shelf holding toiletries, and she chose some scented foam, lathering her body sensuously. The jet was powerful, but reviving, and she twisted and turned under it, feeling some of the tensions of the day seeping away.

She dried herself slowly, her body refreshed and glowing, then took another bath sheet from the pile and wound it round herself, sarong-style, securing it just above her breasts.

If only her tea was waiting, she thought, opening the bathroom door, then, however briefly, life might be perfect.

She walked into the bedroom, and stopped dead, lips parted in shock, and her heart beating an alarmed tattoo.

Because Sandro was there, stretched out across the bed, his coat and tie discarded, and his shirt unbuttoned to the waist.

'Ciao, bella,' he said softly, his eyes lingering on her bare shoulders in undisguised appreciation. 'You look wonderful, and smell delicious,' he went on. 'And now there is this.' He held up the black nightgown with a soft whistle. 'Perhaps marriage may have its compensations after all.'

And as she watched, transfixed, he lifted himself lithely off the bed, and began to walk towards her, the black lace draped over his arm.

# CHAPTER EIGHT

POLLY took a step backwards. She said hoarsely, 'What are you doing here?'

'I want to take a shower,' he said. 'I decided you would probably not wish me to join you, so—I waited.'

She took a breath. 'How—considerate.' Her voice stung. 'Perhaps you'd be even kinder and go to your own room, and use your own shower. I'd like my privacy.'

'So would I, *cara*, but we are both to be disappointed. Thanks to Zia Antonia, all the rooms in the *palazzo* are occupied by other people and will remain so for tomorrow—the day after—who knows?' He paused. 'Also you are under a misapprehension. This is my room—and my shower.'

He paused to allow her to digest that, his mouth twisting in sardonic amusement at her shocked expression.

'The accommodation intended for you is currently taken by my aunt Vittoria, a pious widow with a hearing problem,' he went on. 'She does not like to share either. Also, she snores, which, as you know, I do not.'

He smiled at her. 'But she is certainly leaving tomorrow, so you will only have one night to endure in my company,' he added lightly.

She stared at him, her hands nervously adjusting the towel. 'You really imagine I'm actually going to sleep here—with you?' Her voice rose stormily. 'You must be mad. I can't—I *won't*...'

'You will certainly spend the night with me,' he interrupted, a harsh note in his voice. 'I cannot predict whether or not you will sleep. That is not my concern.'

'Then what does concern you?' She glared at him. 'Certainly not keeping your word.'

He flung exasperated hands at the ceiling. '*Dio*—you think I planned this? That I have deliberately filled my house with a pack of gossiping relatives, including my cousin Emilio, may he rot in hell,' he added with real bite, 'just so that I can trick you into bed with me?'

He gave her a scornful look. 'You overestimate your charms, *bella mia*. You will stay here tonight, without fuss or further argument, for the sake of appearances, because it is our wedding night, and because we have no choice in the matter.

'But let me attempt to allay your obvious fears,' he went on cuttingly. Clasping her wrist, he strode back to the bed, with Polly stumbling after him, tripping on the edge of her towel. He dragged back the satin coverlet, dislodging the huge lace-trimmed pillows to reveal a substantial bolster. 'That,' he said, pointing contemptuously, 'placed down the middle of the bed, should deter my frenzy of desire for you. I hope you are reassured.'

He paused. 'May I remind you, Paola, you agreed to co-operate in presenting our marriage as a conventional one.'

'Yes.' Polly bit her lip. 'But—I didn't realise then what could be involved.'

His smile was thin. 'Well, do not worry too much, *carissima*. There are enough willing women in the world. I see no need to force someone so clearly reluctant.'

He held up the nightgown. 'Although your prudishness hardly matches your choice of nightwear. Why buy a garment so seductive, if you do not wish to be seduced?'

'I didn't buy it,' Polly said stonily. 'It was a present from Teresa.'

'Indeed,' he murmured. 'I never guessed she was such a romantic. Or such an optimist,' he added, his mouth curving in genuine amusement.

'Don't tear it,' he told her mockingly, as Polly made an unavailing attempt to snatch it from him. 'That is a privilege I might prefer to reserve for myself.'

She glared at him. 'Not in this lifetime,' she said defiantly.

'And certainly not unless I wish to do so,' he reminded her softly. 'However, for now, I shall have to console myself with imagining how it might look if you wore it, *bella mia*.' He gave it a last, meditative glance. 'Like a shadow falling across moonlight,' he said quietly, and tossed it to her. 'I must write to Teresa and thank her,' he added with a swift grin, as he straightened the bedclothes.

'And I,' she said coldly, 'shall not.' She swallowed. 'I would like to get dressed now, please.'

His brows lifted, as he scanned the slipping towel. 'You want assistance?'

'No.' She managed just in time to avoid stamping her bare foot on the tiled floor. 'Just some privacy.' She shook her head. 'Oh, can't you see how impossible this all is?'

'I can only see that I shall have to stop teasing you, *cara mia*,' he said with unexpected gentleness. 'Get dressed if you wish, but there is no need for you to face the inquisition downstairs, unless you want to do so. And it is a long time until dinner, when you will be expected to make an appearance, so why not rest quietly here until then? I promise you will not be disturbed,' he added levelly. 'By anyone.'

As she hesitated there was a knock on the door, and a small, round-faced girl came in carrying a tray with Polly's tea. She stopped, her mouth forming into an embarrassed 'o'.

'*Mi scusi, excellenza,*' she stammered. 'I thought the *marchesa* was alone.'

Sandro smiled at her. 'Come here and meet your new mistress, Rafaella.' He turned to Polly. 'I have arranged for this child to become your personal maid, *cara mia*. She is the granddaughter of an old friend, so be kind to her.'

Polly, about to flatly deny any need of a personal maid, saw the girl's eager face, and subsided.

'Once you have had your tea,' Sandro went on, 'I hope she can persuade you to sleep for a while, even if I cannot,' he added wryly. 'And I shall ask her to return at eight to help you to dress for dinner.'

Polly nodded resginedly. 'Thank you. Darling,' she added as an afterthought, and saw his lips twitch before he turned away, heading for the bathroom.

Rafaella set the tray down on one of the old ornamental tables that flanked the bed, then flew to the dressing room, returning with a dark blue satin robe, which Polly awkwardly exchanged for the towel.

'*Parli inglese?*' she asked as the girl folded back the coverlet to the foot of the bed, and plumped up the pillows.

Her face lit up. '*Sì, vossignoria.* I worked for an English family, *au pair*, for two years. I learn much.'

'Yet you came back to work at the *palazzo*?'

Rafaella nodded vigorously. 'It is an honour for me, and for my grandfather, who asked for this post for me, when his *signoria* wished to reward him.'

'Reward him?' Polly queried.

'It was my grandfather who found the *marchese* when his car crashed into the ravine,' Rafaella explained. 'He saw it happen, and ran to help. At first he thought his *signoria* was dead, because he did not move, and there was so much blood, but then he could feel his pulse and knew that he lived, so my grandfather went to the car to rescue the lady.' She shrugged. 'But it was too late.'

Polly winced. 'It must have been a horrible experience for him.'

'*Sì, vossignoria.* He spoke about it to the inquiry, and also to his *signoria* when he was in hospital, but never since. There is too much pain in such memories.'

She bent to retrieve the discarded bath sheet, then straightened, beaming. 'So it is good that the *marchese* is now happy again.'

'Yes.' Polly realised with acute embarrassment that the girl was holding up the black lace nightgown, which must have been entangled in the folds of the towel. 'I—I suppose so.'

She tried to concentrate on her tea, and ignore Rafaella's stifled giggle as she carried the nightdress off to the dressing room.

No doubt the rumour mill at the *palazzo* would soon be in full swing, she thought, swallowing. But at least it would support the idea that this was a real marriage, which would please Sandro.

She put down her cup and turned on her side, shutting her eyes determinedly, and, presently, she heard Rafaella's quiet departure.

It would be good to relax, she thought, burrowing her cheek into the lavender-scented pillow. To recover from the stress and strain of the past days and weeks, and re-focus on this extraordinary new life, to which, for good or ill, she now belonged.

Thanks to the *contessa*, it was proving a more difficult start than she'd anticipated, she told herself, sighing.

For one thing, and in spite of the closed bathroom door, she could clearly hear the sound of the shower, reviving all kinds of past associations, and she pressed her hands over her ears, in an attempt to shut them out.

She didn't want to remember those other times when Sandro had been showering, and she'd joined him, their bodies slippery under the torrent of water, her mouth fierce on his skin, his arms strong as he lifted her against him, filling her with the renewed urgency of his desire.

But the memories were too strong, too potent to be dismissed, and for a moment, as her body melted in recollection, she was pierced once more with the temptation to abandon all pride and go to him.

But it would pass, she thought. It had to. Because she would not be drawn again into the web of sensuality where she'd been trapped before. It was just a moment of weakness because she was tired—so very tired...

And gradually, the distant rush of water became a lullaby that, against all odds, soothed her to sleep.

She had never really dressed for dinner before, Polly thought as she sat in front of the mirror, watching Rafaella apply the finishing touches to her hair. The other girl had drawn the shining strands into a loose knot on top of Polly's head, softening the look with a few loose tendrils that were allowed to curl against her face, and the nape of her neck.

Her dress was a sleek column of black silk, long-sleeved, with a neckline that discreetly revealed the first swell of her breasts, and gave her skin the sheen of a pearl.

She'd kept her make-up deliberately muted, faintly emphasising the green of her eyes, and curving her mouth with a soft rose lustre.

Whatever her inward inadequacies, this time she would at least look the part of the Marchesa Valessi, she thought.

She had hoped that Sandro would be beside her again, to guide her through her second entrance, but Rafaella had told her that he had changed for dinner and rejoined his guests while she still slept.

So, she'd have to brave them all alone.

Sighing under her breath, she rose. 'Rafaella, I'd like to say goodnight to my son before dinner. Can you take me to the nursery, *per favore*?'

'*Sì, vossignoria.* Of course.'

'And that "*vossignoria*" is a terrible mouthful,' Polly went on. 'Maybe we could change it. What did you call your last boss?'

Rafaella looked a little startled. '*Signora*, sometimes, but usually *madame*.'

Polly smiled at her. 'Then that will be fine with me, too.'

'But I was instructed, *vossignoria*, by the *contessa*.'

'And now you're getting further instructions from me,' Polly advised her crisply. 'From now on it's *madame*, and that's final.'

'As you say, *madame*.' Rafaella's agreement was subdued.

Polly was expecting another maze of passages, but the nursery turned out to be only round a corner, and up a flight of stairs.

It wouldn't have been far for Dorotea to come, she thought as she opened the door and walked in.

She found herself in a spacious room lined with cupboards. There was a table in the middle, and a young girl was tidying up, placing toys in a large wicker basket.

Her jaw dropped as Polly entered in a rustle of silk, and she hurried over to a half-open door on the other side of the room, and said something in a low voice. A moment later, Dorotea joined them. She inclined her head stiffly to Polly, then turned to Rafaella and launched herself into a flood of half-whispered Italian, complete with gestures.

Rafaella looked at Polly with an awkward shrug. 'She regrets, *madame*, but your son is asleep. She was not expecting a visit from you. She understood that your duties to your guests came first.'

'Nothing comes before my little boy,' Polly said quietly. 'And I thought it was arranged that she would come and fetch me once he was settled. I have been waiting.'

She paused. 'Clearly, there has been some misunderstanding tonight, but explain to her, please, that we will speak in the morning about Carlino's future routine. And now I would like to kiss my son goodnight.'

Dorotea listened to Rafaella's translation, but it brought no lightening of her expression. And she stood unwillingly aside to give Polly access to the night nursery.

A nightlight in a holder shaped like a shell was burning near his cot, and Charlie was lying on his back, his arms flung wide, his breathing soft and regular.

Polly stood looking down at him, then bent and brushed a strand of hair back from his face with gentle fingers. At the same time she became aware that Dorotea, who'd been watching from the doorway, arms folded across her bosom, was bobbing a kind of curtsy and muttering a deferential '*Excellenza*' as she backed out of the room. And she realised that Sandro had come to join her.

She had never seen him in dinner jacket and black tie before, and the breath caught in her throat, because this new formality conferred its own kind of magnificence. It also set him at a distance, which was all to the good, she told herself.

She summoned a smile. '*Buonasera.* I came to say goodnight. Maybe even goodbye, just in case they tear me to pieces downstairs.'

'They will not do that. They are all eager to meet you.'

She looked back at the cot. 'How—how beautiful,' she said, softly. 'Don't you think so?'

'*Sì,*' he agreed quietly. 'Beautiful indeed.' And she realised that he was looking at her, and turned away as she felt her body quiver in instinctive response, walking past him into the now-deserted day nursery.

He followed. 'But I did not come simply to see Carlino,' he went on. 'I have something for you, *cara mia.*' His hands touched her shoulders, halting her, and Polly felt the slide of something metallic against her throat, and glanced down.

The necklace was nearly an inch wide, a flat, delicate network of gold, studded with the blue-white fire of diamonds. She touched it with a wondering hand. 'Sandro—it's lovely. But there's no need for this.'

'I am permitted to give you a wedding present,' he told her drily.

'I—suppose.' She shook her head. 'But I feel dreadful because I have nothing for you.'

'You don't think so?'

He turned her slowly to face him, then bent towards her, and she felt his lips rest softly, briefly on her forehead. She had not expected that, and his intense gentleness made her tremble.

'My beloved girl,' he whispered. 'You are here with me at last.'

The sudden flash of light from the doorway was a harsh, unbearable intrusion. Stunned and dazzled, Polly pulled free, looking round wildly. 'What was that?'

'My cousin Emilio,' Sandro said with a shrug. 'Armed with a camera, and searching for some moment of intimacy between us to thrill his readers.'

She stared at him. 'You *knew* he was there?'

'I was aware he had followed me upstairs,' he said. 'And guessed his motive. I think we provided what he wanted,' he added, casually. 'And you did well, Paola *mia*. You almost convinced me.'

Hurt slashed at her like a razor. Just for a moment, she'd believed him—believed the tenderness of his kiss.

She said colourlessly, 'I'm starting to learn—at last.'

She paused, taking a steadying breath. 'And while I'm on a roll, why don't you take me downstairs and present me to your family? Because I'm ready.'

'And no more only children,' Zia Vittoria boomed authoritatively. 'In Alessandro's case, it was understandable. His mother was a delicate creature, and no one expected too much, but you seem to be a healthy young woman, and Alessandro's first born is a fine child, in spite of his irregular birth. I commend you,' she added graciously.

Polly, seated at her side, with her smile nailed on, murmured something grateful, and wondered what the penalty might be for strangling a deaf Italian dowager. She was aware of sympathetic smiles around the room, and a swift glance, brimming with unholy mirth, from Sandro.

I should have known it was going too well, she thought grimly.

Dinner in the tapestry-hung banqueting hall had been a splendid occasion. She had sat opposite her husband at the end of a long candlelit table shining with exquisite silver and crystal, and been formally welcomed to the family by Sandro's ancient great-uncle Filippo. Her health had been drunk with every course served, and her neighbours had vied with each other to talk to her, delighted when she'd attempted to reply in Italian. Only the *contessa* had stayed aloof from the talk and laughter round the table, sitting like a marble statue, her mouth set in a thin, unamused smile.

At the reception which followed, Polly had been presented to various local dignitaries, and invited to serve on several charity committees. Sandro, standing at her side, his arm lightly encircling her waist, explained with great charm that, with a young child, his wife's time was limited, but she would consider all proposals in due course.

After which the visitors left expressing their good wishes for the happiness of the *marchese* and his bride, and Polly had felt able to relax a little. Until, that was, she'd found herself summoned by Zia Vittoria, and subjected to an inquisition on her background, upbringing and education in a voice that was probably audible in the marina, even before she tackled Polly's suitability to add to the Valessi dynasty.

When the good lady was finally distracted by the offer of more champagne, Polly seized the opportunity to escape. It was a warm night, and the long windows of the *salotto* had been opened. Polly slipped through the filmy drapes, and out onto the terrace, drawing a shaky breath of relief when she found herself alone.

The air was still, and the sky heavy with stars, just as she remembered. Even before she met Sandro, she had always loved the Italian nights, so relaxed and sensuous.

Polly moved to the edge of the terrace, and leaned on the stone balustrade, inhaling the faint scents that rose from the unseen garden below. Tomorrow, she would explore the *palazzo*'s grounds with Charlie—find the swimming pool perhaps. Take hold of this new life with both hands, and make it work somehow.

As she stared into the darkness, she suddenly became aware of another scent, more pungent and less romantic than the hidden flowers. The smell of a cigar.

She turned abruptly, and saw a man standing a few yards away from her. He was of medium height, and verging towards the plump. Handsome, too, apart from the small, petulant mouth beneath his thin black moustache. And well-pleased with himself, instinct told her.

She met his bold, appraising stare, her chin lifted haughtily.

'Forgive this intrusion, *marchesa*.' His English was good, if heavily accented. 'But I could not wait any longer to meet my cousin's bride. My name is Emilio Corzi.'

'I think we've encountered each other already, *signore*.' Polly paused. 'Earlier this evening—in my son's nursery.'

He laughed, unabashed. 'I hope I did not offend, but the moment was irresistible, if surprising. Not unlike yourself, *vossignoria*,' he added softly. 'I have been watching you with interest, and you have much more charm and style than I was led to believe.'

'Really?' Polly raised her eyebrows. 'I don't need to ask who was doing the leading.'

'You are right, of course.' Emilio Corzi sighed. 'Poor Antonia Barsoli. She has never recovered from the death of that unfortunate girl, Bianca. It must be hard for her to see someone set in her place, especially when Alessandro swore after the accident that he would never marry.' He paused. 'Although she has less reason to be bitter than I have.'

'Ah.' Polly gave him a level look. 'You mean the loss of your inheritance.'

He sighed elaborately. 'It is unfortunately true. His late father had two brothers and a sister, my mother, who produced ten children between them, all girls except for myself, and I was the youngest of three. Alessandro, of course, was an only child, and I dare say too much was expected of him, at too early an age.'

Polly knew she should walk away, but against her better instincts, she lingered.

'Why do you say that?'

'Relations between him and his father were always strained.' Emilio drew reflectively on his cigar. 'And became worse once his mother was no longer there to act as mediator. As you know, she died when he was twelve.' He looked at her, brows raised. 'Or did you know?'

'Of course.' Polly lifted her chin.

'I could not be certain,' he said. 'There are so many areas of his life about which he is silent. Although I am sure he has his reasons.'

'Probably because he doesn't want the details splashed all over your magazines,' Polly suggested shortly.

'But he wrongs me, my dear cousin.' Emilio's tone was plaintive. 'I have not made capital out of his forbidden affair with you—or his secret love-child. I am treating it as a romantic story with a happy ending. My family loyalty is real.' He paused. 'I have not even expressed my doubts in public over the mystery of Bianca DiMario's death. Or not yet anyway.'

'Mystery?' Polly repeated. 'What are you talking about? It was a tragic accident.'

'That was the decision of the inquiry, certainly. But I am fascinated by the reticence of the only witness who was called— Giacomo Raboni.' He smiled at her. 'But after all, his family have served the Valessi faithfully for generations. Who knows what someone less partisan might have said?'

Polly stiffened. 'That is—a disgusting implication. There was a burst tyre on the car. These things happen.'

'But the inquiry was held so quickly,' Emilio countered. 'While Alessandro was still seriously ill in hospital, and unable to give evidence. But perhaps they thought he never would,' he added swiftly. 'It was still possible that he would end his days in a wheelchair, and that there might be permanent brain damage.'

He shrugged. 'But in the end he suffered only some temporary amnesia, and he made a full recovery—to everyone's enormous relief,' he added piously.

'Yes,' Polly said stonily. 'I bet you were thrilled to bits.' She was leaning back against the balustrade, shaking like a leaf, her stomach churning, as she thought of Sandro trapped, perhaps, in a helpless body. Unable even to understand, maybe, that he had fathered a child, let alone hold him or love him.

'But even when he was well again, he was never questioned about that afternoon in the mountains,' Emilio said softly. 'The advantage, I suppose, of being the son of a rich and influential man. And there was much sympathy, too, for my uncle Domenico, who had lost a young girl he cherished as a daughter. So, many questions were left unanswered.'

'Such as?' she demanded curtly.

'What did Giacomo Raboni know, but not speak about? I know he was well rewarded at the time by my uncle. And now, I find, his granddaughter has been given a position of prestige as your personal maid.'

She said hoarsely, 'But gratitude is quite natural. Sandro told me that Giacomo had saved his life. That's quite a service.'

He shrugged. 'I think his silence has been a greater one. And they say too that generosity is often prompted by a guilty conscience.' He lowered his voice conspiratorially. 'Have you ever wondered whether the scar on your husband's cheek might be the mark of Cain?'

'I think you've said enough.' Her tone was ice. 'You're supposed to be Sandro's guest. It would be better if you left.'

He tutted reproachfully. 'You are harsh, my dear Paola. And your loyalty to Alessandro is misplaced, believe me. I am simply trying to be your friend, and one day you may need me.'

'I can't imagine that,' she returned curtly.

'But then did you foresee finding yourself Marchesa Valessi, with Alessandro's diamonds on your hand and circling your throat? I note he has not given you the jewels that have been in the Valessi family for centuries, but these trinkets are valuable enough.'

'Thank you,' Polly said grittily. 'I'll tell him you approve.'

'Oh, no,' he said. 'I do not think you will discuss our conversation with him at all.' He paused. 'So, what will you do when the little Carlo becomes his legal heir, and Alessandro tires of playing husband, and wants you out of his life a second time?'

Shock was like bile in her throat. 'What the hell do you mean?'

He sighed. 'I hoped you would be honest at least. Your days and nights with my cousin are numbered, and you know it. He has never wished to be married. Not to the unfortunate Bianca. Not to you. No one woman will ever fill his need for variety.' His lip curled. 'Do you wish to know the name of his mistress in Rome?'

'That,' she said huskily, 'is it. Go, please. Just pack and—get out.'

There was sudden venom in his voice. 'Did you make him sign a pre-nuptial agreement, or will he make you settle for the same paltry sum as last time's parting price before he sends you home? If so, you may be glad to turn to me. I would pay you well for a personal view of your association with him.'

'You,' Polly said, steadying her voice, 'are completely vile.'

'And he, Paola cara, is totally ruthless, as you must know, else why are you here?' He made her a little bow. 'I will leave you to your solitary contemplation. We shall meet again—once you have learned sense.'

He turned and walked along the terrace, disappearing from view into the darkness.

Polly found she was gasping for breath. She stood, a hand pressed to her throat as she fought for self-control.

She could not stay out here on the terrace forever. Soon, now, she would have to go back inside, and she needed at least the appearance of serenity to fool the sharp eyes that would be watching her.

All the vicious things Emilio had said to her were tumbling around in her head. She might tell herself they were ludicrous, vindictive lies of a disappointed man, but in some ways they seemed like the confirmation of all her worst nightmares.

What had really happened the day Sandro's car went into the ravine? Rafaella had told her that her grandfather refused to speak about it. What had he seen—or heard—that prompted him to silence?

Somehow or other, she thought, I'm going to have to ask him—and make him tell me the truth. Because I need to know.

As for Emilio's comments about her marriage... A little shiver ran through her. He was probably right about that. After all, it was only a means to an end, as Sandro had made clear. And once he had Charlie established as his heir, why would he bother to keep her around? Especially when he had other interests?

*Do you wish to know the name of his mistress in Rome?*

The words ate at her like some corrosive acid.

The fact that there was another woman in his life had not stopped him trying to seduce her back into his bed, she thought, hurt and anger warring inside her. 'A fever in the blood' he'd once called it. And once the fever had been quenched, what then? Had he expected her to be so much in thrall to him that she was compliantly prepared to share him with his Roman beauty?

She bit her lip so hard that she tasted blood. I can't think about that, she told herself desperately. I dare not go there...

But there was another problem, too, that she had to confront. Was it just Emilio or did other members of the family know that he'd tried to pay her off three years before? If so, that was the ultimate humiliation, and she wanted to run somewhere and hide, away from the smiles and sneers that would accompany such knowledge.

But most of all, she wanted to hide from Sandro. And instead she was obliged to go upstairs, and get into one side of the extravagantly wide bed she had to share with him tonight. And be expected to sleep.

Oh, God, she thought, her fists clenching convulsively. It's all such a charade. Such total hypocrisy.

And if I had any guts, I'd get Charlie, and make a run for it back to England, and see how Sandro deals with a scandal like that.

But, realistically, how far would she get? She was here in this—fortress in a foreign country, where he had power, and she had none. Even the money in the bank account he'd opened for her had been transferred to Italy.

She was helpless—and she was suddenly afraid too.

'So, here you are.' Sandro was walking across the terrace towards her. 'What are you doing out here alone?'

She swallowed slowly and deeply, aware of the frantic thud of her heart at the sight of him.

'I needed some fresh air.' She forced herself to sound light and cool. 'Pretending to be pleasant is hard work, and every actress needs an interval.'

'Is it really so hard to meet such goodwill halfway?' he asked unsmilingly.

'I think it exists for Charlie, not myself,' she returned curtly. 'I'm your wife by accident not design, and they must know that.'

He said drily, 'In the eyes of most of my family, you are not yet my wife at all. I am being given embarrassingly broad hints that I should take you upstairs without further delay and rectify the matter.'

'Oh, God.' Polly pressed her hands to her burning cheeks.

'I am truly sorry, *cara mia*.' His voice was suddenly gentle. 'I never meant you to be subjected to this. We had better face them.'

'Very well.' Ignoring his outstretched hand, she walked stiffly beside him towards the open windows of the *salotto*.

'I can give you ten minutes' privacy,' he added quietly. 'But no longer, or Zia Vittoria will be demanding to know why I am not with you, doing my duty by the next generation.'

Her throat muscles felt paralysed, but she managed a husky, 'Thank you.'

In spite of her tacit resistance, Sandro slid an arm round her waist, holding her against his side, as they went into the brightness of the room and paused to meet the laughter and faint cheers that awaited them.

Then she felt his lips touch her hot cheek, as he whispered, 'Go now, *bella mia*.'

The door seemed a million miles away, especially when she had to reach it through a sea of broad grins and openly voiced encouragement. She was aware that people were swarming after her into the hall, watching her walk up the stairs.

She glanced back once, and saw Sandro standing a little apart from them all. He was unsmiling, his eyes bleak, as he looked at her, raising the glass he was holding in a cynical toast. Then he drained the contents in one jerky movement, and went back into the *salotto*.

Leaving Polly to go on, feeling more alone than she had ever done in her life before.

# CHAPTER NINE

THE bedroom was empty, but it was prepared and waiting for her. And, she thought, her senses tautening, for him.

Lamps on tall wrought-iron stands were burning on either side of the bed. The coverlet had been removed and the white lace-edged sheets turned down and scattered with crimson rose petals.

And, she supposed, inevitably, the black lace nightdress was draped across the bed in readiness too.

Well, that she could deal with, she thought, folding it with quick, feverish hands into a tiny parcel of fabric. She went into the dressing room, and stowed it away in her wardrobe in the pocket of a linen jacket against the moment when she could dispose of it for good and all. Otherwise it was going to haunt her.

She also needed an alternative to wear, she thought, rummaging through the exquisitely arranged contents of her lingerie drawer. She decided on a plain ivory satin nightgown, cut on the bias, its neckline square across her breasts, and supported by shoestring straps.

Discreet enough to be an evening dress, she thought as she slipped it over her head after showering briefly in the bathroom. Especially with the diamonds still glittering round her neck. Where they would have to remain, as the clasp resisted all her efforts to unfasten it.

Sighing, Polly shook her hair loose, ran a swift brush through it, and went back into the bedroom.

She was aware the minutes had been ticking past, but she'd still hoped she might be granted a little more leeway than Sandro had suggested. Prayed that it might be possible to be in bed, pretending to be asleep before he came to join her.

But her hopes were dashed, because Sandro was there already, dinner jacket removed and black tie loosened, walking towards the bed. He turned, surveying her without expression as she hesitated in the doorway.

He said, 'Do you not think you are a little overdressed, *bella mia*?'

Her heart skipped. 'What are you talking about?'

His mouth twisted. 'I was referring to the diamonds, naturally.'

She lifted her chin. 'I couldn't unfasten them—and Rafaella wasn't here.'

'She would not risk her life by intruding.' He beckoned. 'Come to me.'

She went slowly towards him, waiting, head bent, while he dealt with the clasp, his touch brisk and impersonal.

'Take it.' He dropped the necklace into her hand.

She said, 'But shouldn't you have it?'

'It was a gift, Paola,' he said shortly. 'Not a loan.'

'I meant—wouldn't it be better in a safe...somewhere?'

'There is a place in the dressing room for your jewellery. Rafaella will show you in the morning.' Sandro turned back to the bed, and began brushing away the rose petals. One of them drifted to Polly's feet, and she bent and retrieved it, stroking the velvety surface with her fingertips.

She said, 'Someone has taken a lot of trouble. Perhaps you were right about the goodwill.'

'The wedding night of a *marchese* and his bride is always a great occasion.' Sandro dragged out the bolster from under the pillows, and arranged it down the centre of the bed. 'How fortunate they will never know the truth,' he added sardonically.

'There,' he said, when he had finished. 'Will that make you feel safe?'

'Yes,' Polly said stiltedly. 'Yes—thank you.'

He walked away towards the dressing room, and Polly switched off her lamp and got hastily into bed. She slid her necklace under the pillow, then lay down, her back turned rigidly towards the bolster. The scent of the roses still lingered beguilingly, and she buried her face in the pillow, breathing in the perfume, and relishing the coolness of the linen against the warmth of her skin.

When at last she heard Sandro returning, she burrowed further down under the sheet, closing her eyes so tightly that coloured lights danced behind her lids.

She sensed that the other lamp had been extinguished, then heard the rustle of silk as he discarded his robe, and the faint dip of the bed as he took his place on the far side of the bolster.

There was a silence, then he said, 'Paola, you are permitted to stop acting when we are alone together. And I know you are not asleep.'

She turned reluctantly, and looked at him over her shoulder. In the shadows of the room, she could see the outline of him, leaning on the bolster, watching her, but she was unable to read the expression on his face.

She kept her voice cool. 'But I'd like to be. This has been one hell of a day.'

'Crowned, I imagine, by your meeting with my cousin Emilio,' he drawled. 'Where did you encounter him?'

Polly, unprepared for the question, hunched a shoulder. 'He happened to be on the terrace while I was there,' she said evasively.

'Emilio does not ''happen'' to be anywhere, *cara*,' he said drily. 'His locations are always intentional.' He paused. 'Did you share a pleasant conversation?'

'No,' she said. 'Not particularly. I hope he isn't a frequent visitor.'

'I believe he comes mainly to see Zia Antonia,' he said. 'Usually when I am not here. As he is leaving early in the morning, he has asked me to pass on a message to you.'

Polly shifted uncomfortably. 'Oh?'

'He sends you his homage,' Sandro went on silkily. 'And hopes that tonight will provide you with wonderful memories for the rest of your life.'

She punched the pillow with unnecessary vigour, and lay down again. 'Well, neither of us are likely to forget it,' she said shortly.

'That is true,' he said. 'But I am surprised to find you on a level of such intimacy with Emilio.'

'I'm not,' she returned heatedly. 'He's a loathsome little worm, and I'm amazed that someone hasn't dealt with him by now.'

'They have tried,' Sandro said drily. 'He has been pushed off a balcony in Lucca, and thrown into the Grand Canal in Venice. And he was nearly the victim of a drive-by shooting in Rome, but it seems that was a case of mistaken identity.'

Polly was surprised into a giggle. 'What a shame.'

'As you say,' he agreed solemnly. 'But, in a way, he can be pitied. For years he has been waiting confidently for me to break my neck on the polo field, be caught in an avalanche or drown while sailing. The car crash must have made him feel that his dream could come true at last.

'Yet here I am with a wife and a son, and his hopes of the Valessi inheritance are finally dashed.'

She put up a hand to her pillow, hugging it closer. Her voice was faintly muffled. 'Is that why you were so determined to take Charlie? To put Emilio out of the running?'

'It played its part. But I wanted him for his own sake, too.' His voice sharpened. 'Paola, you cannot doubt that, surely.'

'No,' she said. 'I—know you did.'

It was almost her only certainty, she thought. Emilio's vile insinuations were still turning like a weary treadmill in her brain, reminding her yet again just how tenuous her position was. And how easily she might lose everything in the world that mattered to her.

And in spite of the warmth of the night, she gave the slightest shiver.

He noticed instantly. 'Are you cold? Do you wish for a blanket?'

'It's not that.' She sat up, making a little helpless gesture. 'I—I just don't know what I'm doing here—why I let myself do this. I don't understand what's happening.'

He was silent for a moment, then he said wearily, a trace of something like bitterness in his voice, 'Currently, you and I, *cara mia*, are about to spend a very long and tedious night together. When it is over, we will see what tomorrow brings, and hope that it is better. Now, sleep.'

He turned away, and lay down with his back to her, and, after a pause, she did the same.

Time passed, and became an hour—then another. Polly found herself lying on the furthermost edge of the bed, listening to Sandro's quiet, regular breathing, scared to move or even sigh in case she disturbed him.

She felt physically and emotionally exhausted, but her brain would not let her rest. She was plagued by images that hurt and bewildered her, images of fear and isolation, but she found them impossible to dismiss, however much she wanted to let go, and allow herself to drift away into sleep.

At one point, she seemed to be standing at one end of a long tree-lined avenue, watching Sandro, who was ahead of her, walk-

ing away with long, rapid strides. And she knew with total frightened certainty that if she allowed him to reach the end of the
avenue, that he would be gone forever. She tried to call out, to
summon him back, but her voice emerged as a cracked whisper.

Yet somehow he seemed to hear, because he stopped and looked
back, and she began to run to him, stumbling a little, her legs like
leaden weights.

She said his name again, and ran into his arms, and they closed
round her, so warm and so safe that the icy chill deep inside her
began to dissolve away as he held her.

And she thought, This is a dream. I'm dreaming... And knew
that she did not want to wake, and face reality again.


When she eventually opened her eyes the following day, that same
feeling of security still lingered, and she felt relaxed and strangely
at peace.

The first thing she saw was that the bolster was back in its
normal place, and that the bed beside her was empty. She was
completely alone, too, with only the whirr of the ceiling fan to
disturb the hush of the room. Sandro had gone.

Well, she thought, I should be grateful for that.

She sat up, pushing her hair back from her face. It was very
hot, she realised, and the shutters at the windows were closed to
exclude the molten gold of the sun. At some moment in the night,
she'd kicked away the covering sheet, but her satin nightdress was
clinging damply to her body.

She glanced at her watch, and gasped. No wonder the temperature was soaring—the morning was nearly over. She felt as if
she'd slept for a hundred years, and that, if she left this room, she
would find the passages choked with cobwebs.

And, as if on cue, there was a knock on the door and Rafaella
came in carrying a tray.

'*Buongiorno*, madam.' Her smile was wide and cheerful.

Polly spread her hands helplessly. 'It's almost afternoon!' she
exclaimed. 'Why did no one wake me?'

'The *marchese* said that you needed to sleep, and should not be
disturbed,' Rafaella returned demurely, her eyes straying to the
tray she had just placed on the bed.

Polly followed her gaze, and saw that in addition to the orange juice, the fresh rolls, the dish of honey, the bowl of grapes and the silver coffee pot, there was a red rose lying across the snowy tray cloth, and a folded note beside it.

Swallowing, she reached for it. It said simply, *'Grazie, mi amore,'* and was signed with his name.

Polly realised she was blushing to the roots of her hair, and hurriedly crushed the paper in her hand. Everyone in the *palazzo*, she thought, would know about his message by now, and the re-membered passion implied in its words.

It was simply another brick in the wall of pretence around their marriage, and she knew it, but that didn't make it any easier to take.

She had also seen the faintly puzzled glance that the girl had sent the ivory nightgown.

Maybe I should have left the black one shredded on the floor, she thought ruefully. Silenced any lingering doubts that way.

She cleared her throat. 'Where—where is the *marchese*?'

'He has been bidding goodbye to his guests, madam. Now he has gone down to the port with his son and the *bambinaia*.' She beamed. 'The little Carlo wished for ice-cream, I think.'

'His father has a short memory,' Polly commented crisply. 'Charlie, ice-cream and a car ride could be a lethal combination.'

'Ah, no, *signora*. The *marchese* was also ill on journeys when he was a *bambino*, and Dorotea has her own special remedy,' Rafaella reassured her cheerfully. 'Shall I pour *signora*'s coffee?'

Dorotea? Polly thought, as she sipped the strong brew. Then where was Julie?

'The *maggiordomo*, Teodoro, sends his respects to *vossignoria*,' Rafaella reported when she returned from running Polly's bath. 'The *marchese* has instructed him to show you the *palazzo*, and he awaits your convenience.'

'Oh,' Polly said, slowly. 'Well, please thank him for me. It will be my pleasure.' She paused, spreading a roll with honey. 'I was also thinking, Rafaella, that I would really like to meet your grand-father.' She made her tone casual. 'Thank him for all he did for the *marchese*. Could you arrange that for me?'

'It would be his honour, *signora*,' Rafaella's dark eyes shone. 'But at the moment he is away, visiting my sister in Salerno, who is expecting her first child. When he returns, perhaps?'

'That would be fine,' Polly agreed. 'I'll hold you to it.'

An hour later, bathed and dressed in a knee-length white skirt and a sleeveless navy top, she made her way to the nursery, hoping that Charlie might be back. Instead, she found Julie sitting alone at the big table, listlessly leafing through the pages of a magazine.

'Oh.' Polly checked at the sight of her. 'So you didn't go to the port.'

Julie sighed. 'Dorotea may not speak much English, but she made it plain I wasn't wanted,' she said wryly. 'Instead, I've been cleaning out these already spotless cupboards.'

Polly frowned. 'Doesn't she realise you're here to be with Charlie?'

'That's the problem. Apparently there's only one way to look after his excellency's son, and it's not the way I do it. And the Contessa Barsoli was here earlier, asking when I planned to go home.' She looked squarely at Polly. 'I think my coming here was a big mistake.'

Polly forced a smile. 'I'm hardly the flavour of the month with them either. I was only just allowed to say goodnight to him yesterday,' she added candidly, then paused. 'But please hang in there, Julie. I'm sure things can only get better.' And mentally crossed her fingers.

Teodoro was waiting in the hall for her, still looking anxious, but his face cleared a little when Polly spoke to him in his own language. Overall, she thought afterwards, the tour of the *palazzo* went well, although there were too many rooms, too many glorious works of art on the walls, too many priceless tapestries, statues and ceramics on display to be assimilated all at once. And most of the furniture in everyday use would have graced any museum. Becoming familiar with it all would be a life's work. And her days here were limited.

If she had a criticism, she thought, it would be that it all seemed incredibly formal and curiously lifeless. Everything appeared to have its own place, which it had occupied for centuries.

The exception was Sandro's study, and the small office which adjoined it, staffed by a severe woman with glasses called Signora Corboni. This was where the work was done, Polly surmised, surveying the computers and fax machine, and metal filing cabinets, but even here the past intruded in the shape of a massive antique desk.

And she had never seen so many fireplaces. Every room seemed to have one, and the largest often had two. But there was no central heating, so logs would be burned to dispel the chill and damp of an Italian winter.

There was only one door locked against her. The room, Teodoro told her with faint embarrassment, occupied by the *contessa*. And Polly smiled and shrugged to indicate that there was no problem— that the *contessa* was an elderly woman entitled to her privacy.

Teodoro had clearly been keeping the best until last, flinging the final door open with a flourish. 'And this, *vossignoria*, this is all for you.'

It was far from the largest room she'd been shown, yet her flat in England would probably have fitted into it quite comfortably. And comfort was the theme, with a carpeted floor, two deeply cushioned sofas covered in a blue and cream floral design flanking the stone hearth, and matching curtains hanging at the large window.

'Oh.' Polly knelt on the window seat, looking down over a sloping riot of dark green trees and shrubs to the azure sea beyond. 'Oh, how lovely.'

Teodoro beamed in satisfaction, and began to point out the other amenities, which included a television set, a state-of-the-art music centre with a rack of CDs, and a tall case stocked with the latest English fiction and non-fiction titles.

There were no old masters on the walls, but some delightful water-colours. There were roses filling the air with scent on a side-table, and the ornaments, although undoubtedly valuable, had clearly been selected for their charm.

'This was the favoured room of the *marchese*'s late mother, may God grant her peace,' Teodoro said, crossing himself devoutly. 'Messere Alessandro ordered it to be specially prepared for you. He wished you to have somewhere quiet and private for yourself alone, to sit and read, perhaps, or play music.'

And be out of his way? Polly wondered wryly. But, whatever Sandro's motives, she couldn't deny her pleasure in the room, or fail to appreciate the thought that had gone into it.

She said quietly, 'That's—very kind of him.'

He nodded, pleased. He indicated the telephone standing on a small, elegant writing desk. 'If you wish to make a call, our switchboard will connect you. And if there is anything else *vossignoria* requires, be gracious enough to pull the bell by the fireplace.'

After that there were more practical matters to be dealt with. There were food stores and the wine cellars to be inspected, plus the laundry and the bakery to be visited.

The *palazzo* was a little world of its own, she thought, and pretty much self-sufficient, probably dating from the days when it was regularly besieged by its enemies.

Not a lot of change there, she thought ironically as she refused lunch, but gratefully accepted Teodoro's offer of iced lemonade served on the terrace.

She had just seated herself in a cushioned chair under the shade of a sun umbrella when Sandro appeared, walking up the steps from the garden.

He was wearing shorts, and an unbuttoned cotton shirt, his feet thrust into canvas shoes, and was carrying an excited Charlie on his shoulders.

'*Ciao.*' His greeting was casual, but the look he sent her was curiously watchful. 'Did you sleep well?'

She forced a smile. 'Better than I could have hoped. And you?'

He said laconically, 'I survived.' And lowered Charlie down to the flags.

The little boy came rushing to Polly. 'Mammina, I went in a boat, with *big* sails.' Waving arms indicated a vast expanse of canvas. 'And a man give me a fish all of my own. Doro says I can eat it for supper.'

Polly sent Sandro a surprised look. 'What's this?'

'I took him to meet an old friend of mine, called Alfredo.' Sandro poured himself some lemonade. 'When I was a young boy, I used to escape whenever I could down to the port, and Fredo would take me fishing with him. A pleasure I would like Carlino to share.'

'But he can't swim,' Polly protested. 'Supposing the boat had capsized?'

Sandro shrugged, his face hardening. 'Supposing we had all been abducted by aliens?' he countered impatiently. 'And I intend to give him his first swimming lesson later today, after siesta.' He paused. 'Perhaps you would like to come and make sure his life is not endangered again.'

She said stiffly, 'I suppose you think I'm making a fuss about nothing.'

'Yes,' he said, 'if you think I would allow harm to come to one hair on his head.'

Biting her lip, she turned back to Charlie and gave him a big hug. 'So, tell me about your fish, darling. What colour is it?'

He gave it frowning thought, then, 'Fish-coloured,' he decided.

Sandro's lips twitched. *'Avanti,'* he said. 'Let us go and find Doro, *figlio mio*. It is time you had a rest.'

'Let me take him,' Polly said quickly. 'To Julie.'

'But I am already going upstairs,' he said. 'So there is no need for you to do so. Unless, of course, you wish to share the siesta with me,' he added with touch of mockery.

'Thank you,' Polly acknowledged, stonily. 'But no.'

His mouth twisted. 'You seemed to find it enjoyable once.'

'Perhaps,' she said. 'But I really don't need to be constantly reminded of my mistakes—especially those in the distant past.'

'Last night is not so distant, *cara*,' he said softly. 'And you slept happily in my arms for most of it.'

Polly put her glass down very carefully. 'What are you talking about?'

'Think about it,' he advised, then swung Charlie onto his hip and went indoors, leaving her staring after him, alarm clenching like a fist inside her.

He was teasing her, Polly told herself, pacing backwards and forwards across her living room. For reasons of his own, he enjoyed needling her—seeing how far he could push her before the explosion came. That was all it was. She was sure of it.

And yet—and yet...

She couldn't forget that curious feeling of well-being that had surrounded her when she'd awoken that morning. How rested she'd felt. How completely relaxed.

And remembered, too, those times when they were lovers that he'd joined her in bed when she was already asleep, and she'd woken to find herself wrapped in his arms, her head tucked into the curve of his shoulder, and her lips against his skin. And, smiling, had slept again.

There was a strange familiarity about it all.

Oh, no, she groaned silently. Please—no...

And, all too soon now, she had to face him again, she thought glumly. She couldn't hide away anywhere, so the only thing she could do was bluff it out. Pretend that nothing had happened, which might even be true, and never refer to it again.

She was halfway to the door, when it opened abruptly and the *contessa* came in.

So much for privacy, Polly thought wryly.

She said, politely, '*Buongiorno, contessa.* Is there something I can do?'

The older woman stared around her for a long moment, then turned back to Polly, smiling stiffly. 'On the contrary, dear Paola. I came to make sure that you had everything you wanted—in your new domain.'

She gave the room another sharp, appraising look. 'I confess I have not visited it since Alessandro gave orders for its total renovation. I—I find it painful to see the changes, indeed I can barely recognise it, but I know I must not be a foolish old woman.'

Polly said quietly, 'I don't think anyone would ever see you in that light, *contessa*.' She paused. 'Were you very close to Sandro's mother? I didn't know.'

'Close to Maddalena?' the older woman queried sharply. 'I knew her, of course, but we were never on intimate terms. No, I was speaking of my cherished Bianca, who was also given this room by Alessandro's father as her personal retreat. She loved it here.' She sighed deeply. 'Now every trace of her has gone, even the portrait of her that my cousin Domenico had painted.' She paused, and a note of steel entered her voice. 'I am astonished that your husband should have so little regard for his father's wishes.'

'I'm sorry you feel like that,' Polly said, caught at a loss. 'Maybe you should take up the matter with Sandro himself.'

'My poor Bianca.' The *contessa* swept on regardless. 'How much she loved him—and what she endured for his sake. And how soon she is forgotten.' And she sighed again.

'I'm sure that's not true,' Polly told her quietly. 'I know he has the greatest respect for her memory, *contessa*.'

'Dear child, you are kind to say so. But the evidence makes that so hard to believe. She was such an innocent, and her only sin was to love Alessandro too much. And because of that—she died.'

She shook her head with the appearance of someone labouring under more sorrow than anger.

'He drove too fast—always. And that terrible day, he was in a temper—a wicked, dangerous rage. He had quarrelled with his father, so Bianca followed him, like the angel she was—insisted on going in the car with him to reason with him. To persuade him to return and make peace with his father.'

Her voice broke a little. 'Only for her, there was no return. He was too angry—too reckless to judge the bend correctly, and the car went into the ravine.

'He was never made to answer for what he had done, of course. His own injuries saved him from possible charges.

'But it is guilt he feels, my dear Paola—not respect—and that is why he has had every remnant of my poor Bianca's presence removed—even her portrait.'

She paused, looking keenly at Polly, who was standing with her arms wrapped round her body in an instinctive gesture of defence. 'I am sorry if I grieve you, but it is as well you should know the truth.'

Polly said quietly, 'I am sure my husband blames himself just as much as you could wish, *contessa*.'

The older woman's tone was almost purring. 'But call me Zia Antonia, I beg you. We cannot be strangers. Your position in this house is hardly an enviable one,' she added. 'Alessandro is so—unpredictable, and I fear you may find yourself much neglected. I hope that when problems arise, you will know you can always turn to me.'

'Thank you,' Polly said. 'I—I'm very grateful.' *Or am I?* she asked herself silently as she watched the *contessa* walk to the door, bestow another thin, honeyed smile and leave. *It's like feeling obligated to a cobra that's already bitten you once.*

But the *contessa*'s words had left her shaking inside. She was clearly implying that Sandro was guilty of manslaughter at the very least.

This, coupled with Emilio's comments about a possible cover-up at the official inquiry, painted a frightening picture, and one Polly did not even want to contemplate.

If he had been recklessly speeding and made a fatal error of judgement which caused the accident, then surely he had been

well-punished for it. *The mark of Cain,* she thought, and shuddered.

But, at the same time, the power of the Valessi family was being
highlighted for her in an awesome way, she realised unhappily.

Money was waved, and things happened. A girl who could
prove a nuisance was dismissed back to her own country. An
eyewitness to a car crash was persuaded to doctor his account of
the tragedy to protect the heir to a dynasty. An expensive court
action was threatened, and that same heir acquired a wife and
child.

He would have hated the scandal of a court appearance, she
thought. If I'd listened to my mother and stood up to him, maybe
he'd have backed off. And I would not be here now, torn apart
by doubts. Tormented equally by my fears and longings.

She looked down at the glow of the diamond on her hand. A
symbol of a fever in the blood? she wondered. Or a cold flame
that would consume her utterly, reducing her to ashes? As it might
have destroyed Bianca three years earlier, she thought, and shivered.

And once she had gone, would she be so easily forgotten too?

There was a tap on the door, and Teodoro appeared.

'Please excuse me.' He inclined his head respectfully. 'But the
*marchese* is asking for you to join him at the swimming pool. I
should be happy to show you the way, *marchesa*, if you will
accompany me.'

'Yes,' she said, and took a deep breath. 'Yes, of course.'

She got slowly to her feet, pushing her hair back with a me-
chanical gesture. Life went on, and whatever her mental turmoil,
it seemed she was required to join Sandro, and needed to obey the
summons. Accept the situation that had been forced upon her, she
thought, and all its implications.

Because, after all, what other choice did she have?

And, straightening her shoulders, she reluctantly allowed
Teodoro to escort her from the room, and out into the sunlight.

# CHAPTER TEN

THE pool was an oval turquoise set in creamy marble, created, Polly guessed, out of a former sunken garden and reached by a series of shallow steps, which wound their way downwards through banks of flowering shrubs. And where Teodoro left her to make the rest of her way alone.

As she descended, she saw that the pool was surrounded by a broad sun-terrace with cushioned loungers and parasols, and, at the far end, there was a flamboyant piece of statuary, depicting some sea god surrounded by leaping dolphins.

And with equal flamboyance, a large inflatable duck with a coy smile and long eyelashes was bobbing quietly at the pool's shallow end.

Sandro was stretched out under one of the umbrellas, reading. He was wearing a pair of brief black trunks, which set off his lithe, bronzed body in a way that made her heart skip a momentary beat. His only other covering was the pair of designer sunglasses which he removed at her approach.

'Ciao.' He surveyed her with a faint frown. 'Are you all right?'

'Never better,' Polly lied too brightly. She looked around her. 'What—what a wonderful spot this is. And so peaceful.'

'I think the peace will be broken when Dorotea arrives with Carlino,' he said drily.

'Dorotea?' Polly asked, her own brows creasing, seating herself on an adjoining lounger. 'Why not Julie?'

He shrugged. 'Perhaps she is still learning her way about—or tired from the events of yesterday.'

'Yes,' she said. 'Perhaps.' She hesitated. 'I should apologise for my failure to join you this morning, and say goodbye to your guests. I hope no one was offended.'

'I explained you needed your rest,' he said. 'They understood completely.'

Faint colour invaded her face. 'Oh, I expect you made sure of that.'

136

'It was hardly a lie,' he said. 'You did not sleep well, because
you were clearly troubled by bad dreams. Otherwise, why would
you have spoken my name and reached for me, as you did?'

Her flush deepened. She said coldly, 'I wasn't aware of it, believe me. And I've had nightmares before,' she added.

'Not,' he said softly, 'when you have been in bed with me,
*carissima*.'

She bit her lip. 'Perhaps not. But there was no need for any—
intervention on your part.'

'Well,' he said lightly, picking up his book again, 'it will not
occur again. From tonight, you will sleep alone, *bella mia*. I have
given the necessary orders.'

'Thank you,' she said. 'My own bedroom as well as a personal
living room. What luxury.' She paused. 'But can I ask not to be
allocated another shrine to Bianca?'

His gaze sharpened. 'What are you talking about?'

'Your cousin Antonia visited me earlier. She was upset about
the changes you'd made to your mother's room—especially the
removal of Bianca's portrait.'

'I will tell Teodoro to rescue it from storage,' he said. 'And
hang it in her own suite, if it means so much to her. But she
already maintains a shrine to Bianca,' he added coldly. 'It is on
the mountain road at the place where the car went over. There is
a photograph, with a candle burning in front of it, and fresh flowers
which she places there regularly. I am sure she would show it to
you, if you asked.'

She said, 'I'll bear it in mind.' She paused. 'Not that it matters,
but don't your servants find it a little strange that we're having
separate rooms?'

'They are not paid to question my decisions,' he drawled. 'And
they will not find it so extraordinary. My parents and grandparents
had the same arrangements, and probably every generation of my
family before that.

'And you are also under a misapprehension,' he added. 'You
will not be moving. You will continue to sleep in the master bedroom, which is quite free of any connection with Bianca.' His tone
was expressionless. 'As far as I know, she never entered it.'

She said uncertainly, 'But surely that's your room, and you
should keep it.' She tried to smile. 'After all, you're very much
the master here.'

'I can sleep anywhere,' he said. 'And besides, I shall be away from the *palazzo* a great deal.'

'You will?' She looked at him uncertainly.

'*Naturalamente*. My work involves a great deal of travelling, and this trip has been planned for a long time.' He slanted a look at her. 'If circumstances were different, I would take you with me, *cara*. But I cannot guarantee there will always be convenient bolsters in our accommodation.'

'Not that they seem to make much difference to you,' she flashed.

He hunched an indifferent shoulder. 'I held you, Paola, while you slept, and because you seemed to need comfort. If you wish me to apologise for that,' he added deliberately, 'you will wait forever.'

He looked her over. 'You are not dressed for swimming. You do not intend to join your son in the pool for the first time?'

She bit her lip. 'I didn't bring any swimwear with me. I—I suppose Teresa thought there was no need...that I would buy something when I got here.'

'It's not a problem.' He pointed to the pair of changing cabins that stood on the opposite side of the pool. 'You will find a selection there. I hope there will be something to your taste.'

'Or yours anyway,' she returned coolly.

He picked up his book. 'Then keep your clothes on,' he said with cool indifference, 'if you do not want to swim. And also if you do not care about the disappointment to Carlino,' he added silkily, offering the killer blow.

Oh, but she did want to swim. The sun seemed to be pouring its full intensity into this secluded marble bowl, and she could feel the sweat trickling down her body. The thought of cool water against her skin was irresistible.

She said, 'I care very much, and you know it. I—I'll go and change.'

Feeling self-conscious, she crossed to the women's cabin, but a swift glance backwards revealed that Sandro was absorbed in his book again.

The swimwear was displayed in a cupboard, a whole row of bikinis on padded hangers. There was one in black, and the rest were in a range of clear, pretty colours. To her surprise, all of them were in her size, and, even more astonishing, none of them were nearly as revealing as they might have been.

The violet bikini she eventually picked had sleek, simple lines, with cups that lifted and enhanced her breasts without undue exposure, and briefs that discreetly skimmed her hip bones. She slipped on the gauzy jacket that matched it, and slid her feet into white canvas mules before venturing outside again.

Sandro watched her walk towards him, his face enigmatic. 'I am glad at least one met with your approval,' he commented.

'They were all—lovely.' She hesitated. 'And not what I'd expected you to choose for your ladies.'

Sandro sighed, and put down his book. 'I chose them for you, Paola, this morning at the marina. You, and no one else,' he told her with a touch of harshness. 'This is my home, and I have never invited my "ladies", as you call them, here for poolside orgies, whatever you may believe.

'Finally, you are my wife,' he added cuttingly. 'And, in theory, I am permitted to see you in private in any state of undress I wish. In public, however, I prefer a certain decorum. Do I make myself clear?'

She bent her head. 'Perfectly. It's all down to appearances again.'

His smile was cynical. 'Of course, *cara mia*. Because appearances are all we have. So accustom yourself, as I am doing.'

He paused. 'And now try to smile, because here comes our son.'

Against all the odds, thought Polly as she pulled herself out of the water and reached for a towel, the session in the pool had turned out to be one of the happiest times she could remember in her life.

To her surprise, Charlie, his armbands securely in place, had taken to the water as if he belonged in it, and his wide-eyed enjoyment of this new environment had prompted a more relaxed response from herself as well. They played with a ball in the shallow end, and after some rowdy splashing games Polly steered her son carefully round the pool on the back of the duck, as he squealed with delight. Afterwards, she watched and encouraged as Charlie, under Sandro's patient guidance, managed his first uncertain swimming strokes.

It was, however, apparent that Sandro was strictly avoiding any but the most fleeting physical contact with herself, which created a few moments of awkwardness.

The only other drawback was the presence of Dorotea, who sat with her knitting at the poolside, uttering faint cries of alarm at intervals, in the apparent belief that Charlie was about to be allowed to drown by his negligent and uncaring parents.

If she really found it all so nerve-racking, why on earth hadn't she let Julie, who had swimming and life-saving qualifications, bring him down to the pool instead? Polly wondered with faint irritation.

As it was, Dorotea could not wait to get her charge out of the water and towelled down, as she clucked over him.

My mother all over again, Polly thought wryly. And something I shall have to watch.

Charlie was furious to discover that the inflatable duck would not be permitted to accompany him back to the *palazzo* or sleep with him that night, and threatened a tantrum. But Sandro diverted this by reminding the little boy that he was to have his special fish for supper, and that the duck might steal it from him. Besides, he added, improvising rapidly, the duck would also miss his pool, and keep them all awake during the night with his homesick quacking.

Polly, vigorously rubbing her dripping hair, watched Charlie depart, his hand in Dorotea's.

She glanced across at Sandro, who was also drying himself. She said on impulse, 'He's going to miss you terribly while you're away.'

'This time it is unavoidable, but it will not be for long,' Sandro said. 'And next time he will not miss me at all, because I shall take him with me.'

Polly folded the towel she'd been using with immense care.

She said, 'I'm sorry. What are you saying? Because I don't think I quite understand.'

'It is perfectly simple, *cara*,' he drawled. 'My next trip is a much shorter one, and I intend Carlino to accompany me.'

Polly looked at him, stupefied. 'But he's only a baby,' she whispered.

'He will not be asked to make any boardroom decisions.' Sandro tossed his towel aside and sat down on the lounger, raking back the tousled dark hair.

'It's still ludicrous,' she protested. 'You—you can't take him away.'

He smiled faintly. 'And who is going to stop me? You, *bella mia*?' He shook his head. 'I don't think so.'

She took a deep breath. 'Why are you doing this?'

'Because I love his company,' he said. 'And I wish to strengthen the bond between us, now that it has been established.'

'But I've never been without him for more than a night,' Polly said desperately.

'Then you are fortunate,' he said with sudden harshness. 'I have already missed too much of his life, and I do not mean him to grow up a stranger to me, as I was to my own father for so long.'

She went over and knelt beside him, her hands gripping his arms. 'Sandro.' Her tone was pleading. 'Don't do this to me, please. Or to him. He's too young.'

His face expressionless, he freed himself gently but inexorably from her clasp.

'My mind is made up,' he said. 'He would be travelling with me tomorrow, but my arrangements are already made.'

'Including a trip to Rome, no doubt.' The words were out before she could stop them.

His brows lifted. 'Rome, yes,' he said, with faint mockery. 'That is unmissable, of course. Afterwards—Milan, Florence, Turin and Venice. The next time will involve a simpler route.'

She stayed on her knees, looking up at him. She said huskily, 'Let me go with you.'

For a long moment he was silent, then very slowly and with infinite care his finger traced the curve of her breast above the cling of the soaked bikini cup, then slid under the strap, pulling it down without haste from her shoulder.

He said quietly, the topaz eyes intent and watchful, 'But when do you offer your company, *carissima*? In a few weeks with Carlino? Or tomorrow—alone—with me? On a honeymoon?'

The vivid sunlight seemed to enclose them both in a golden breathless cloud, where she could hear nothing but the trembling hurry of her own heart. Feel nothing but the burn of his touch on her cool, damp skin. See in his eyes the urgency of another, deeper question that she dared not answer.

She longed to tell him 'Yes', she realised dazedly, and with shame.

Because she knew that tiny tendrils of sensation were uncurling at his touch, arousing potent memories of her nakedness explored and exquisitely enjoyed. Igniting the urgent need to yield herself once more to the pleasure of his hands and mouth. To lose herself, trembling, in the totality of his powerful masculinity. A woman reunited with the only man she had ever known. Ever wanted.

Her nipples ached to be free of their flimsy covering and offered to the balm of his tongue.

She wanted to give up the struggle, and surrender. To forget the unhappiness of the past, and abandon the remnants of her pride to the passionate delight of the moment.

Instead she snatched, drowning, at the last vestige of sanity and self-respect she possessed. Because a moment in time was all he might have to give her. And she could not bear to be taken and then discarded once again on a whim.

Especially when he had just made it more than clear that it was only their child he wanted and valued.

He said softly, 'Paola, I need you to answer me.'

'I'm sure you know already,' she said. 'It has to be—Charlie, and always will be.'

Hand miraculously steady, she hitched her bikini strap back into place, and got to her feet.

'After all, a business trip is scarcely a honeymoon, *excellenza*,' she went on with forced lightness. 'And, as you say, your arrangements for tomorrow are already made—including some I am sure you would not wish to alter. And for which I would be—surplus to requirements.'

Tell me it's not true, her heart cried out to him silently. Say that you want me, and only me. That you love me. Beg me—just once—please—please...

But: 'How understanding you are, *cara*,' he drawled. 'The perfect wife for a man who does not wish to be married.'

'I wish,' she said, 'that I could pay you the same compliment. Say that you're the ideal husband for a reluctant wife.' She paused. 'And now perhaps you will excuse me?'

She turned away, walking to the changing pavilion, but before she had gone three yards Sandro was beside her, swinging her round to face him.

'Tell me one thing.' His voice was soft and savage. 'Who will you reach for in the nights ahead, when the bad dreams come?'

She tore herself free. 'No one,' she answered hoarsely. 'A lesson I should have learned three years ago, because all my bad dreams are about you, *signore*.' She paused. 'Now let me go.'

His mouth curled. 'With pleasure, my sweet wife. Enjoy your freedom, because it is all you will have from me.'

He went back to his lounger, and lay there face downwards, and motionless, pillowing his head on his folded arms.

Suddenly, getting back to the *palazzo* seemed a safer option than retrieving her clothes, and Polly found herself going up the stone steps two at a time, as a voice in her head whispered breathlessly, It's over—finished—done with.

And wishing with all her heart that she could feel relief, instead of the desolation that stalked her like a shadow through the late-afternoon sun.

The *palazzo* without its master was a different proposition altogether, and Polly became aware of that within forty-eight hours of Sandro's departure.

Following the afternoon at the pool, he had not joined her for dinner, informing her through a bewildered Teodoro that he had an engagement in town. And the next morning he was gone almost before the sun was up, so there was no opportunity to say goodbye.

Polly gathered from Rafaella that a courteous reluctance to disturb her through his early departure had been used to explain his move to another bedroom. She also realised, almost at once, that the excuse had fooled nobody, and that being regarded as the *marchese*'s unwanted bride was not an enviable situation to be in.

How else to explain the none-too-subtle shift in attitude by the rest of the household almost as soon as Sandro had gone? The thinly veiled hostility she'd encountered in the nursery seemed to have spread through the *palazzo* like a miasma.

The food she was served was often cold, her attempts to speak Italian were ignored, her bell left unanswered, and once, in a mirror, she'd caught a glimpse of one of the maids making the sign to ward off the evil eye behind her back.

It was no comfort to realise that Julie was faring even worse. She saw hardly anything of Charlie, being designated instead to hand-wash and iron all his clothes, and even his bedding, in between scouring the nursery itself.

And when Polly told Dorotea firmly that this had to stop, and Charlie's things must be sent to the laundry, so that Julie could bring the little boy down to the pool each afternoon, she was met with shrugs and looks of incomprehension.

And each time Polly herself entered the nursery, she could feel the resentment in the air.

Even Rafaella seemed oddly subdued, and it was hard to get a smile out of her.

Perhaps she resents working for someone who's a *marchesa* only in name, and a second-class citizen in reality, Polly thought wryly.

But it wasn't just the attitude of the staff that she found difficult to take. It was missing Sandro.

She thought of him all the time, found herself listening for his step, and the sound of his voice. She had no idea when he was to return, and there was no one she could ask.

Least of all himself, she acknowledged, even though he telephoned the *palazzo* each day to speak to Charlie. On the occasions when he asked to speak to her too, their exchanges were cool and stilted.

Strangers, she thought achingly. With nothing to say to each other.

But even living a separate existence under his roof was preferable to his continuing absence, she thought. And her imagination worked overtime in picturing where he was, and what he might be doing. And with whom...

The nights were the worst. In spite of the summer heat, the vast bed she occupied seemed as wide and chilly as a winter ocean, and sleep was a deep pit of loneliness which swallowed her up, then released her, restless and unrefreshed when morning came. And often, when she woke, her face was wet with tears.

She wished with all her heart that she'd been the one to move out. Everything that belonged to him had been scrupulously removed, but it had made little difference. His presence still seemed to linger, invisible but potent.

He had been gone nearly a fortnight when Polly received a pleasant surprise—a flying visit from Teresa, Ernesto and the twins, who had come to visit his parents in Naples.

They were clearly stunned to discover Sandro's absence, but quickly concealed their shock under a flood of chatter and laughter.

Polly knew that Teresa would have picked up immediately on her wan face and shadowed eyes, but that good manners would keep her from asking awkward questions.

But when Ernesto was down at the pool with the children, and Polly was alone with Teresa in her living room, she did confide in the other girl about her staff problems, and saw her frown.

'Your Italian is good,' she said. 'And will become better with practice. So, there should be no misunderstandings—especially with Dorotea. She has worked at the *palazzo* longer than anyone, and is devoted to the Valessi family. You are the mother of Alessandro's heir, so she should be your greatest supporter.' She patted Polly's hand. 'I will go and ask for some coffee and almond cakes to be brought, and see what I can find out.'

When she returned, her face was solemn. 'They believe they are going to lose their jobs,' she said. 'That you intend to replace them all with your own servants from England, and that Julie is only the first of many.'

'But that's complete nonsense.' Polly stared at her, aghast. 'I haven't got any servants in England, for heaven's sake. And Julie's here on a strictly temporary basis. In fact, I'm surprised she hasn't walked out already.'

She shook her head. 'And even if I wanted to make changes— which I don't—Sandro would never allow it. Surely they know that?'

Teresa shrugged. 'They know only that he is a man with a new bride,' she commented drily. 'And that you have powers of persuasion with him that they lack.'

She hesitated. 'Dorotea has been the most deeply hurt. She believes you think her too elderly to have charge of Carlino, and too old-fashioned in her ways, and that is why she will be the first to be replaced.'

'No wonder it's like walking into a brick wall whenever I go near the nursery,' Polly said bitterly. 'Oh, God, how can this have happened?'

Teresa chose her words carefully. 'It is clear to me, Paola, that these rumours have been started by someone with authority, whose word they feel they can trust. I think you have an enemy, *cara*,' she added gently.

Polly had been staring at the floor, but now her head came up sharply. 'Don't tell me,' she said with sudden grimness. 'The *contessa*.'

'It seems so. She has offered to be their champion, and fight their cause with you. No doubt she is already telling them that you are intransigent, and will make no concessions.

'You need to do something, Paola, before they walk out,' she added candidly, 'and Alessandro returns to find his house deserted.'

'Perhaps I'm the one who should leave,' Polly said in a low, unhappy voice. 'I'm clearly out of my depth here. I thought they just despised me because I didn't know how to be a *marchesa*.'

'But you have one great advantage over any lies that Antonia Barsoli tells,' Teresa said quietly. 'You are Alessandro's chosen wife, and they love him.' She smiled encouragingly at Polly. 'Make it clear their jobs are not threatened, and fill that big nursery with more babies for Dorotea to cherish, and they will love you too.'

Easier said than done, Polly thought, forcing a smile of agreement. On both counts.

She was smiling again when she waved them off a few hours later, but she felt bleak as she went slowly back indoors. For a while, she'd been let off the hook, and allowed to put her troubles aside to enjoy their company.

Now her temporary reprieve was over, and her problems were crowding round again. But at least she now knew what she was up against, she thought. And Teresa's advice had been practical as well as bracing, so she had a plan of action too.

It had done her so much good to have them here, and she'd extracted a serious promise from them to come for a proper visit later in the summer. If, of course, she was still here, she amended with a pang.

However, just for a few hours, she hadn't felt quite so isolated, and she missed them all badly now that they'd gone back to Naples.

Nor was she the only one.

Charlie, Julie reported ruefully, had screamed blue murder when he realised the twins were leaving, and had subsequently cried himself to sleep.

'He really needs other children to play with on a regular basis,' she added, with a swift sideways glance at Polly, who flushed, guessing that the other girl was thinking in terms of brothers and sisters for him.

Clearly, because she was part of the opposition, any gossip about the separate rooms had passed her by completely.

Perhaps, as time went on, she would establish some kind of social life, Polly thought, trying to be hopeful, and meet other young mothers whose children could provide Charlie with companionship.

Meanwhile, she would simply have to go on enduring all these none-too-subtle hints, she told herself and sighed.

The next morning dawned overcast and heavy, with even a hint of thunder in the air.

Good day for starting a different kind of storm, perhaps, Polly thought as she drank the tea that Rafaella had brought to her bedroom.

As the girl emerged from the dressing room with the pale blue linen trousers and matching jersey top that she'd been asked to fetch, Polly gave her a quick smile.

'Has your grandfather come back yet from Salerno?' she asked. 'Because I'd still like to talk to him.'

'I have not forgotten, *madame*.' There was a faintly evasive note in Rafaella's voice. 'I will ask again.' She paused. 'Shall I run your bath now?'

'Yes—please.'

Polly took another reflective sip of tea. It sounded as if Giacomo had already been approached and returned a negative response, she thought, troubled. Which seemed to suggest that he might well have something to hide over Sandro's accident.

For good or ill, I need to know, she told herself.

In the mail that was brought to her living room later that morning was a postcard from Cornwall. 'Just like old times,' ran the message. 'Keep well. Be happy.' The handwriting was her father's, but her mother had signed it too, she noticed thankfully.

She took out the notes that she'd made the previous day with Teresa's help, and read them through several times, committing them to memory, before she put them in the empty grate and set fire to them.

Then she rang for Teodoro. 'Will you tell all the staff that I wish to see them in the *salotto* at three o'clock?' she instructed quietly. 'And I mean everyone.'

'Even Dorotea? The little Carlino is upset because he cannot swim today, and she plans to take him out in the car this afternoon.'

'Certainly Dorotea,' Polly said crisply. 'Julie can look after my son.'

'*Sì, Vossignoria.*' He hesitated, studying her with worried eyes. 'Is there some problem?'

She smiled at him. 'Nothing that can't be fixed, I hope. Three p.m., then.'


Teodoro had done his work well, because the *salotto* seemed full of people when Polly entered.

She had decided not to change into more formal clothes, because that might look as if she was trying too hard. Instead, she had simply combed her hair and applied some colour to her lips.

She stood in front of them all, her back to the open door, and spoke slowly using the Italian phrases that Teresa had written down for her. 'I have called you here today to clear up a serious misunderstanding. Some of you may have heard a rumour that I plan to take your jobs from you, and have you dismissed from the *palazzo*. I wish to set your minds at rest, and assure you that there is no truth in this story, and I cannot understand where it has come from, or why it has been spread in this malicious way.'

She heard faint gasps from her audience, but went quietly on. 'I am sorry that none of you felt able to come to me and ask if it was true, but we are to a large extent still strangers to each other. I intend to change that, and take on much of the everyday management of the household myself.'

More gasps, and louder.

'One thing I must make clear at once,' she continued, raising her voice a little above the whispering that had also broken out. 'In the last few weeks, the life of my little boy has changed completely. He has a new environment to learn, and a new language, too.'

She paused. 'Julie, who came with us from England, is not simply a *bambinaia*, but a friend who is helping him come to terms with all these puzzling changes. But it was always the plan of the *marchese* that Dorotea, who cherished him in childhood, should ultimately take full charge of his son in turn. And this is my wish, also.'

She looked directly at Dorotea, who was staring back, her mouth working, and her hands twisting in her white apron.

'My husband, the *marchese*, has a demanding career,' Polly continued. 'And I wish him to have a peaceful and well-run home to return to. I hope we can work together to achieve this, but anyone who cannot accept my regime is, of course, free to leave.'

She smiled around her, keeping it positive. Letting them see she expected their co-operation. 'Although, naturally, I hope you will all stay. And that you will bring any future difficulties straight to me. Because I am the mistress of the house.'

But it appeared she had lost them, because nearly all eyes were looking past her to the door behind.

And then she heard Sandro's voice, cool and slightly mocking. '*Bravo, marchesa.* I am impressed.'

She swung round, her heart thumping, and saw him, leaning against the massive doorframe, watching her steadily with a smile that did not reach his eyes.

# CHAPTER ELEVEN

THE almost agonised leap of her heart at the sight of him stilled and died. She checked the impulsive step towards him she'd been about to take, waiting rigidly instead for him to come to her side.

As he did, his cool gaze sweeping the room, his hand lightly clasping her shoulder. 'So,' he said, 'I suggest that anyone wishing to remain in our employ gets back to work—*subito*.'

Polly had never seen a room empty so quickly or silently.

'Teodoro,' Sandro added as the majordomo approached, 'be good enough to bring us coffee—in the *marchesa*'s own living room, I think, if you permit, *cara mia*?'

As if she had any real choice in the matter, thought Polly, finding herself led gently but firmly by the hand to the room in question.

Sandro waved Polly to one of the sofas, and seated himself opposite, long legs stretched out in front of him as he loosened his tie. He looked tired, she thought, and he needed a shave.

She looked down at her clasped hands. 'I wasn't expecting to seé you.'

'I did not anticipate returning so soon.'

She cleared her throat. 'Did—did you have a successful trip?'

'So far,' he said. 'Unfortunately, it was curtailed before I reached Rome.'

'Oh.' She felt a stab of fierce pleasure. 'Why was that?'

'Because last night I received a telephone call from Teresa and Ernesto telling me that you had problems here, and might need me.'

She looked at him, stunned. So, they knew where to find you, she thought, biting her lip. And I didn't.

'Therefore, I came to you at once,' he went on. 'Only to find you coping admirably alone.'

She said, 'It's kind of them to be so concerned, but they've already been of great help. They—they shouldn't have dragged you into this. Interrupted your trip.' She shrugged. 'Really, it was all pretty trivial. A storm in a teacup.'

His mouth twisted. 'If it is like the storm outside, Paola *mia*,' he said as a sudden flash of lightning illuminated the room, followed almost at once by a reverberating clap of thunder, 'then it may get worse before it is better.'

He paused. 'So, has your rallying call halted the revolution, *cara*?' he asked softly. 'Or are there still matters to be dealt with?'

She met his gaze with as much composure as she could muster. 'I think it's—settled.'

'Ah,' he said. 'Then Zia Antonia is at this moment packing her bags.'

She swallowed. 'No, of course not. I—I couldn't do that.'

'But you are the mistress here,' he said. 'I heard you say so.'

'Yes.' Her hands tightened on each other almost painfully. 'But perhaps I was presuming too much.'

'Or not enough,' he returned drily. 'While I have been away, I have had time to think, and I realise that the situation here cannot be allowed to continue.'

Before she could even ask what he meant, the door was flung open and the *contessa* came in, all smiles.

'*Caro* Alessandro.' He rose at her entrance, and she reached up to embrace him. 'But what a wonderful surprise for us all. I should have been here to greet you, but I was resting in my room. This weather—so dreadful. I shall be fortunate to avoid a migraine.'

She turned to Polly, a reproving note in her voice. 'But, my dear child, you have ordered no refreshment for your husband on his return. A little remiss of you, if you will forgive me for saying so.'

'I am sure she will do so,' Sandro said quietly. 'And coffee is being brought, so do not concern yourself.'

The *contessa*'s tone became steel covered by honey. 'But I must express my anxieties, my dearest cousin. Your household is in my charge after all, and yet my maid had to inform me of your arrival.' She tutted smilingly. 'She also informs me that our dear Paola summoned all the staff to a meeting a little while ago, to harangue them on the subject of loyalty. If she had issues to raise on that or any other matter, then surely she should have come to me first.'

The smile she bestowed on Polly was pure acid. 'One must make allowances for your inexperience, dear girl. You are not accustomed to dealing with servants, of course. But, in future, there is certainly no need to indulge in such…ludicrous histrionics—or to send for your husband, while he is away on important business, and involve him in a purely domestic matter.

'I hope Alessandro is not too angry with you,' she added on a teasing note that set Polly's teeth on edge.

'I am not angry at all,' Sandro corrected her courteously. 'And nor did Paola send for me. I had other reasons for my return.' He moved across to Polly and put his arm round her, drawing her close to his side.

'I felt, you understand, that I had left my bride alone for too long, and could not bear to spend another night away from her. A very different domestic matter,' he said softly.

Polly looked down at the floor, aware that every drop of blood in her veins had moved to her face and was tingling there.

The *contessa*'s little laugh was husk-dry. 'Why, Alessandro, how marriage has tamed you,' she said. 'You have become quite a romantic, *caro mio*.' She paused theatrically. '*Dio mio*. Tell me that I have not intruded on a private moment.'

Sandro smiled back at her. 'Not,' he said softly, 'while the key for that door remains unaccountably missing. Perhaps you would have the goodness to search for it again.'

Just open, Polly told the floor silently. Just open and swallow me—please.

'In fact,' Sandro went on remorselessly, 'you may bring my wife all the keys. She can hardly embark upon her new duties without them.'

The delicate blusher that the *contessa* wore was suddenly like a stain on her white face. Her drawn breath was a hiss.

'You intend *her* to manage the *palazzo*. A girl from nowhere, without family or position? A girl for whom you sacrificed my Bianca, and broke your father's heart? And whose only accomplishment has been to bear your bastard?'

Her strident laugh broke in the middle. 'Are you insane? You see for yourself that she cannot handle your servants. And who will ever accept her?'

'I have,' Sandro said with deadly quietness. 'Nothing else is necessary.' He paused. 'Ever since Paola came here you have attempted to undermine her, but each time she has proved to be more than your equal. Today was one such moment. Nor will I allow her to endure your insults any longer.'

He looked at the older woman, his mouth hard and set. 'My father offered you a home, and I acceded to his wishes and permitted you to remain, setting convenience against my better judgement. But my tolerance is now exhausted.'

'No,' she said hoarsely. 'No, Alessandro. You cannot do this.'

He went on as if she had not spoken. 'Out of respect for my father, I shall provide you with a house. I shall also consult with my lawyer on a suitable supplement to your income. But you must and will leave Comadora.'

'But I helped you find her.' Her fingers were twisting together like claws. 'I searched for this—*sciattona* in England because you still wanted her.'

'No, *contessa*,' Sandro said softly, 'you discovered somehow that I wished to find her, and told Emilio. What did you do, I wonder? Listen at a door? Read my correspondence?' He shook his head. 'It would not be the first time.

'And Emilio sent you to England on his own behalf, hoping to buy lurid details of my affair with Paola, and discredit me at last.' He shrugged. 'But, unluckily for both of you, I guessed what you were doing, and found her first. So you had to pretend you had been working for me all the time.'

His mouth twisted. 'How galling that must have been. How much had Emilio offered for your services?'

Her thin body was as taut as a wire. 'I would have done it for nothing,' she spat back. 'How could I have known you would forget everything that was due to your name, and marry your discarded whore?'

There was a terrible silence. Polly turned away, feeling sick, her hands pressed to her burning face. Sandro walked to the fireplace and reached for the bell rope, but as he did so there was a knock on the door, and Teodoro came in with the tray of coffee.

He checked instinctively, his glance darting from one to another, but Sandro beckoned him forward. 'Please escort the *contessa* to her room,' he said. 'She is unwell. Call her doctor, and tell her maid to stay with her.'

Teodoro set the tray on a side-table, and offered the *contessa* a deferential arm which she ignored, walking slowly and stiffly to the door. Where she turned.

'You will be sorry for this.' Her tone sounded almost conversational. 'In the past I have argued against Emilio's wish to have the inquiry into Bianca's death reopened. But no longer. This time, *marchese*, you will appear and answer for what you did. And your loyal accomplice, Giacomo Raboni, will be made to tell all he knows—in public. Emilio will see to that.'

Another lightning flash lit up the room. In its momentary glare, Sandro's face looked carved from granite, the scar livid against his cheek.

He said, 'If he hopes to buy Giacomo, he is wasting his time.'

The *contessa* shrugged. 'Everyone has their price, my dear cousin,' she said softly. She sent Polly a malevolent glance. 'Including, if you remember, the little gold-digger you call your wife. Where will she be, I wonder, when you come out of jail?'

Teodoro, his face rigid with shock, seemed to grow another six inches in height. He took the *contessa*'s arm without gentleness and hustled her from the room.

The thunder roared again, and rain began to fall, huge, heavy drops beating a tattoo on the terrace, and hurling themselves in gusts against the window.

Polly sank down on one of the sofas, because her legs would no longer support her. Resting her elbows on her knees, she buried her face in her hands and waited for the shaking to stop.

Eventually she became aware that Sandro had come to sit beside her, and she raised her head and looked at him.

She said in a small, quiet voice, 'That was so—terrible.'

'I am sorry, Paola.' He spoke gently. 'You should not have had to endure that. I did not realise she was so near the edge.' His hand covered hers and she realised he was trembling a little too.

She said on a rush, 'I—I should go up to the nursery. Charlie may be frightened of the storm.'

'In a moment,' he said. 'But stay with me now. We need to talk.'

'Yes.' She ran the tip of her tongue round her dry mouth. 'I—I suppose we must.' She paused. 'I always knew the *contessa* didn't like me,' she said slowly. 'But—it was more than that. It was hatred. Not just for me—but also for you.'

His mouth tightened. 'Until now, I only saw the bitterness, and thought I understood. When she came here twenty years ago, I think she believed that my father would eventually offer her marriage. Only he had no such intention. His relationship with my mother had brought happiness to neither, and, after her death, he was content with an occasional discreet liaison.

'When Antonia saw she had nothing to hope for from him, she diverted all that fierce energy into preparing Bianca as a bride for me. Perhaps she felt her own thwarted dreams would be fulfilled by the next generation. But it was not the usual matchmaking that older women sometimes indulge in. Even as young as I was, and as careless, I sensed there was something wrong. Something obsessive—and dark. Just as I felt...' He paused. 'Well, that is not important. Let me say that I began to spend as little time as possible at Comadora.'

'But why did your father go along with her scheme if he saw how you felt?'

Sandro hesitated. 'He saw marriage as a business arrangement, not a matter of emotion,' he told her slowly. 'Also I believe he felt guilty, so his encouragement was a form of recompense to Antonia for having disappointed her so deeply himself.'

Polly thought of the portrait of the late *marchese* which hung at the top of the stairs, remembering the harsh lines of the dark face beneath the grizzled hair, the thin mouth and piercing eyes that she felt followed her as she passed. Not a man, she thought, who looked as if he ever suffered from remorse, and she repressed a shiver.

'When the accident happened to Bianca, the *contessa* must have felt as if she'd died herself,' she said quietly. 'Perhaps we shouldn't blame her too harshly. Especially...' She stopped hurriedly, aware that she'd been about to say *when there are so many questions over what really happened*.

'Especially?' Sandro had noticed her hesitation.

She said, 'Especially when you have lost someone that you love so much.' She remembered the weeks after her return to England. The greyness of her life as one bleak day followed another. The nights she'd spent in bitter weeping, her eyes and throat raw with grief and bewilderment. Her stunned sense of isolation, caught as she was between her mother's anger and her father's disappointment.

'She'll feel as if she's in an abyss,' she went on, half to herself. 'With no way out, and no one to turn to. Facing an eternity of emptiness.'

Her own turning point had come when she'd felt the first faint flutter of her baby moving inside her, she realised. And from somewhere she'd found the strength to reclaim her life and sanity.

If there hadn't been Charlie, she thought, I could have ended up like the *contessa*, corroded with anger and bitterness.

He said with faint grimness, 'Almost you persuade me, *cara*, but not quite. She cannot remain here.'

'But you can't make her go,' Polly said passionately. 'Can't you see she means what she says? She and Emilio will rake up everything that happened three years ago and use it against you. You know that they will.'

He was very still suddenly. And when he moved, it was to release her hand.

He said quietly, almost conversationally, 'You speak, *cara*, as if I had something to fear. Is that what you think?'

'How do I know what to think?' The loss of the gentle clasp of his fingers round hers made her feel suddenly bereft. 'All I hear is that the inquiry wasn't told everything. That Rafaella's grandfather, who found you, is sworn to secrecy. My God, you've just admitted as much.' She swallowed. 'So I have to believe you have something to hide—and that the *contessa* and your vile cousin will move heaven and earth to uncover it. And once these things start, who knows where they can lead?'

'Clearly you imagine they could lead to prison,' Sandro drawled. 'Unless I decide instead to submit to blackmail. Neither option has much appeal, *bella mia*. And I would not be much of a man if I were to choose either of them without a fight.

'But then you do not have a very high opinion of me, anyway,' he added with a shrug. 'Is that why you have been trying to persuade Giacomo to meet you through Rafaella? And why you have had no success?

'Unfortunately for you, whenever an attempt is made to contact him, he immediately informs my lawyers, and they tell me. And that, my loving wife, is one of the other reasons I decided to make an early return, to suggest that you waste no more time on these fruitless enquiries.

'But then, what does it really matter?' He got to his feet, stretching lithely. 'Except that I am once again the villain,' he added mockingly. 'But that is something I shall have to live with.'

He paused. 'And now I am going to shower and change,' he

went on. 'Under the circumstances, I shall dine in the town tonight. I would not wish to spoil your appetite by forcing you to eat with a murderer.'

'I never said that,' Polly protested. 'I never would.'

His smile was grim. 'But I swear it must have crossed your mind, *mi adorata*. And the knowledge of that might turn my stomach too.'

As he strode to the door, she said huskily, 'Sandro—please. I just need to know the truth.'

'Truth,' he echoed contemptuously. 'It is just a word, Paola, like so many others. Like love, for example, and loyalty. Like honour and faith. Just words to be used and forgotten, as we will eventually forget today ever existed.' He inclined his head curtly, and was gone.

Polly sat staring at the closed door. She knew she should go after him, pour out all her doubts and fears—all her confused emotions. Make him listen. Make him, somehow, understand.

He had clearly expected her to trust him without question, but how was that possible when she was still dealing with the nightmare of the past, and his betrayal?

We both loved him, she thought wretchedly. Both Bianca, and myself. And he wanted neither of us. The only difference is that I survived, and she didn't. The margin is that small.

And I still love him, no matter what he does, or what he is. And I know now that beyond logic, beyond reason, I always shall, because I can't help myself. He's part of me—my flesh, my blood, the pulse of my heart. Because, in spite of everything, I only feel safe with his arms around me.

And, like the *contessa*, that's a tragedy I have somehow to endure.

She gave a long, shaking sigh. The abyss was back, it seemed, and deeper than ever. And with as little hope for escape.

After a while she got up wearily, and went to the table where the forgotten coffee waited. It was still hot, and it provided her momentarily with the jolt she needed.

She and Sandro might be a million miles apart, but upstairs was a child who might need her.

When she reached the nursery she paused, taking a deep breath before she went in. If she walked into the usual wall of resentment, she wasn't sure she could bear it.

Dorotea was there, seated in one of the big rocking chairs that flanked the hearth, knitting busily, while opposite her sat Julie with Charlie on her lap, fast asleep.

The older woman looked up at Polly hovering in the doorway, and her plump face creased into an equally hesitant smile.

She got to her feet, indicating respectfully that Polly should take her seat, then signalled to Julie to transfer the little boy to his mother's arms.

This safely achieved, Dorotea stood for a moment, and patted Polly awkwardly on the shoulder as Charlie murmured drowsily and pushed his small round head against the familiar curve of her breast. '*Bene,*' she said. 'Is good now, *vossignoria, sì*?'

'*Sì,*' Polly agreed, her throat tightening. 'This—is good.'

Dorotea beckoned to Julie, and they both disappeared into the night nursery, leaving Polly alone with her child. Leaning back, eyes half closed, she listened to the storm retreating over the hills. Just the act of holding Charlie quietly seemed to offer a kind of peace amid the turmoil of emotions that assailed her.

Whatever Sandro might feel about her, she told herself, whatever darkness there might be inside him, his love for Charlie was unqualified and beyond doubt, and she could cling to that. Because even if her husband never smiled at her again—never touched her—their son remained an indissoluble link between them.

She was suddenly aware she was no longer alone, and, glancing round, saw Sandro standing in the doorway, watching her, his mouth hard, the dark brows drawn together.

She wanted to speak, but what could she say? Tell him that as long as they were together, nothing else mattered? But they were not together, and how could they ever be, when there was so much to divide them?

Unless you came to me now, she thought, her heart in her eyes as she looked back at him. Unless you held us—your wife, and your child. And if you would promise to try and love me a little as you love him. Then I wouldn't care about anything else.

Surely—*surely* he could feel the yearning in her, the unassuaged and aching need, and show her a little mercy—couldn't he?

But just as her lips pleadingly framed his name, he turned away and left as silently as he'd appeared.

And Polly sat where she was, forcing back the tears that were bitter in her throat, because she could not allow Charlie to wake and find her crying.

She spent a restless, unhappy night, and woke late the following morning, to the sunlight and an incongruously flawless sky.

'Buongiorno, madame.' Rafaella appeared with coffee as if on signal. 'It is so beautiful today with no storm.' She beamed at Polly. 'The marchese asks if you will honour him by joining him at breakfast. And wishes you to know that Signor Molena will be there also.'

'Molena?' Polly queried, feeling the name should mean something.

'His signore's avoccato,' Rafaella explained.

'Oh,' Polly said in a hollow voice, recalling that terrible afternoon at her mother's house. 'The lawyer. I—I remember.'

'Sì, the lawyer.' Rafaella said the word with care, and smiled again. 'Today, vossignoria is to meet with my grandfather,' she added with real excitement. 'His excellency has said so.'

Polly stared at her. 'Your grandfather?' she said slowly. 'Are you serious?'

'Certamente, madame.' The girl paused. 'Also the contessa goes with you,' she added more hesitantly.

'I see.' Polly digested that apprehensively, not understanding at all. 'Is she—well enough?'

She had questioned Teodoro haltingly about the contessa's condition the previous evening, and been told that the doctor had paid her a lengthy visit, and administered a sedative. Also that a nurse would be coming to spend the night, and that a transfer to a private clinic the next day was also being considered.

Polly, wincing inwardly, had given him a quiet word of thanks.

But if the contessa was well enough to go out, maybe a less rigorous solution would be found, she thought.

She popped into the nursery on her way downstairs to kiss Charlie good morning, and wished she could have lingered there forever.

When she finally reached the door of the sala da pranzo, she had to force herself to open the door and go in.

'Good morning, cara,' Sandro rose politely. 'You remember Alberto, of course.'

'It is a pleasure to see you again, *marchesa.*' Signor Molena bowed politely, and she murmured something in reply.

Why was he there? she wondered as she helped herself to a slice of cold ham she would never eat, and poured some coffee. Had he been summoned to tell her that her brief, ill-starred marriage was over?

She sat pushing the meat round her plate, while the two men talked quietly, their faces slightly troubled.

But the coffee put heart into her, and when Sandro said abruptly, 'If you have finished breakfast, Paola, we will go,' she was able to rise to her feet with a semblance of composure.

There were two cars parked in front of the house, and Polly saw that the *contessa* was being helped into the second of them by a brisk-looking woman in a white uniform.

The older woman looked bent and ill, and for an instant Polly quailed. Then she felt her arm taken firmly, and Sandro was guiding her towards the leading car.

She hung back, looking up into his face, searching in vain for some sign of softening.

'Sandro,' she whispered. 'Please—we don't have to do this.'

'Yes,' he said quietly, 'we do, *cara mia.*'

'But it's none of my business—I see that now. And I'm sorry— so sorry to have interfered.'

'It is too late to draw back,' he told her harshly. 'Only the truth will do for my cousin, and for you, it seems. This is what you wanted, and this is what you will get. So, *andiamo.* Let's go.'

She sat rigidly beside him in the back of the car, her hands clenched together, as Signor Molena took his place beside the chauffeur, and the cars began to move forward.

And above the whisper of tyres on gravel, she could hear a small voice in her head repeating 'Too late' over and over again, and she was afraid.

# CHAPTER TWELVE

THE dusty road in front of them climbed steeply and endlessly. They had passed through several tiny villages where the main streets were passable by only one vehicle at a time, but all signs of habitation were now behind them.

Polly had gone down to the town and visited the marina several times, but this was the first time she had been driven up into the mountains behind Comadora, and she was too tense to take real stock of her surroundings.

After the rain, the air was clear, and the creamy stone of the jagged crags, heavily veined in shades of grey and green, seemed close enough to touch. It was a landscape of scrub and thorn, stabbed in places with the darkness of cedars. Above it a solitary bird wheeled, watchful and predatory.

She found she was shivering slightly, and broke the silence. 'Is this the road to Sorrento?'

'One of them.' He did not look at her, and she could see his hand was clenched on his thigh.

I've made him do this, she thought bleakly. Made him confront whatever demons are waiting in this desolate place, and he'll never forgive me.

They had been travelling for about ten more minutes when the chauffeur began to slow down. The car rounded a sharp bend, and Polly gasped soundlessly as she saw that immediately beyond it the ground fell away, and she was looking down into a deep gorge with a glimmer of water far below.

They pulled over to the rough verge on the opposite side of the narrow road, and stopped.

Sandro turned to Polly, his face expressionless. 'Come,' he said, 'if you wish to see.'

After the fuss she'd made, she thought wretchedly, she could hardly tell him it was the last thing she wanted, so she followed him out into the sunlight. In spite of the heat, she felt cold.

Sandro's face was rigid, the slash of the scar prominent against his dark skin. Alberto Molena came to his side, talking softly, encouragingly, and eventually he nodded curtly and they crossed the road together, and stood looking down into the depths below.

She did not go with them. Her eyes had detected a flash further along the road, as if the sunlight was being reflected back from glass. She could see a smudge of colour too, and guessed this was the shrine that Sandro had mentioned.

There was nothing unique about it. Polly knew that they were seen all over the Mediterranean where bad accidents had occurred. But none of the others had carried any meaning for her.

Slowly, almost reluctantly, she went to face one of her own demons. Bianca had indeed been a beautiful girl, her face heart-shaped, and her eyes dark and dreaming. The only jarring note was struck by a set, almost hard look about the mouth, but Polly supposed she could not be blamed for that.

Knowing the man you love feels nothing for you in return can do that to you, she thought sadly.

Also in the elaborate frame was a small plaster figure of a saint, with an unlit votive light in front of it, and a vase of slightly wilted flowers.

She heard a step, and, glancing round, saw the *contessa* approaching, leaning heavily on a cane.

'Get away from here.' The older woman's voice was harsh, almost metallic. 'You are not fit to breathe the same air that she did.'

She turned and stared malevolently at Sandro, standing motion-less on the edge of the drop, only yards away. Polly's heart missed a beat, and she was just about to cry a warning when they were joined by the nurse, who took the *contessa*'s arm gently but firmly, murmuring to her in a soothing tone.

Polly crossed the road and stood at Sandro's side. She said in a low voice, 'Coming here may have been a bad idea. I think your cousin's getting agitated.'

'She has been here many times before,' he said stonily. 'Unlike myself.'

She looked at him, shocked. 'Is this the first time—since the crash?'

'The first, and I hope the only time. We came here solely to meet Giacomo Raboni, so that you could see what happened at this place through his eyes.' Sandro paused. 'He speaks little

English, but Alberto will translate for you—if you can trust his accuracy,' he added with a touch of bitterness.

'Yes,' she said, 'of course I can.'

She looked down. Just below the edge, the ground, littered with rocks and boulders of all sizes, sloped steeply away for about a hundred yards before reaching a kind of rim, beyond which it disappeared into infinity.

The kind of drop, she thought, that nightmares were made of, and shuddered.

She said, 'Will Signor Raboni be long? I'd like to get away from here.'

'It has always been a bad place,' Sandro told her quietly. 'But it is part of the truth which is so important to you.' He paused. 'And you will not be detained here much longer. Giacomo is coming now.'

She heard a rattle of stones behind her and turned. A man was coming down the hill, half walking, half sliding, an elderly dog scrabbling beside him.

Giacomo Raboni was of medium height, and stout, wearing ancient flannel trousers, a collarless shirt and a cap pulled on over curling white hair. He had a mouth that looked as if it preferred to smile. But for now, his expression was faintly grim.

He gave the *contessa* a measuring look, then turned his head and spat with great accuracy, just missing the dog. Then he turned shrewd dark eyes on Polly, telling her without words that she wasn't the subject of his whole-hearted approbation either.

He took Sandro's offered hand and shook it warmly. He said gruffly, 'You should not be here, *excellenza*. Why not let the dead girl sleep?'

Sandro's voice was harsh. 'Because, my old friend, she still poisons my life as she did when she was alive.' He paused. 'You agreed to keep silent to protect the living, and spare them more grief. But my father can no longer be hurt by what you saw, and the Contessa Barsoli has tried to use your silence to damage me, and my marriage, so she is no longer worthy of my consideration.'

He threw back his head. 'But my wife is a different matter, so it is time to speak, if you please, and tell her what happened here. And slowly, so that Signor Molena can tell her what is said.'

Giacomo Raboni gave a reluctant nod. He said, 'I had been on the hill that day, looking at my goats. A neighbour had told me that two of them seemed sick. As I came down the track, I heard the sound of a car. As it came round the corner, I recognised it as the car which belonged to the Signore Alessandro. But it was being driven strangely, swerving from side to side, and I could see why. There was a passenger beside him—a girl, but not in the passenger seat, you understand. She was leaning towards him—clinging to him, it seemed.'

He stared at the brink, frowning. 'At first I thought it was love play between them, and that they were fools, bringing their games to such a dangerous road. Then I realised that the *marchese* was not embracing her, but struggling, trying to push her away, and control the car too.'

He turned his head and looked steadily at Polly. 'At that moment, *vossignoria*, I knew that your husband was fighting for his life. Because she was not reaching for him, but trying to grab the wheel. I think, also, she went for his eyes, because he flung up an arm to defend himself, and in that instant she turned the car towards the edge of the cliff.'

'Oh, God,' Polly said numbly. 'Oh, no.'

'As it went over, I heard her scream something. Then there was the sound of the crash, and I ran.

'I saw that the car had hit a rock, but glanced off it and continued down. It had reached the brink, but there it ran into a dead tree so it could go no further.

'But the *marchese* had somehow been thrown clear. I climbed down to him and realised he was badly injured. There was much blood and his pulse was weak.'

He paused. 'I realised too that the girl was still in the vehicle, and that the engine was running. The tree was a spindly thing, old and brittle, with shallow roots. It could not hold the car for much longer, so the *signorina* was inches from death.

'I went down to her, careful not to fall myself. The driver's door was open, and she was lying across the seat. She too was terribly injured, but I reached in to her, tried to take her hands to pull her free before the tree gave way.

'I spoke to her—called her Signorina Bianca, but she seemed barely conscious, and it was plain she did not know who I was. In her pain, she looked at me with eyes that saw nothing, and whispered something.

'She thought she was speaking to the *marchese*—that he was

with her still, and she repeated the same words she had used before.'

His own voice was hushed with the horror of it. 'She said, ''If I cannot have you then no one will.'' And with her last movement, she put her foot on the accelerator and sent the car over the edge.'

Polly stood rigidly, her hands pressed to her mouth. Then the *contessa*'s hoarse voice broke the silence. 'You're lying,' she accused, her face twisted. 'The *marchese* has paid you to say these terrible things.'

He drew himself up with immense dignity. 'The *marchese* has paid me with nothing but his regard. All this I would have said at the inquiry, but he knew the distress it would give his father, who loved the Signorina Bianca and was already a sick man. For his sake and no other, we allowed it to become an accident. And, for the honour of the Valessi, I have kept my silence until now.'

His voice became deeper, more resonant. 'But I, Giacomo Raboni, I tell you that the Signorina Bianca tried to murder the Signore Alessandro. And I saw it all.'

There was a terrible keening noise from the *contessa*, who had sunk to her knees in the dust.

'No,' she was moaning. 'It cannot be true. Not my angel—my beautiful dove. She never harmed anyone—or anything in her life.'

'No,' Sandro said, harshly. 'That is the real lie. There were stories about her—rumours of cruelty from the moment she came to Comadora. A dog that belonged to one of the grooms tied up in the sun and left to die without water or food because it left paw-marks on her skirt. The pony my father bought for her which threw her, and mysteriously broke its leg in its stall soon after.

'And the convent school she attended. Did you know that the superior asked my father to remove her? Or how much he had to give to the chapel-restoration fund for her to be permitted to remain? He insisted of course that the nuns were mistaken.'

He shook his head. 'All I knew was that she'd repelled me from the first. And nothing my father could have said or done would have persuaded me to make her my wife.'

The *contessa* was weeping noisily. 'It cannot be true. She would never have harmed you. In spite of your cruelty and indifference, she loved you. You know that.'

He said grimly, 'I knew that she was obsessed by me. And that she was determined to become the Marchesa Valessi. Between you, you forced me away from my family home, and drove a wedge between my father and myself. Unforgivable things were done at your instigation.'

'No,' she moaned. 'No, Alessandro.'

Polly said softly, 'Sandro—she's in real pain. No more, please.'

He looked at her sombrely, then went reluctantly to the *contessa*, and lifted her to her feet. He said more gently, 'Just the same, I would have spared you this knowledge, as I did my father, if you had not started your insidious campaign against my wife— the whispers at the party you organised with such kindness, the rumours among the staff, all stemming from you.

'But Paola emerged triumphantly from each trap you set for her. How that must have galled you. But it is all over now. There are no more secrets, unless you choose to keep from Emilio what you have heard today. Can you imagine what a feast he would make of it—what the headlines would say about your beloved Bianca?'

A shudder went through her. She looked up at him, her face suddenly a hundred years old. 'I shall say nothing,' she told him dully. 'All I can ask, Alessandro, is a little kindness.'

'There is the house on Capri,' he said. 'You have always liked it there. Alberto will examine your financial circumstances and make suitable arrangements for your comfort. Now he will escort you back to Comadora.'

She nodded with difficulty, then took his hand and kissed it.

Polly watched Signor Molena offer his arm, and lead her back to the car. Saw it turn carefully, then go back towards Comadora.

Leaving her, she thought, to travel alone with Sandro. She stole a glance at him, and saw that he was staring down at the crash site again, his eyes hooded, his face like a mask.

He said quietly, 'There is nothing there. No sign that anything ever happened.'

Only that scar, she thought. The one you will carry forever.

She wanted to go to him. To take his face in her hands, and kiss the harshness from his mouth. To offer him the healing warmth of her body.

But she didn't dare.

I made him face this, she thought. I made him remember the unthinkable—the grotesque. The fear and the pain. And how can he ever forgive that? How can he ever forgive me?

She swallowed. 'Sandro—shall we go home?'

'Home?' he queried ironically. 'You mean that huge empty house I visit sometimes, that stopped being home after the death of my mother?'

'But it could be again,' she said. 'It has to be—for Charlie.'

His sigh was small and bitter. 'Yes,' he said. 'At least I have my son.'

He walked away to where Giacomo Raboni waited. They spoke quietly for a moment or two, then embraced swiftly, and the old man, whistling to his dog, went back the way he had come.

On the journey home they sat, each in their separate corners, the silence between them total.

At last Polly could bear it no longer. She said, 'Is the chauffeur's glass partition soundproof?'

'Yes,' he said. 'Completely.'

She hesitated. 'Then may—may I ask you something?'

'If you wish.' His tone was not encouraging.

'What was Bianca doing in your car that day?'

'You imagine I invited her for a drive?' he asked bleakly. 'I had just had a bad interview with my father—one of the worst. He had done something I could not forgive, and I needed quickly to put it right. Bianca must have been listening at the door as she often did, because when I went out to the car she was there in the passenger seat, waiting for me.

'I told her to get out—that I had no time for her little power games—but she refused. I had no time to argue, and to put her bodily out of the car would have been distasteful, so I had to let her stay. Although I warned her that I was not returning, and she would have to make her own way back to Comadora alone.

'She began bragging to me almost at once about her power over my father. Said that I could run away, but in the end he would make me marry her or strip me of my inheritance. Leave me with an empty title. Then she became amorous—said she would give me pleasure in ways I had never had before. She even described some of them,' he added, his mouth curling in contempt.

'I was fool enough to let her see my disgust, and she began to get angry in a way I had never seen before. She began to talk about you—said filthy, obscene things, becoming more and more hysterical. Finally she was screaming at me that I belonged to her. That she would kill both of us rather than lose me to another girl. That was when she began trying to seize the wheel.

'Even then I did not realise she was serious, may God forgive me. I thought she was just being—Bianca. The one that only I seemed to see.'

He shook his head. 'I was shouting back at her—telling her I was going to throw her out of the car if she didn't stop.' His mouth tightened. 'That was when she attacked me with her nails, as Giacomo said. And the rest you know.'

Polly said in a small voice, 'Do you think she was mad?'

He shrugged. 'I have asked myself that a thousand times. If so, she hid it well with everyone but me.'

'Yes.' Polly swallowed. She said with a touch of desperation, 'Sandro, I'm so sorry—for everything.'

'There is no need,' he said. 'The *contessa* had nursed her delusions for too long, and it was time the truth was told. So do not blame yourself.'

He sounded kind but remote, and her heart sank.

But she mustered a smile. 'Thank you. That's generous.'

'Is it?' he asked, an odd note in his voice. 'But then, Paola, you ask for so little.'

And there was silence again.

Back at the *palazzo*, there was an air of shock that evening. The *contessa* had gone by private ambulance for a few days' rest at a clinic, and it was apparent that she would not be returning.

Alberto Molena stayed for dinner, and, although conversation was general over the meal, it was clear there were pressing matters to be discussed. So Polly was not surprised when courteous excuses were made over coffee, and the two men retired to Sandro's study, and remained closeted there.

Polly listened to music for a while in an effort to calm herself, then went upstairs to her room and sat by the window. She had plenty to think about. Questions that still remained unanswered, but which could be more complex than she'd believed.

Sandro had been on his way back to Sorrento when the accident had happened, she thought. And he'd spoken of some 'unforgivable' action of his father. What had the old *marchese* done to prompt such a reaction? she asked herself.

And why was Sandro coming to her, if he intended to end their affair? It made no sense. Especially as Bianca was clearly con-

vinced that their relationship was still a threat to her, and Sandro
had not denied it during their fatal quarrel.

The man who had visited her, scaring her with his oblique
threats and offering her money to leave—who had sent him? Was
it really Sandro, as she'd always believed? For the past three years,
she'd looked on it as the agonising proof of his cruel betrayal.
Now, suddenly, that certainty was shaken to its foundations.

I have to know, she thought. I have to put the last missing pieces
in place—even if I don't get the answers I want, and all my worst
fears are confirmed. But I can't just barge in, asking questions.

Somehow, she knew, she had to bridge the distance between
them. And there was one sure way to do that, she thought, warm
colour rising to her face.

How did they manage these things in the old days? she wondered, sending the huge bed a speculative look. Did the then
*marchese* announce over dinner that he would be visiting his wife
later? Or did the *marchesa* send a note to her husband, requesting
the pleasure of his company in bed? Or was there simply a look—
a smile—any of the covert signals that lovers had always used?

Whatever, she didn't think any of that would work in her own
situation. Maybe the direct approach would be best.

She went into the dressing room, and retrieved the black lace
nightgown from her jacket pocket, before taking a long scented
bath.

A shadow over moonlight, he'd once called it, she thought,
looking at herself in the mirror, and the most blatant evidence of
her wishes that she could ask for.

She put on a satin robe in case she encountered a lurking ser-
vant, and made her way, barefoot, to his room.

She drew a deep, steadying breath, then knocked swiftly and
went in. Sandro was there. He was in bed. And he was alone.

In fact he was propped up by pillows, frowning over a sheaf of
papers he was reading. He glanced up at her entrance, his expression changing to total astonishment.

'Paola? What is it? Is there something wrong?'

She'd planned what to say, but the words were sliding round in
her brain. 'It's Charlie,' she blurted out at last.

He sat up. 'Is he ill?' he demanded, his voice sharpening in
alarm.

'No,' she said. 'As far as I know, he's fast asleep. But he's lonely. He was so happy when the twins were here, and he really needs children near his own age around him.'

She swallowed, her fingers nervously playing with the sash of her robe. She said, 'You said I never asked for anything. So—I was thinking—maybe he should have brothers and sisters.'

She stole a glance at him under her lashes, hoping for some reaction, but she was disappointed. Sandro's face was expressionless.

'Indeed?' he said politely, after a pause. 'So what do you suggest—adoption, or some scientific trick in a laboratory?'

She hadn't expected that either. 'No, of course not.' She made a small helpless gesture. 'I thought that you—that I...'

She ran out of words, so she slipped off the robe and let it drop to the floor, allowing him to assimilate the full effect of the cobweb of lace that was the only covering for her nakedness.

He looked at her very slowly, his hooded gaze travelling over her from head to foot.

He said quietly, 'Are you really so desperate for another child? Then take that thing off and come here.'

She'd thought he would get out of bed, and come to her. That he'd tear the gown from her with his own hands as he'd once suggested.

But she obeyed him, quickly, almost nervously sliding under the sheet he'd turned back for her. Knowing with a kind of sick certainty that this was not going according to any plan of hers.

He pushed the papers to the floor and turned to her, the topaz eyes sombre as he looked down at her.

Once he kisses me, she thought desperately, it will be all right. I can make it all right...

But Sandro did not kiss her. His hands slid down her body in an almost perfunctory caress, then moved under her flanks, lifting her towards him. She was already aroused, wildly receptive to even the prospect of his possession, so there was no physical barrier to his invasion of her body, which was wordless, clinical and immediate.

And as she lay beneath him, stunned, it was apparent that it was also going to be over very quickly. He cried out once, harshly, and she felt the scalding heat of his climax. Then he rolled away from her and lay, his chest heaving as he recovered his breath, one arm across his eyes.

When he spoke his voice was muffled. 'I hope I have performed my duties as stud satisfactorily, *marchesa*. I trust, also, that your wish for conception will be granted, as I would not wish to undergo this experience a second time.'

'Is that—that all you have to say to me?' The husky words were forced from her dry throat. Her bewildered, unsatisfied body was aching for the fulfillment he had never before denied her. Burning for him to *love* her.

'No,' he said, '*cara mia*.' He made the endearment sound like an insult. 'I could think of much more, but you would not wish to hear it, believe me. And now perhaps you will leave me to sleep.'

She was dying inside, but somehow she managed to reach her robe, and huddle it round her before she fled.

Too late, she thought, her heart thudding, as she almost fell into her own room and slammed the door shut behind her. He had told her it was too late as they left the house that morning. But she hadn't understood. Or had she just been deliberately blind and deaf?

Now comprehension had finally dawned, and with it a heartbreak that threatened to destroy her utterly. And she pressed herself against the unyielding hardness of the heavy door, and let the fierce agony of tears have their way with her.

# CHAPTER THIRTEEN

POLLY got into the rear of the limousine, placing the bouquet of flowers she'd been given on the seat beside her, then leaned forward to wave a smiling farewell to the women who'd thronged out of the restaurant to see her depart.

As the car threaded its way through the narrow streets crowded with tourists, she leaned back and closed her eyes, kicking off her high-heeled sandals and wriggling her toes, the nails enamelled in an elegant pale pink to match her fingers.

Teresa had advised her well, she thought, looking down at the deep blue of her silk suit. Whatever else might be wrong with her life, at least she dressed well.

Today she had been the guest of honour at a charity luncheon in aid of a local children's home, and she'd made a small speech at the end of it in her increasingly fluent Italian, and been warmly applauded.

She took lessons several times a week with a retired schoolmaster, who lived with his plump, cheerful wife in a small white-painted villa on the edge of town. Usually they sat under an awning on the patio, and when work was finished the *signora* would serve coffee with tiny almond *biscotti*, often accompanied by a glass of her home-made *limoncello*.

The first time it had been offered, Polly had felt wrenched in half, remembering with vivid poignancy how Sandro had once teased her about making the delicious citrus liqueur for him. But she had smiled gallantly, and praised it extravagantly, to the delight of her hostess.

But then smiling radiantly, and behaving with grace and modesty, were all part of the public persona she was establishing. A façade behind which she could hide the lonely, heartsick girl that she was in reality.

It was almost three weeks since her humiliated flight from Sandro's bedroom. And it had taken every ounce of courage she possessed to face him the next day, instead of staying in her room, pleading a headache.

And when they had finally met, she was able, somehow, to match his cool politeness with her own. She had even found herself painfully wondering what had happened to the nightgown she'd left on the floor, but she did not mention the subject.

Which was how it still was, she thought, her mouth twisting. Nothing was ever mentioned. She and Sandro were like satellites, pursuing their separate orbits round the small, beloved moon that was Charlie.

By mutual, if tacit, consent, they were never alone together. She went down to the swimming pool with their son only in the mornings, when she knew Sandro would be working in his study, or out. And she was thankful that he respected her privacy. The thought of being caught by him in a bikini, or any other form of undress, made her shrivel inside.

And in the afternoons, after siesta, she remained in the shade of the terrace so that he could have Charlie to himself.

The little boy could swim like a fish now, and he was also learning, under his father's supervision, to ride the pony that was kept at one of the farms.

Although Sandro was not always at Comadora. She was kept abreast of his schedule by Signora Corboni, who was not nearly as dour as she looked, and who presented her with a printed list of his engagements each week, including the occasions when he would be away from the *palazzo*. Polly knew this was only so that she could make the appropriate domestic arrangements, and not because Sandro wished her to keep track of him. And she could not help noticing painfully that two of these absences had been spent in Rome.

But with each day that passed, she found she was learning more and more about her new life, and becoming absorbed into the established routine at the *palazzo*.

For instance, she had soon discovered that Sandro had far more than a hotel chain and the family's banking and corporate interests to occupy him. The Valessi estate owned acres of olive and citrus orchards, together with vineyards, and even a small quarry. In addition, the farms produced enough fruit and vegetables to supply most of the local tourist facilities.

When Sandro was at home, many of the lunches at the *palazzo* were working affairs, where she was expected to act as hostess, and, although she did not understand all that was being discussed, she picked up enough to take an intelligent interest. And invariably she was rewarded by a brief, formal word of thanks from Sandro as their guests departed.

She knew that was probably just for the sake of appearances, but it was a crumb of comfort to be cherished, all the same.

On the downside, there'd been a few moments of nightmare embarrassment the previous week when she'd felt obliged to seek him out and tell him that there would be no baby after all.

Sandro had been at his desk, making notes in the margin of some report, and his pen had stilled momentarily. Then he'd said with remote courtesy, 'My regrets for your disappointment,' and returned to his report.

And she had turned and left the study, and gone to talk to the cook. Because life went on, and people had to be fed and welcomed, even if she felt she was breaking up emotionally.

So, she told herself with bitter self-mockery as the car turned onto the long hill that led up to the *palazzo*, I shall become known for my good works—and Charlie, poor babe, will remain an only child.

Hardly enough to fill her days, she thought with a stifled sigh. While she could not even bear to contemplate the long, restless, driven nights that were already her torment.

She knew that most of the people who saw her in her chauffeur-driven car and designer clothes thought that she had nothing else in her life to wish for.

Only Polly knew that the Valessi family now had another closely guarded secret—her total estrangement from the only man she had ever loved.

On arrival at the *palazzo* she went straight up to her room, where Rafaella was waiting for her. She took Polly's flowers to place in water, and waited for her to change out of the suit, so she could restore it to its usual pristine condition.

Polly took a quick shower and changed into a jade-green halter-necked sun-dress, which was cool and decorous at the same time. Then she collected her sunblock, and the book she was reading, and made her way towards the stairs and her intended destination of the terrace.

She was halfway down the wide sweep, when she heard a man's

voice in the entrance hall below, and hesitated, finding herself oddly reluctant to proceed any further. For one thing, this was not the usual time of day for visitors, she told herself. For another—there was something disturbingly familiar about the visitor's smooth tone, as if he was someone she should recognise.

Moving cautiously to the balustrade, she leaned over and looked down.

She saw him at once, talking to Teodoro. A tall, well-dressed man with a smile that seemed to have been painted on his thin mouth. As he spoke he was hunching his shoulders, spreading his hands to emphasise a point, and always that smile—quite unforgettable and still with the power to scare her even three years on.

She would have known him anywhere, she thought. It was the man who'd told her to leave Sorrento—and who'd offered her Sandro's pay-off. And who was now here at the *palazzo*.

Suddenly her stomach was churning, and she lifted a hand to her mouth to stifle her startled cry of recognition. And as she did so the bottle of sunblock fell, and rolled down the stairs.

Both men turned and looked up at her, so her planned retreat was impossible. Cursing her clumsiness, she made herself walk down the rest of the stairs, moving slowly and gracefully, steadying her breathing with an effort. Teodoro had retrieved her sunblock, and returned it to her with a respectful bow. Polly thanked her mechanically, knowing that the other man's flat dark eyes were devouring her.

'So,' he said in English. 'The charming Signorina Fairfax. Or should I say—the Marchesa Valessi? An honour I had not anticipated.' The smile widened. 'Your ladies' luncheon was expected to last longer, I think.'

The significance of that was not lost on her. I'm not supposed to be here, she thought, stiffening.

She turned to Teodoro. 'Does this person have business here?' she asked in Italian, with an assumption of coolness.

'*Sì, vossignoria.* He had an appointment with the *marchese*, but his *excellency* has not yet returned from his own lunch engagement.'

'You do not ask why I am here,' the other man intervened mockingly. 'But perhaps, *marchesa*, you already suspect the nature of my business with your husband. After all, it would not be the first time.'

Polly lifted her chin. 'My husband sees a great many people, I do not question his business with them—or his choice of associate.'

Teodoro was regarding her round-eyed, having never heard his mistress speak so dismissively to a visitor before.

She looked stonily back at him. 'Please show the *marchese*'s—guest to the *salotto*.'

'I already know my way,' he said. 'But I thank you for your graciousness.' He paused. 'Would a cold drink be possible?'

Polly said, 'Will you see to it, *per favore*, Teodoro?' She walked away, her head high, but she was quaking inside, and a block of ice seemed to have settled in the pit of her stomach.

The terrace was altogether too accessible from the *salotto*, she realised, so she walked down into the gardens, finding a secluded stone bench under a flowering hedge, and sinking onto it.

So it was true after all, she thought with desolation, her hands clasping the edge of the bench so tightly that her knuckles turned white. He had been working for Sandro after all, and any lingering hopes that she might have misread the situation were stone dead.

And now he had returned, which could only mean that Sandro had decided to put an end, once and for all, to the tragic farce their marriage had become. And with unbelievable cruelty, he'd summoned his stooge, all over again, to conduct the negotiations and offer her a final settlement.

Go away and keep quiet, would be the ultimatum once more, as it had been three years ago.

But this time there was Charlie to put into the equation, and the kind of deal she might be offered made her feel sick with fear.

He would stay in Italy, of course, because this was a battle she could not fight without weapons. All she could hope for was to be allowed to spend time with him on some regular basis. Surely Sandro would permit that, and not send her off into some kind of limbo of isolation and misery.

The *contessa*, she knew, was now installed in the house on Capri, with a nurse-companion. Was similar accommodation being planned for her somewhere? They said, she thought numbly, that Ischia was very beautiful...

She heard someone moaning, and realised that the low, desperate sound was coming from her own lips.

Had Sandro decided it was time for her to be finally dismissed

from his life when she'd told him that she was not pregnant by
that brief, soulless coupling a few weeks earlier?

But what difference did it make? she asked herself, wrapping
her arms round her shivering body. Even if she was expecting
another child, it would only win her a temporary reprieve at best.

She rose, and began to pace up and down the flagged walk,
suddenly unable to keep still. Needing to do something—
anything—while her raging, unhappy mind tried to find its focus.
A way forward into a future that was no future at all.

But she would not wait meekly to be told, she thought with
sudden determination. If it killed her, she would take matters into
her own hands and leave with some kind of dignity.

And she would take nothing from him except the right to see
Charlie. That, surely, he could not deny her...

The *salotto* was empty when she returned to the *palazzo*, and
Teodoro was just coming from the direction of Sandro's study,
having presumably delivered the unwelcome guest to his host.

He gave her a wary look, and she couldn't blame him. She'd
behaved with an outstanding lack of hospitality, and she probably
looked like a madwoman.

She laid a detaining hand on his sleeve. 'Teodoro, so silly of
me. I've forgotten the name of my husband's visitor.'

His expression changed to astonishment. 'It is Signor Ginaldi,
*vossignoria*. The *avvocato* from Salerno.'

'Of course,' she said. '*Grazie.*'

A lawyer, she thought. Why hadn't she guessed? Sandro was
bound to have more than one. There was Alberto Molena, the
acceptable, trustworthy face of the law, and, in the shadows, this
other to do his dirty work.

She forced a smile. 'Will you be good enough to tell me when
he's gone? I—I need to talk to the *marchese*.'

'Of course, *vossignoria*.' He paused. 'And a package came for
you earlier, which I have placed in your living room.'

A package, Polly thought. She wasn't expecting to receive anything. And surely it couldn't be divorce papers already? Wasn't
there some minimum time for a marriage to exist before it could
be legally dissolved? Maybe this was another point for Sandro to
consult his shady lawyer about—whether the process could be
hurried on in some way.

She closed the living-room door, and stood looking round her.

My room, she thought, her throat tightening. Created specially for me. But why—when he must have already known I would not be staying? Why pretend that he cared—even this much?

The package was lying on a side-table, a large padded envelope addressed to her in her mother's handwriting. Polly picked it up, frowning a little, weighing it in her hand. This was the first direct communication she'd received from Mrs Fairfax since she'd arrived in Italy.

She'd written to both her parents, of course, and she telephoned several times a week, but conversation with her mother was still faintly stilted, and confined to strictly neutral subjects.

Oh, God, she thought, wincing. What would her mother say when she came back without Charlie? Her father had said only last week that she seemed to be recovering from her depression, but this latest blow was bound to have a profound effect on her.

And what consolation can I possibly offer? she wondered.

She sat down and opened the envelope. A sheet of folded notepaper fell out, followed by another package, wrapped in plastic and heavily taped.

Her mother had written,


Dearest Polly,

This is not an easy thing for me to tell you, but it has to be done. After you came back from Italy three years ago, these letters began arriving, sent on by the travel company you used to work for.

I realised, of course, that they must be from *him*, and I opened the first ones and read them. My excuse was that I saw how unhappy he'd made you, and I didn't want him to cause more misery and disruption in your life. But that wasn't all of it. It was obvious that he wanted you to come back, and I knew I couldn't bear to part with you or the baby you were expecting. I told myself that I had a right to see my grandchild born. That he'd had his chance, and blown it, as people say these days.

The letters continued coming for months. I meant to burn them because you seemed to have accepted the situation and settled down. And I didn't want your father to find out about them either, because I knew he'd say I must hand them over.

When your husband came here, one of the first things he asked was why he'd never received a reply to any of them. I tried to tell him that we hadn't received any letters, but I can't be a very good liar because he guessed immediately. He was terribly angry, and very bitter, but I begged him not to tell you, because I was afraid you would never forgive me. And he eventually agreed he would say nothing to you if I didn't fight him for Charlie. It was the hardest thing I've ever had to do, but I see now I deserved it.

Some of the letters were heartbreaking, Polly, and I had to stop reading them, but I had no right, even so, to keep them from you. There were things in them that you needed to know. And maybe you still do, because I can tell from your voice that you're not as happy as you make out.

While we were in Cornwall I told your father everything, and he was very shocked. He said I had to make things right between you both, and that is what I'm trying to do now.

He has forgiven me, bless him, and I hope so much, darling, that you'll feel able to do the same one day. And your husband too, perhaps.

Darling, I'm so truly sorry.

Your loving mother.

Polly snatched up the packet and began to tear it open, her carefully manicured nails snapping as she wrestled with the tape, until she reached the bundle of airmail envelopes inside.

About five of them had been opened, in all, but each of the letters had been carefully inscribed by her mother with the date it had been received.

The first one began abruptly,

Paola,

I have to tell you that I am in hospital in Naples. I have been in a bad car crash, and will have to remain here for several more weeks. There is an English nurse working here on an exchange, and she is writing this for me, because I can do very little for myself, except lie here and think. And my thoughts are not happy. I have known for some time that you have left Sorrento, and no

one will tell me where you have gone. But the company you
worked for has said it will forward this to you, so I can only hope
it will reach you.

Forgive me for not writing before, my dearest love, but when I
first recovered consciousness I could remember little of what had
happened. However my memory has slowly returned, and with it
came you, my blessed girl.

The specialists also feared that I had damaged my back so severely
that I might never be able to walk again, and I knew I could not
keep you to your promise of marriage if I was to spend the rest
of my life in a wheelchair.

I know now that I shall make a full recovery, but it will take time,
which would pass more quickly if you were with me. Please write
or call me, and come to me soon.

                                          Your Alessandro.

'Oh, dear God,' Polly whispered. She slid off the sofa onto her
knees, the flimsy blue envelopes cascading round her.

The next one was in his own shaky handwriting.

My darling, why have I not heard from you? If it is the money
that my father gave you to leave, I promise it does not matter to
me. I know how ruthless he can be, and how confused and miserable he must have made you. It was the last thing he told me
before the accident, and we quarrelled terribly. I swore to him that
if he had truly forced you to leave, I would never see him or speak
to him again. And that I would find you wherever you had gone,
and make you my wife.

In the letters that followed he told her his real identity, and all
about Bianca, and the accident, holding nothing back, she discovered with incredulity. He wrote,

It has been decided that for the sake of the family name, none of this should be made public. Also my father is very sick, and any more shocks could kill him. He has asked me to forgive him for sending you away, and we are better friends than we were. I hope you can forgive him too, as he accepts now that I shall always love you, and is ready to welcome you as a daughter.

He ended, 'My dear love, this silence from you is more than I can bear.'

'Sandro,' Polly whispered, tears pouring down her face. 'Oh, *Sandro*.'

She tore open more envelopes, scanning the increasingly desperate words.

'My face was torn by a piece of rock,' he told her at one point. 'The doctors say I should have plastic surgery, but I know that if you were only here to kiss me, I would be healed.'

And later:

I think of you night and day, my sweet one, and pray for you to come back to me, but God doesn't seem to hear me. If you no longer want me, be merciful and tell me so. With each day that passes, it becomes more difficult to hope.

And eventually the desperation faded, and the anger and bitterness began. And the reproaches.

I see now that you never loved me. That my father was right when he said that you had found out somehow who I was, and decided to make money from your knowledge. You should have held out for a better price, Paola. The lovely body you gave me was worth far more than that pittance.

And at last:

My father has died, may God give him peace, and I am now the
Marquis Valessi. I am also enough of a fool to still want you.
Even now, if you came to me, I would take you, although not as
my wife. And if the thought of my scarring revolts you, you can
always close your eyes, and think of the financial rewards.
But I shall not ask again.


'Yet you did,' Polly wept aloud, rocking backwards and forwards on her knees. 'In spite of everything, you came to find me.
Oh, God, if I'd known—if I'd only known...'

She suddenly heard the unwelcome sound of the door opening.
She looked round, her eyes blurred with tears, and saw Sandro in
the doorway, staring at her, his lips parted in shock.

If she'd been humiliated the other night, it seemed nothing to
what she felt now. She'd intended to walk out of the *palazzo*, and
his life, with her head high, commanding his grudging respect if
nothing else.

But, at this terrible moment, Polly knew exactly what she looked
like. Because she did not cry prettily. Her face would be blubbered
with tears, her nose running and her damp hair plastered to her
forehead. And when she sobbed out loud, her mouth looked like
a frog's.

'What the hell are you doing here?' She choked on the words.

'Teodoro said you were asking for me.' There was no harshness
in his voice, or arrogance. He sounded uncertain—bewildered.

'But I was coming to you, not you to me.' She glared at him,
and actually hiccuped as she did so. 'So will you please get out?'

But instead, he walked towards her. Sank to his knees beside
her, his hands framing her wet, snuffling, desperate face.

'Paola,' he said gently. 'What is it?'

She tried to think of a lie, but somehow, with his eyes looking
tenderly and gravely into hers, only the truth would do.

'You loved me,' she burst out, her voice breaking. She gestured
wildly at the scattered letters. 'You really loved me, and I never
knew,' she ended on a little wail.

'I loved you the first moment I saw you.' He produced an exquisite linen square, and began to dry her white, unhappy face.
'You know that.' As he moved he heard the rustle of paper under

his knee, and glanced down. His brows snapped together. 'Where did you get these?' he demanded abruptly.

'My mother sent them. She wanted me to know how you'd really felt after I left. And that you hadn't sent me away—only it's too late—too late.' And she began to sob again.

'*Mi amore*,' he said softly. '*Mi adorata*. What are you talking about?'

'You're going to send me away,' Polly said wildly. 'You're going to ask that man to tell me—to get rid of me. I—I saw him earlier, waiting for you. Waiting for his orders. But from you, this time, not your father.'

She tried to swallow. 'And I'll go—really. I won't make a fuss, I promise—except that I'm doing that already, I suppose, but you weren't meant to see me like this, so it doesn't count.'

'Paola,' he said, cutting through her confused ramblings. 'My beloved, my angel. How can I send you away? It would cut the heart out of my body.'

'But I saw him,' she gulped. 'The lawyer—your lawyer, who threatened me and tried to pay me that money. And you think I took it.' She began to grope for the appropriate letter. 'But I didn't.'

'I know you did not,' he said quietly, capturing her hands and holding them in both of his. 'As he has just been persuaded to admit. He deceived my father, and he deceived me. And he has never been my lawyer. He is simply a creature of the *contessa*'s that my father used once as an intermediary. You need never think of him again.'

'But what happened to the money?' She stared at him.

'I believe that he and the *contessa* divided it between them,' he said drily. 'Alberto has found unexplained funds deposited to her credit around that time.'

'The *contessa* a thief?' Polly took his handkerchief and blew her nose. 'Surely not.'

He shrugged. 'For years, Teodoro has suspected her of—er—creative accountancy with the *palazzo*'s finances. But forget her too,' he added firmly. 'And tell me why you have been crying.'

She bent her head. 'Because you were alone and in pain all those months, and I didn't know.'

'How could you,' he said, 'when you did not get my letters?' He paused. 'Would you have come to me if you had known?'

'Yes,' she said, and tried to smile. 'Even if I'd had to walk all the way over broken glass.'

He said softly, 'My sweet, my beautiful girl.'

She kept staring at the floor. 'That's not true,' she said gruffly. 'When I cry I look like a frog.'

'Do you?' There was the breath of a smile in his voice. He bent and kissed her lightly and tenderly on the lips. 'Then now you are a princess again. And I will try very hard to give you no more cause for grief.'

He got lithely to his feet, pulling her up with him, then seated himself on the sofa with her on his knee, held close in his arms.

He looked deeply into her eyes. 'Paola, is it true? Do you love me?'

'I never stopped,' she admitted shakily. 'Although God knows I tried.'

'I cannot blame you for that,' Sandro said ruefully. 'I tried hard myself, but it was impossible. And I knew that despite anything you might do, I was condemned to love you always, until death, and beyond. So, at last, I came to find you.'

She smoothed the collar of his shirt, not looking at him directly. 'But what about your mistress in Rome? Your vile cousin Emilio told me about her.'

'That was over a long time ago,' he said, adding grimly, 'As Emilio well knows.' He hesitated. 'But she was not the only one, *cara*. See, I confess everything, but it was a time when I thought you were lost to me forever. My father had just died, and my life was hell. But all it taught me was that you were my only love, and always would be.'

She looked up into the dark face, her eyes questioning. 'Then why—*why*—that other night…?'

He was silent for a moment, then he said slowly, 'Because I was angry, and I wanted you very badly. That is a dangerous combination in a man, *cara mia*.

'When I saw you standing there, I thought paradise was mine at last. I looked at you, longing for you to tell me that you loved me—or at least that you desired me. One kiss—a touch of your hand—and I would have been yours.

'But you spoke only of Carlino—his happiness, his need for a playmate, as if that mattered more, somehow, than you being in my arms, a woman with her man.

'It was as if my being exonerated of Bianca's death had convinced you that I was a suitable candidate for fatherhood again. I felt as if I was some tame stud, to be used only when required. And that my needs and emotions were immaterial.

'And frankly I found that unbearable—an insult to my manhood, and everything I felt for you. But I was also scared that anger might get the better of me, and I would lose all control and treat you in a way we could both regret for the rest of our lives.

'So I told myself, *Bene*—if that is all she wants, it is all she shall have. Until afterwards, when I saw your wounded eyes.' He drew her closer repentantly. 'I was afraid that I had hurt you too much—driven you away forever.'

'But I'd been scared too,' she whispered. 'In case you rejected me. I knew how much you loved Charlie, and thought he might prove a link between us. A way to approach you.'

'And do you know why I love him so?' Sandro asked quietly. 'Because he reminds me of you, when we first met—so innocent, so trusting, so unstinting in affection. And he wanted to be with me, even though I was being shunned by you.'

Polly sighed. 'And I thought you only wanted him. That I was just here on sufferance.'

His mouth twisted. 'More suffering than sufferance, I think, *bella mia*. Living with you has been heaven and hell. Heaven to hear the sound of your voice, see your smile, breathe, sometimes, the fragrance of your skin—your hair.

'But hell to be aware of all these things, and yet be denied the right to hold you in my arms at night.

'I should have told you. I came back early from that trip principally because I could not bear to be apart from you another day.'

'I dared not believe you,' she said. 'I couldn't risk having my heart broken a second time.'

He said softly, 'So, are you prepared to take that risk now, *carissima*? To be my wife, and face whatever our lives bring at my side?'

'Yes.' She smiled into his eyes. 'I'm ready to do that, *caro mio*. My dear love.'

He carried her in his arms out of the room, and up the broad sweep of the staircase.

'So much for public decorum,' she teased breathlessly.

'At least you are still wearing your clothes.' His answering grin was as mischievous as a boy's.

But when they were alone and the door was not merely closed but locked, Polly saw the stark hunger in his eyes, and knew a fleeting moment of fear, in case he demanded more than she had the power to give.

Then his hands descended on her bare shoulders, and her body exploded wildly in the sheer shock of recognition. And of overwhelming, aching need.

He bent his head, and his lips parted hers deeply and sensuously. His arms tightened round her, crushing her breasts fiercely against his hard chest.

When the long kiss ended, they were both breathless. Then he reached for her again. They undressed each other, swiftly, almost frantically, tearing at buttons and zips, ripping recalcitrant fabric away. And the years of separation faded into oblivion as Polly lay naked in his arms at last in the sunlit warmth of the afternoon.

Their mouths feverishly explored the familiarity of flesh and bone, seeking unforgotten pleasures, reviving the shuddering sweetness of touch, their voices whispering—urging.

His tongue was liquid fire against her taut nipples, his fingers like silk as they found the molten, eager core of her and lingered, creating their own exquisite torment.

'Do you remember?' he murmured against her lips. 'The things you once said to me?'

'I've forgotten nothing.' Her voice was a husky purr.

'Then say them now.' He whispered, as his body slid into hers with one powerful thrust. He was not gentle, but she did not wish him to be so. His claim on her was as total as her surrender to him, and she gloried in it, her body arching against him, drawing him ever more deeply into the moist heat of her. Closing round the pulsating length of him, and making him groan with pleasure. And all the time, her lips whispered against his skin, until time ceased to exist, and her voice splintered hoarsely into rapture. Speech was impossible, overtaken by her incoherent, delirious cries of delight.

And, as he came in his turn, Sandro cried out her name as if it had been dragged from the very depths of his being.

Afterwards, they lay wrapped together, sated and languid. 'Am I forgiven?' he whispered.

'For the other night?' She stretched herself against him bonelessly, smiling against his shoulder. 'Far too early to tell, *excellenza*.'

'*Dio mio*. You have other penances in mind?'

'Enough to last for the rest of our lives.' Polly sighed luxuriously. 'And only an hour ago, I thought I would never be happy again.'

'I always hoped, *mi adorata*,' Sandro said drowsily. 'Even when it seemed all hope was gone.'

'Now we have something better than hope,' she told him gently. 'We have each other. Forever.' And she pressed her lips tenderly to his scarred cheek.

If you enjoyed what you just read,
then we've got an offer you can't resist!

# Take 2 bestselling
# love stories FREE!
# Plus get a FREE surprise gift!